ABERRANT
BEHAVIOR

Jim Lively

TREATY OAK PUBLISHERS

PUBLISHER'S NOTE

This is a work of fiction. None of the characters or events is based on actual people, living or dead, or their lives or circumstances. Any similarities are a coincidence and purely unintentional.

Printed and published in the United States of America

TREATY OAK PUBLISHERS

ISBN-978-1-943658-53-4

Available in print and digital from Amazon

DEDICATION

To Paulette.
Thank you for your support, creativity, spirit of
adventure and sense of humor.

CHAPTER ONE

"Mr. Mahoney, do you have a final witness to call?"

"Yes, Your Honor. I would like to ask Mrs. Simon to take the stand."

The judge said, "Mrs. Simon, please come forward."

Mrs. Simon made her way to the front of the courtroom.

"Mrs. Simon, would you please raise your right hand? Do you promise to tell the whole truth and nothing but the truth, so help you God?"

"Yes, Your Honor."

"Please take the stand."

Mrs. Simon was a petite woman in her late forties, with blonde hair and ice-blue eyes. She was much younger than her husband.

The judge said, "Mr. Mahoney, you may question your witness."

"Thank you, Your Honor." He shuffled some papers on the table in front of him and pulled out a legal pad. "Mrs. Simon, would you please state your entire name for the record?"

"Jamie Lynn Simon."

"Now, Mrs. Simon, can you please tell me your relationship to the insured, John Simon?"

"Yes. He's my husband."

"Can you please tell the court about your husband's condition?"

"He suffers from a rare cancer. He will die if the insurance company won't cover a procedure that he desperately needs to save his life."

"Can you share with us what insurance company denied the coverage?"

Mrs. Simon pointed in the direction of Charles Pierce. He was the legal counsel representing Mutual Indemnity Insurance Company, a health insurer. Sitting next to Charles was one of the company's vice presidents. Before she could respond, Charles said, "Objection, Your Honor. Mutual Indemnity Insurance Company has already stipulated that it provided the health coverage for Mr. Simon."

"Sustained," the judge said.

Mrs. Simon looked at the judge. "They're so evil, they won't even let me say their name."

The judge winced. "Mrs. Simon, please do not volunteer testimony." He turned to face her legal counsel. "Mr. Mahoney, you're aware that this is an extremely narrow issue you're litigating. It boils down simply to whether Mutual Indemnity Insurance Company abused its discretion in denying coverage for a specific medical procedure for Mr. Simon. Are you intending to show that Mrs. Simon has testimony relevant to this issue?"

"Yes, Your Honor," Mr. Mahoney replied. "Mrs. Simon was an advocate on behalf of her sick husband, along with her doctors, and pleaded that this procedure be approved. She had extensive dealings with the insurance company."

The judge nodded. "OK, proceed."

"Mrs. Simon, let's jump straight to the procedure. We have already heard testimony from Mr. Simon's treating physician that in his opinion, the procedure in question was medically necessary. You're not a doctor, so I'm not going to ask your opinion of whether you thought it was medically necessary. But I'm going to ask, were you informed how much it would cost?"

"Objection," Charles said. "There is no relevance between the cost and whether Mutual Indemnity Insurance Company abused its discretion in denying coverage for the procedure."

"Overruled. Please continue, Mr. Mahoney."

Mrs. Simon glared at Charles. "Yes," she said. "The molecular genetic type of procedure is kind of unusual and unique. It, along with other treatment required, would cost in the neighborhood of a million dollars."

"So that's the cost, whether you paid for it or Mutual Indemnity Insurance Company paid for it, correct?"

"Yes. We couldn't afford to pay that kind of money, though."

"Mrs. Simon, what does your husband do for a living?"

"He's a manager at a construction company."

"I see. I assume he makes a good living?"

"Along with my job, we have a comfortable life."

"And what do you do for a living?"

"I work part-time for a friend who is a veterinarian."

"Do you think that on your salaries, you could afford to pay for this procedure out of pocket?"

"Heavens no."

"So I'm assuming that the only way for Mr. Simon to get this procedure performed is for the insurance company to pay for it?"

"Yes. That's why we have been paying expensive premiums all these years."

"Did you ever discuss the cost of the procedure with anyone at Mutual Indemnity?"

"Yes. That's how I found out how much it would cost."

"So Mutual Indemnity Insurance Company knew the cost but declined to provide the coverage?"

"Yes." Mrs. Simon dabbed her eye with a tissue.

"How did that make you feel?"

Charles stood immediately. "Objection. How Mrs. Simon felt is irrelevant."

"You heartless bastard!" Mrs. Simon screamed.

"Mrs. Simon, you can't make outbursts like that," the judge told her. "If you continue, I will be forced to cut off your testimony. I'm going to sustain the counsel's objection."

She began to sob.

"Mrs. Simon, let me rephrase the question," Mr. Mahoney said. "How did Mutual Indemnity Insurance Company inform you of the cost of the procedure?"

"The caseworker assigned to my husband's case told me. She described that the procedure is currently considered experimental by the Mutual Indemnity Insurance Company Medical Review Board, although that could change at any time. The Medical Review Board members often change their decision on whether to cover a procedure after it has been successfully tested and performed several times. The board isn't going to cover a procedure until it has been proven to be effective according to its protocols. The caseworker said she had seen the board deny a procedure for one patient and then turn around six months later and approve it for another patient."

Charles said, "Objection. Mrs. Simon cannot testify for the caseworker. Hearsay evidence."

"Sustained."

Mrs. Simon buried her head in her hands.

"Mrs. Simon, you're going to have to get control of yourself," the judge said.

She lifted her head. "Don't you see what they're doing? They won't pay for the procedure because it's so damn expensive. That's the only reason they denied it. They're going to let my husband die."

The judge motioned to Mr. Mahoney. "Counselor, I'm going to cut off Mrs. Simon's testimony if she has one more outburst."

Mr. Mahoney said, "Mrs. Simon, do you need a break to compose yourself?"

She waved her hand. "No, I'm OK."

Mr. Mahoney continued. "Mrs. Simon, as far as you know, has the procedure been performed successfully in other countries?"

Charles objected. "Counsel has not laid a foundation that Mrs. Simon is an expert to testify on any type of medical procedure or whether it has been performed successfully."

"Your Honor, I'm not asking her to give an expert opinion. I want her to give her opinion as the wife of a very sick man."

"Overruled," the judge said. "You may answer the question, Mrs. Simon."

"Yes, I learned about the nature of the molecular genetic therapy procedure from my doctor. He gave me some literature to read on the subject. Also, I have researched the procedure on the internet. It has been performed successfully in Sweden,

Norway, and Finland. The success rate for the patient to recover fully is greater than seventy percent."

"So as the wife of a very ill man, you're quite naturally wondering why his insurance company will not cover the tried-and-true procedure, is that correct?"

Charles again objected. "Counsel is leading his witness."

"Sustained."

"But, Your Honor, it's the truth," Mrs. Simon said. "Why won't they pay for the damn procedure that has been proven to be successful?"

"Mrs. Simon, I have warned you about your outbursts. Mr. Mahoney, do you have many more questions for the witness?"

"I'm almost done, Your Honor, if you will bear with me. Mrs. Simon, can you tell us how you learned Mutual Indemnity Insurance Company was going to deny paying for the procedure?"

"I received an impersonal form letter from someone I didn't know from the company. It had a bunch of legalese, but I got the gist that they weren't going to pay for it."

"So your caseworker didn't inform you?"

"That's correct. I couldn't believe it. I thought caseworkers were supposed to work with the families. Instead, I received a letter from some stranger."

"Mrs. Simon, your doctor testified earlier that no one from Mutual Indemnity ever contacted him about the medical necessity of the procedure prior to denying it."

Charles said, "Objection. The doctor's testimony speaks for itself."

Mrs. Simon squirmed uncomfortably in her chair.

"Sustained," the judge said. "Counsel, if you want to refer

to the testimony of the doctor, we can have the court reporter read it back. But I don't see how the doctor's testimony is relevant to Mrs. Simon's testimony."

Mr. Mahoney said, "Let me phrase the question this way: Mrs. Simon, did you ask your doctor to intervene on your behalf with Mutual Indemnity Insurance Company?"

"Yes. He said everyone he talked to associated with Mutual Indemnity was an incompetent idiot, and at no time did anyone ask him for his opinion about the medical necessity of the procedure."

Charles said, "Objection. Hearsay evidence. Mrs. Simon can't testify for the doctor."

"Sustained. Mrs. Simon, your counsel's question was whether you asked the doctor to intervene on your behalf with the insurance company. Please restrict your answer to the question asked."

Mrs. Simon started sobbing. "This is so wrong. How can you be so obtuse? It's so obvious why the company won't pay for the procedure."

The judge banged his gavel on the desk. "Mrs. Simon, I have repeatedly warned you about your outbursts. I am going to call a thirty-minute recess."

* * *

FORTY MINUTES LATER, THE JUDGE reentered the courtroom. The bailiff said, "All rise."

Everyone stood until the judge reached the bench and said, "Please be seated. Mr. Mahoney, do you have more questions for your witness?"

"Your Honor, I just have a few more questions."

The judge said, "Mrs. Simon, please take the stand again. You remember that you're still under oath." Mrs. Simon looked pale and was clutching a tissue as she settled into the witness chair. Her ice-blue eyes were red around the edges.

Charles felt so sorry for her.

"Now, Mrs. Simon, did you ask your doctor to contact Mutual Indemnity Insurance Company and discuss the necessity of the procedure he was recommending?"

"Yes."

"To the best of your knowledge, did he do so?"

"Yes. He tried to talk to the insurance company's medical director or someone on the board that makes these decisions."

"As far as you know, was he successful?"

"No."

"So as far as you know, no one with Mutual Indemnity was even willing to talk to him?"

"That's correct."

"Mrs. Simon, how's your husband today?"

"He's extremely ill. His condition seems to be deteriorating every day."

"In your opinion, would he be well enough to testify in court?"

Mrs. Simon teared up. "No, he has around-the-clock caregivers. He can barely get out of bed. There's no way that he would be strong enough to testify."

"I see. So you're the last hope to plead his case for him so that he might have a chance of living?"

"Objection. Counsel is leading his witness."

"Sustained."

Mr. Mahoney said, "I have no more questions, Your Honor."

The judge looked at Charles. "You may question the witness, Mr. Pierce."

Mrs. Simon glared at Charles with her ice-blue eyes.

Charles grimaced, set down his pen, and said, "One moment, Your Honor." He turned to the Mutual Indemnity vice president seated next to him and whispered, "This is your last chance. Are you sure the board can't be persuaded to cover this procedure?"

"I have strict marching orders to stay the course," he whispered.

"This case might lead to some bad press for the company."

"I'm aware of that, and the board is too."

"The board merely has to tweak the protocol, and this woman's husband has a chance of living."

"No, our decision is final."

Charles turned back around and faced the judge. "Thank you, Your Honor. I have no questions for this witness."

The judge said, "You may step down, Mrs. Simon." He waited for her to return to a seat behind the bar. "Mr. Mahoney, you may proceed with your closing argument."

"Thank you, Your Honor. As the court is aware, in these types of cases, it is incumbent on the plaintiff to prove that the defendant, Mutual Indemnity Insurance Company, abused its discretion in denying the coverage under the terms of its health insurance policy. The court has heard the testimony of Dr. Walter Steele, a board-certified oncologist and the plaintiff's physician. He is the head of the Oncology Department at Presbyterian Hospital of Dallas and well versed in these types of cases. As he testified, he has assisted fellow oncologists in Europe in successfully performing this molecular genetic therapy procedure. We have testimony from Fred Davis, the chairman of the Mutual Indemnity Insurance Company Medical Review Board, that there is no board-certified oncologist presently serving on its review board. The same board that denied coverage for the molecular genetic therapy procedure because in the board's determination, the procedure is considered experimental. Wouldn't a prudent decision-maker want to make a fully informed decision? How can the decision be informed about the treatment for cancer when no oncology specialist serves on the board or even as a consultant to the board?

"Dr. Steele further testified that he tried repeatedly to talk to someone in authority at Mutual Indemnity Insurance Company to plead his patient's case that this procedure was not experimental and was necessary for Mr. Simon to have a chance at living. He was blocked every which way by the defendant. Wouldn't a fair decision-maker want to hear what the patient's doctor has to say? Especially a doctor with Dr. Steele's credentials? There appears to be no investigation or deliberation by the Mutual Indemnity Insurance Company Medical Review Board into how the procedure is performed or its rate of success. No, the board relied on an antiquated medical protocol to deem this procedure as experimental. Could it be that the defendant had already decided that it was not going to cover the procedure because of its cost? A million dollars is quite a hit to the bottom line, even for an insurer the size of Mutual Indemnity Insurance Company.

"Undisputed evidence has been offered that this procedure has been proven successful in various countries in Europe by both Mrs. Simon's testimony and medical documents introduced by Dr. Steele into evidence. To deny the procedure on the grounds that it is experimental is outrageous. When you consider the conduct of the company's medical review board, along with the cost of the procedure, I cannot fathom how the court could not find that the defendant abused its discretion in this case. You can see the effect it has had on Mrs. Simon. If all these factors combined don't constitute abuse of discretion, then I don't know how the court could ever find a defendant insurer liable for abuse of discretion. We respectfully request that the court find in favor of the plaintiff and insured, Mr. Simon, and that Mutual Indemnity Insurance Company be found liable for all expenses related to covering the costs of the molecular genetic therapy procedure, coupled with any other treatment recommended by Mr. Simon's health-care professionals. I rest, Your Honor."

The judge motioned to Charles. "Mr. Pierce, you may proceed with your closing argument."

Charles rose to his feet. He wondered why he chose this line of work. This was a nasty business. He hated defending rich insurance companies from those needing health care. "Thank you, Your Honor. Quite simply, an insurance company cannot be shown to have abused its fiduciary discretion under the evidence presented in court. Fred Davis, the chairman of the Mutual Indemnity Insurance Company Medical Review Board, offered into evidence the protocol duly adopted by the board that is controlling here. According to Mutual Indemnity Insurance Company protocol 521, a medical procedure will be denied as experimental until it has been performed successfully in the United States in accordance with the laws and regulations of this country. The Mutual Indemnity Insurance Company

Medical Review Board adhered to that protocol in this case. The courts have consistently held that if an insurer demonstrates that it has followed its written medical protocol, and the decision to deny coverage was based on that protocol, then it cannot be found to have abused its discretion. The plaintiff has provided no evidence to counter Mutual Indemnity Insurance Company's evidence that the defendant's protocol was followed in this case. Furthermore, the plaintiff has not offered one shred of evidence that the procedure in question has been performed in this country. It doesn't matter if it has been performed with success elsewhere. Whether the defendant failed or refused to have any contact with the plaintiff's doctor is not relevant to the issue of whether it abused its discretion in this matter. The fact that no oncologist currently serves on the Mutual Indemnity Insurance Company Medical Review Board is not relevant to its decision to deny based on protocol 521. We request that the court find that the defendant did not abuse its discretion in denying coverage for the procedure in question and thus cannot be liable under its insurance policy for any payment related to the procedure. I rest my case, Your Honor."

Charles sat down. He was curious to see if the judge was going to rule in favor of his client now or take a break first. This decision was going to devastate poor Mrs. Simon. She would have no recourse.

The judge cleared his throat. "Before I announce my ruling, I want to take a moment to address Mrs. Simon. I'm so sorry for all you and your husband are experiencing. The last thing you want is the stress of suing your husband's insurer and testifying in court. I'm completely sympathetic to all you must be going through with your husband's illness. My wife is a cancer survivor. Mrs. Simon, these types of cases allow the court almost no wiggle room. By that, I mean the federal statute governing health insurance of this type is pretty cut and dried. The insurance lobby is incredibly powerful and pretty much dictates to Congress how to write the laws governing them. You have heard both legal counsels refer to the abuse of discretion as a standard to be proved. Although it may seem confusing to a layperson, it is very difficult for a plaintiff to prove that an insurance company abused its discretion in denying a benefit under these circumstances. As a judge, though, I am bound by law to follow the legal court opinions that have already heard and ruled on this issue."

The judge pointed at Charles. "Mr. Pierce, I couldn't practice your kind of law if my life depended on it. I don't know how you're able to sleep at night."

Charles did have trouble sleeping at night.

The judge wiped his brow. "This court finds in favor of the defendant, Indemnity Mutual Insurance Company. However, because I do have some discretion in this area, I will not award court costs and attorney fees to the defendant."

Charles shot a glance over at the plaintiff's table. Mr. Mahoney had his arm around Mrs. Simon. She was crying. Charles packed his papers into his briefcase. The vice president sitting beside him said, "Congratulations, Charles. Good job." He extended his hand toward Charles.

Charles ignored it. "You know what? I think it's time for me to retire." He walked over to where Mr. Mahoney and Mrs. Simon were seated. He said, "Mrs. Simon, I am truly very sorry that this decision may affect your husband's health."

She looked up at Charles with fiery, ice-blue eyes full of

tears. "There's a special place in hell for you!"

"I understand your feelings." Charles started to say more and decided against it. He could feel tears welling up in his eyes. That was it. He was finished. *This was my last case.*

CHAPTER TWO

Simon v. Mutual Indemnity Insurance Company was indeed Charles's last case. He spent a few weeks tying up loose ends before leaving his practice. His first months of retirement were spent adjusting to his new life. Charles eventually fell into a daily routine. Mornings were devoted to reading the newspaper, getting a little exercise, and making breakfast for his wife, Charlotte, who was still working. In the afternoons, he would search the internet for exotic places that he and Charlotte would never visit. In the evenings, Charles would drink wine and watch movies until he fell asleep. He could sense that his new lifestyle was grating on Charlotte's nerves. They were growing further apart, even though they were spending more time together.

On the morning of March 7, 2017, Charlotte said, "Charles. What has happened to you? Look at how you spend your day. Are you happy with what you've become?"

"Not really."

"I'm not happy."

"Well, I'm sorry that my retirement is so upsetting to you."

"It's not just that. There's more. We need to have a serious talk tonight."

"OK. Fine."

Charlotte left for work, and Charles settled into a chair with a cup of coffee and the newspaper. He was flipping through the paper and came to the obituary section. At the bottom of the second page was a brief obituary:

> John Carl Simon, 1956–2019. Mr. Simon is survived by his loving wife, Jamie Lynn Simon. The family asks that contributions to the American Cancer Society be made in lieu of flowers.

Damn it! That poor woman must be devastated, he thought. First, she was subjected to that brutal trial. It was her only hope that her husband would get his procedure paid for by the insurance company. She had walked into the courtroom thinking that justice would prevail. He had certainly done his part to make sure that it wouldn't.

Charles deposited the newspaper in the trash and pulled out his phone to check his email. In the in-box was a message from Wayne Sanders with the subject "Happy Hour." It read:

> Hey Charles, I was so happy to learn of your recent retirement. Listen, are you free for happy hour tonight? I know it's late notice, but I thought it might be fun to go to one of our old law school haunts. Yes, I am referring to Peggy's. Believe it or not, the old dive is still open. Drop me an email or give me a call. Wayne.

Charles had not talked to Wayne in forever. *How did he even know that I was retired?* Charles agreed to meet him at 7:00 p.m. at Peggy's. He wondered if he should let Charlotte know that he was going to be out tonight. He decided not to tell her because it would only upset her. He'd just text her from the bar.

* * *

Wayne and Charles caught up on old times. Charles glanced at his phone; it was 9:00 p.m. "Oh crap. I forgot to text Charlotte." Quickly, he drafted a text to let Charlotte know that he would be home no later than 10:00 p.m.

Wayne and Charles ordered another cocktail. "How's Charlotte doing?"

"OK, I think. She doesn't approve of my new lifestyle as a retiree, though."

"Why do you say that?"

"Since I quit practicing law, I haven't decided what I want to do with the rest of my life. So I tend to mope around the house during the day and drink heavily at night. What's not to like?"

Wayne laughed. "I think I have to side with the wife of my old law school buddy here. Ever thought about doing some part-time pro bono work? That might give you a meaningful outlet to pursue. At a minimum, it'll get you out of the house and likely back in Charlotte's good graces."

"Well, my only expertise is defending wealthy insurance companies. I'm not sure how I could use my skills in a productive way to help the little guy. Did you by chance see the obituaries this morning?"

Wayne swirled the drink in his glass. "No. Remember, I'm not retired. I don't have time to read the newspaper. If I did, I sure as hell wouldn't read the obituaries. Why do you ask?"

"In the last case that I tried, I was counsel for the Mutual Indemnity Insurance Company. It was being sued by a John Simon, who had coverage under one of its health policies. The company refused to pay for a procedure it deemed to be experimental. However, the procedure has been performed successfully many times in Europe. Technically, it was the correct legal decision under the policy's medical protocol. Morally, it was a terrible decision. Mutual Indemnity Insurance Company could have easily changed the protocol and paid for the procedure."

"I take it this procedure is expensive?"

"Around a million dollars."

"Ouch. That would have been a blow to the bottom line."

"That's what the plaintiff's attorney argued. John Simon's obituary was in the paper this morning. He was the plaintiff in the case. That, my friend, is why I quit practicing law." Charles took a final swig of his citron vodka and soda. "Wayne, it's been fun catching up, but I better go. Very strange that Charlotte hasn't responded to my text."

Wayne stayed at the bar to savor the final remnants of his cocktail, and Charles exited Peggy's. He handed the valet his ticket and checked his phone. He was puzzled that he hadn't received a response from Charlotte. The valet pulled up, and Charles took a step toward his car and stumbled. He regained his balance and slipped a five-dollar bill to the valet.

"Are you OK to drive home?" the valet asked.

"I'm fine. I haven't had that much to drink. Just clumsy."

The valet shut the door after he was settled in the front seat. "Be careful," he said. "The place is crawling with cops."

"Thanks. I will."

Charles slowly pulled out of the parking lot and onto the adjoining street. There were some flashing lights a couple of blocks ahead. As he drove past, a police officer was conducting a sobriety test on a young woman. Charles drove the short commute back to his house without incident. When he arrived, it appeared that all the lights in the house were turned off. He assumed that Charlotte must have gone to bed. Relieved that he could put off any confrontation until the morning, Charles parked the car in the garage and opened the back door that led to a narrow hallway into the kitchen. One of the under-the-counter lights in the kitchen was left on, giving him enough light to see his way. Stopping at the refrigerator, he reached in and grabbed a bottle of water and took two quick mouthfuls. He then walked into the adjacent living room. The lights were turned off, but he could see a shadowy figure in the middle of the room from the moonlight filtering through the window. Charles retraced his steps to the entrance, located the light switch, and flipped it on.

Oh my God, Charlotte! What did you do? No, no, no!

Charlotte's limp body was hanging from one of their bedsheets, tied to the overhead beam that ran the length of the room. Charles dropped his water bottle and rushed over to Charlotte. Her eyes were black and motionless, staring straight ahead. Frantically, he untied the sheet and lowered her body to the floor. Charles fell to his knees and clasped her wrist, searching for a pulse. Charlotte's skin was stone cold. Charles started crying and pounding the floor with his fists. *How could this happen?*

Somehow, he managed to stand up and locate his phone. His hands were trembling so much that he had difficulty dialing

911. Charles walked to the front door, switched off the light, and exited the house. The branches on the trees were gently swaying in the night breeze, causing shadows to dance across his front lawn.

It seemed like an eternity before he heard sirens in the distance. Minutes later, an ambulance and a squad car pulled up in front of the house. Two men from the ambulance came running up the sidewalk. Charles remained seated. "She's in there, to the right." They hurried past him into the house. The exterior windows to the living room glowed a dim yellow as the men switched on the lights. A single officer ambled slowly up the sidewalk.

"Are you the one who called nine-one-one?"

"Yes."

"What's your name, sir?"

"Charles Pierce," Charles stammered.

"Mr. Pierce, my name is Officer Belton." She handed Charles her card. "What happened here, Mr. Pierce?"

He sniffed and rubbed his eyes. "I came home tonight and found my wife hanging in the living room."

"I see. What time was that?"

"I guess about thirty minutes ago."

"Before seeing her tonight, when was the last time you saw her?"

"This morning before she went to work."

"Did she seem distraught or depressed?"

"I don't think I would say she was either distraught or depressed. I do know, though, that she was not happy with my new lifestyle."

"What do you mean?"

"I recently retired from practicing law, and I've been in kind of a funk for a while. She seemed frustrated that I was not doing more with my life."

"You had no prior indication she might commit suicide?"

Charles started shivering even though it wasn't that cold. "None whatsoever."

One of the men emerged from the house. "Officer, do you want to secure the scene?"

"Yes," the officer said. "Excuse me, Mr. Pierce."

Charles continued to sit on the front porch, staring at the blinking lights on top of the ambulance. One of the men sprinted past him to the ambulance and returned with a body bag.

"Do you need me to go inside?" Charles asked.

"Wait for the officer. It's her call."

A few more minutes passed, then Officer Belton walked out of his house.

"Mr. Pierce, one of the paramedics said your wife was clutching this paper in her right hand." She handed Charles the crumpled paper. "Does this mean anything to you?"

Charles unfolded the paper and read the words out loud that Charlotte had scribbled: "Tell me about Jamie."

What? Jamie? Who the hell is Jamie? "No. I'm clueless."

"You don't know anyone named Jamie?"

"No. I have no idea what this note means. Did she leave any other note? Maybe we should check her computer."

"This note was all we found. The homicide detectives are on their way. They'll likely seize the computer."

"Homicide detectives? My wife wasn't murdered!"

"I understand. But it's standard police procedure."

Two detectives and the CSI squad arrived in three vehicles. Dressed in dark suits, the detectives walked up the sidewalk. The officer handed one of them the note and said, "Everything is now secure. Two paramedics are inside. When they were checking the victim's vitals, they discovered that she was clutching this note. They are awaiting your directions before removing the body."

Each detective read the note. One of the detectives and the CSI squad went into the house. The other detective began questioning Charles about all his actions that day—whether he and Charlotte had a fight, if he knew anyone named Jamie. They went over the same subjects time and time again. Charles suspected the detective wanted to make sure he didn't change his story. It was now 1:00 a.m., and the CSI squad and detectives seemed satisfied they had done all they could. The detectives suggested Charles check into a hotel somewhere and get some rest.

He never spent another night in that house. A few weeks later, one of the detectives contacted Charles to tell him that the investigation was closed. Neither Charlotte's computer nor her friends or coworkers had been able to shed any light on the meaning of her note. Apparently, she wanted the answer to that mystery buried with her.

CHAPTER THREE

"Mrs. Simon?"

"Yes, I'm Mrs. Simon. Who's calling?"

"Ma'am, my name is Bob Westbrook with Bankers Life Insurance Company. Do you have a moment?"

"If you're trying to sell me insurance, then no. I recently lost my husband. The last thing I need is life insurance."

"No, ma'am, I'm not calling to sell you insurance. But I do have some information pertaining to your late husband."

"Information?"

"Were you aware that your husband purchased a whole-life policy back in April of 2001? He insured himself for a substantial amount and paid the entire premium in one lump sum."

"No, I was not aware that he had an insurance policy. Is this some kind of a sick joke?"

"No, ma'am. This is no joke. He purchased the policy."

"Really? How did John have that kind of money to purchase an insurance policy? Wait a minute. Did you say he purchased the policy in 2001?"

"Yes, ma'am, on April twenty-ninth, 2001, to be exact."

"That was the year his mother passed away and left him several hundred thousand dollars. He told me he invested it and lost it all in the stock market."

"Well, ma'am, he didn't lose it all. Because he purchased a whole-life policy that is now worth a million dollars."

"Are you serious?"

"Quite."

"Am I the beneficiary?"

"Yes, ma'am. That's why I'm calling you. I need you to sign some authorization forms so that I can transfer the money to you. Due to the large amount of the proceeds, I would recommend you have it direct deposited into your banking account. If you will give me your email address, I will send you the forms to review and sign."

Mrs. Simon provided her email and concluded the conversation with Mr. Westbrook. She wondered why her husband did not tell her about the policy. What could've possibly been the point? Why did he say he lost it all in the stock market? John was an old, lovable fool. If they could have had this money while he was alive, they could have paid for that damn procedure.

CHAPTER FOUR

Mrs. Simon sat down at her kitchen table with a cup of coffee to read the morning newspaper. She unfolded it and read the headline in the local news section: "Attorney's Wife Commits Suicide."

Mrs. Simon took a sip of coffee and perused the article. She set the newspaper on the table, closed her eyes, and said out loud, "How do you feel now, you bastard? I do pity that poor woman, though. I guess the trauma of her husband having an affair with the mysterious Jamie was too much for her to handle. I wonder if the police found my emails to Mrs. Pierce? She probably deleted all of them. Little did she know that all I wanted was for her to divorce that son of a bitch. I told you, Charles Pierce, there's a special place in hell for you. Losing your wife is only the beginning."

An hour later, Mrs. Simon pulled into the parking lot of her employer, Dr. Samantha Graves, DVM, veterinarian. She opened the door to the clinic.

The receptionist said, "Good morning, Jamie."

"Good morning, Frida. Is Dr. Graves in?"

"No, she doesn't have any appointments until ten o'clock."

Mrs. Simon checked her watch. It was 9:45 a.m. She didn't

have much time. She said, "I'm going to go neaten up the lab until she gets here."

"OK."

Mrs. Simon entered the lab next to the examination room. She tried to recall where Samantha kept the ketamine. It had been administered to a dog last week. Samantha had cautioned how she had to be careful. It only takes a few drops on the dog's tongue to help it relax, she'd said. Too large a dose could kill the dog. Mrs. Simon remembered asking if it would have the same effect on humans. She said absolutely and then explained how some people even used small dosages of ketamine recreationally. Mrs. Simon had immediately thought that this would be perfect for dealing with Charles Pierce. She fingered all the medications until she came to a brown bottle. She held it up to the light. The label read "100 mg ketamine."

Mrs. Simon was careful not to take the whole bottle. Samantha would be suspicious. She found two empty vials, filled them, and screwed the caps on tightly. They contained enough ketamine to kill a small army. The front door to the clinic buzzed as it opened. Mrs. Simon slipped the vials into her purse and pretended to be organizing some trays on the counter. Dr. Graves opened the door to the lab.

"Good morning, Jamie."

"Good morning, Samantha."

"It's your last day, Jamie. I didn't expect you to have to work today. Frida has your final paycheck ready whenever you want to leave."

"Thank you, Samantha. You're a dear friend. I don't know what I would've done without you when John was ill." Mrs. Simon wiped a tear from her eye. "You always supported me, even when I was too distraught to come to work. I'll always be so grateful for your friendship and kindness."

"We've known each other for a long time, Jamie. You can't get much closer than sorority sisters."

"So true. Remember, you were going to become a physician, and I was going to marry the richest boy on campus."

Samantha laughed. "Yes. I came to realize that I loved animals more than people."

"Well, you were closer to hitting your target than me. I ended up marrying John Simon. He was a decent and sweet man, but no millionaire."

"That may be, but with that life insurance policy, you are now a millionaire."

"I just didn't figure that I would have to wait until I was a widow to have some money. Life can be crazy."

"So what are your plans? Are you going to travel?"

"Perhaps. I haven't decided yet."

CHAPTER FIVE

Three months after Charlotte's death, Charles had relocated from his hotel room into a small apartment in downtown Dallas. He'd almost abandoned driving his car. At first, he rarely left his apartment. He stewed there, thinking of Charlotte and the note she had left. He kept going over in his mind, *Who is this Jamie she mentioned?* It was more of a luxury prison than a place to call home. His friends encouraged him to see a psychiatrist. They told Charles that he was becoming too reclusive. He declined most invitations for dinner or drinks. Eventually, though, he learned that living downtown had its perks. When Charles did venture out, he could walk around the corner of his building and choose from a dozen places to eat or drink. One day he walked into a restaurant called the Wine Therapist. It soon became his favorite retreat.

On Thursday afternoon, June 15, 2017, Charles opened the door to the Wine Therapist. The bottom metal frame of the glass door dragged on the threshold. That phenomenon occurred every time the door opened. Instinctively, the Wine Therapist regulars would glance over at the entrance to see who was coming in. He took two steps inside, allowing his eyes to adjust to the low-level lighting. It appeared he was the only customer. The Wine Therapist was managed by Rachel, a lovely brunette in her early fifties.

"I was wondering if you were going to stop by today," she said.

"Of course. It's Thursday, isn't it?"

"Yes, but sometimes you stand me up." As was their brief tradition, Rachel would come from around the bar and give Charles a tight hug. He was not sure what he enjoyed more, a hug from Rachel or the cold glass of chardonnay she would soon be pouring for him.

Rachel brought over two bottles of chardonnay. She said, "I know you prefer an oaky flavor. Take a taste and see which one you like. The first one is from France, and the second is from California."

Charles swirled the wine in his glass and tried one and then the other in a second glass. "The Renaldo Chardonnay is definitely my favorite."

"I knew you were going to choose the California chardonnay over the French one."

"Now, how would you know that I would pick the California one?"

"Because the French white burgundies have too much *terroir* for you."

"Too much what?"

"*Terroir* is all the environmental factors that influence the taste of the grape. This is strictly regulated. US wines are more about science."

"I see. You should be a wine sommelier."

Rachel smiled. "I prefer just managing the Wine Therapist." She filled Charles's glass almost to the brim.

"Rachel, you always give me a generous pour."

"I call it a VIP pour."

Charles heard the door drag on the threshold and turned to see who was intruding on their conversation. A young man studied the wine bottles on the wall for a few moments before sitting at the opposite end of the bar.

Rachel waited for him to get settled before asking, "Do you need a wine menu?"

"Yes. Thank you."

Charles stared at him while he was reading the menu. He wondered where he had seen that guy before. He looked familiar.

Rachel asked, "Made a decision?"

"Yes, I'll have a glass of the Structured pinot noir."

Charles watched as Rachel poured the man's wine. She said, "Is this your first time here?"

He cast a quick glance in Charles's direction and said, "Yes. Quaint place."

She said, "My name is Rachel. I manage the bar. Let me know if you need anything."

Charles said, "Not only does she manage the bar, but she's a hell of a self-taught psychiatrist, and she pours a healthy glass of chardonnay." He toasted Rachel with his glass.

Rachel said, "Oh hush, Charles. Don't scare off new customers."

Charles took a sip of his chardonnay as Rachel disappeared into the kitchen. He suddenly knew where he had seen that guy. He had been in the lobby of Charles's apartment building that morning. "Excuse me. Do you live at the Heights, by chance?"

"No."

"Sorry. I thought I saw you in the lobby this morning."

"Wasn't me." The man leaned on his hand, which shielded his face. "People are always mistaking me for someone else."

"Is that right?"

"Miss, may I have my check?" he asked.

Rachel appeared from the kitchen. "It's eleven dollars even," she said.

He stood up and placed a five and a ten on the bar. "Keep the change." The man turned his back to Charles and walked out the door.

"He hardly touched his glass of wine," Rachel said. "Strange guy."

"Yes. What's weird is that I'm certain I saw him in the lobby of my apartment this morning. But he denied he was there. Why would he do that?"

Rachel emptied his glass in a sink behind the bar. She said, "Maybe he was in your apartment building but incognito."

"What do you mean?"

"Maybe he was there seeing his mistress. Or maybe he was following somebody."

Charles finished off his glass of wine. Rachel said, "I assume you'd like another."

"You read my mind."

Rachel poured another full glass of wine and scooted it in front of him.

Charles said, "Come to think of it, I think I saw that guy another time. He was sitting down the bar from me at the Iron Skillet one morning. That's spooky."

"Do you think he's following you?"

"Why would anybody want to follow me?"

"Maybe because of your wife's suicide? He could be a cop."

"No. They told me her case was closed. Very strange."

"Charles, did your wife have insurance?"

"She had some. Why do you ask?"

Rachel came closer to Charles and lowered her voice even though they were the only people in the bar. "I had a friend whose husband died mysteriously. The cops cleared her of any wrongdoing long before the insurance company did. They followed her around for almost a year after her husband's death."

"Are you serious?"

"I'm very serious. It unnerved her."

"Was her husband insured for a lot?"

"About half a million dollars."

Charles finished off his glass of wine. "That's a significant sum. Charlotte only had a small amount of insurance through her company. I used it to pay for her funeral."

Rachel looked at Charles's glass. "I'm guessing you don't want another one?"

"No. I'm done. Thank you, as always, for the wine and therapeutic conversation."

"Anytime."

CHAPTER SIX

"Hello?"

"Hello, Mrs. Simon. This is Frank."

"Hello, Frank. Do you have something for me?"

"Yes, I'm afraid that I've got some bad news."

"What is it, Frank?"

"I think our target made me this afternoon. I tailed him to a wine bar downtown, and he and I were the only customers. He engaged me in conversation. I was in the lobby of his apartment building this morning. Apparently, he spotted me. I denied it, but he was certain he remembered seeing me."

"I see. What was the name of this wine bar?"

"It's called the Wine Therapist. He's visited it every Thursday afternoon for three straight weeks. Today was the first time I've been inside. Generally I wait outside for him because there aren't many people in there during the day. I didn't want him to recognize me. Today, I decided to take a chance. That was a mistake. I can tell you a few things that I learned while there, though. Our target appears smitten with the woman who manages the place. Her name is Rachel. Also, our target drinks chardonnay."

"Interesting. That could be useful. I may have to pay a visit to the Wine Therapist."

"Mrs. Simon, I'll write up a detailed report about it and several of the target's preferred choices for dining, drinking, and other interests. But it wouldn't be wise for me to continue to tail him."

"I understand, Frank. You've done a hell of a job. Tell me how much I owe you when you deliver your report. I'll make out a check."

"It'll be ready by tomorrow afternoon."

"OK, Frank."

"Mrs. Simon, may I ask what you are going to do with all this information on the target? Of course, you are under no obligation to tell me."

"Frank, I think it's only prudent I keep my plans to myself."

"I understand, Mrs. Simon. You know how to contact me if you should ever need my services again."

"Goodbye, Frank."

Mrs. Simon mixed herself a vodka and tonic. She was anxious to get her hands on the report.

CHAPTER SEVEN

The doorbell rang. Mrs. Simon answered the door.

"Hello, Frank. Please come in."

"Thank you, Mrs. Simon. Here's the final report on the target. It's got a lot of details that are probably not of any use, but I wanted to be as thorough as possible."

"I understand, Frank. I'm confident your report will prove to be very useful. Here's your check. Will you please keep all this confidential?"

"Yes. Definitely."

"By the way, Frank, I may need you to do a little more work on this case in a bit. It will not involve you having to tail Charles Pierce, though."

Frank shifted his feet. "Absolutely. Just say when and what you need done."

After Frank left, Mrs. Simon sat down and pored over every detail in the report. It provided a thorough description of all Charles Pierce's activities and the places he liked to frequent. Every other Wednesday evening at 7:00 p.m., he went to happy hour at a members-only reception held at the Nasher Sculpture Center. On the second Tuesday of every month at 7:00 p.m., he attended a lecture series held at the Dallas Museum of Art.

And he went to the Wine Therapist every Thursday at about 4:00 p.m. He had season tickets to the Dallas Modern Dance Society and regularly attended dance performances. The next two performances were Saturday, November 11, at 8:00 p.m., at the Wyly Theater and December 9 at 8:00 p.m. at the Winspear Opera House.

Mrs. Simon's first plan was to pay the Wine Therapist a visit this Monday and get a feel for the place on a day that Charles didn't usually come in. She needed to make sure that she was not too conspicuous in case Charles showed up. Mrs. Simon wanted to make sure that Charles did not recognize her. She doubted if he even remembered what she looked like. After all, the only time he had seen her was when she testified at the trial. Her hair was blonde then. She surmised that he would not expect her to be a natural gray. Mrs. Simon had aged since that trial. She opted to wear tinted glasses to conceal her eyes. She went online and became a member at the Nasher Sculpture Center, the Dallas Museum of Art, and the Dallas Modern Dance Society. She thought, *Charles Pierce is going to have another art patron join him for these various events.* Surely, she would have an occasion to get close enough to spike his drink.

On July 10, 2017, Mrs. Simon entered the Wine Therapist at 4:00 p.m. She wore heavily tinted tortoiseshell glasses and her gray hair pulled into a tight bun. Mrs. Simon stared at her reflection in the window. She was satisfied with her disguise. She opened the door and peered inside. A man and a woman were seated at one end of the bar. Mrs. Simon decided to sit toward the middle of the bar, leaving a couple of seats between her and where Charles usually sat, according to Frank's report. A woman behind the bar was watching her. Mrs. Simon suspected that the woman must be Rachel, the manager.

As soon as she was settled, the woman walked over to her. "May I bring you something, or would you like to see the wine menu?"

Mrs. Simon looked up at Rachel. "May I see it please?"

Rachel placed a menu in front of Mrs. Simon.

She opened it. Frank's report said that Pierce had ordered chardonnay. There were two listed. One from California and the other from France. Mrs. Simon wondered which one Charles Pierce had ordered. She said, "Excuse me. Can you help me pick a chardonnay, please?"

"What kind of chardonnay do you like? Do you like those that are more citrus or oaky?"

Mrs. Simon pretended to be confused. "I'm not sure. Is there one that is more popular?"

Rachel leaned on the counter in front of Mrs. Simon. "I tend to find that men prefer oak, whereas women prefer the citrus. The oaky chardonnay is from California, and the other one is French."

Mrs. Simon set the menu down. "I like to be different. I'll go with the oaky one, then. It's the California wine, right?"

Rachel smiled. "I admire a woman who goes against the norm. Yes, it's a Renaldo Chardonnay from Sonoma Valley. It's slightly buttery and very oaky."

She poured Mrs. Simon a glass of Renaldo Chardonnay.

"Do you always serve these two types of chardonnay?"

"We change the menu about every three weeks, depending on our stock."

"So if I came in last week, then you would've served me the Renaldo?"

"Yes, if you wanted an oaky chardonnay. By the way, my name is Rachel. I'm the manager here." She extended her hand.

Mrs. Simon thought it more discreet to use her middle name. "My name is Lynn. Nice to meet you." The women shook hands.

"Is this your first time here?"

"Yes. I happened to be downtown and saw your sign. I was thinking a glass of chardonnay would hit the spot."

"Great. Thank you for coming in."

Mrs. Simon took a sip of her wine. "Do you get a regular crowd here?"

"Yes. I see some of the same customers every week. One woman comes in almost every night after work before her long commute home. Most of my regulars are men, though."

"Interesting. Well, maybe I'll become a regular."

Rachel wiped the bar. "Well, Lynn, I hope you do. You'll meet some interesting characters and enjoy some exquisite wine along the way. Do you live downtown?"

"No, but I'm downtown several times a week, running errands." Mrs. Simon slowly drank her glass of wine. She listened to the banter between Rachel and the couple. Mrs. Simon felt like this initial visit had gone well. Not only did she check out the layout, but she made an important connection with Rachel. When she came in the next time, she'd blend with the other regulars. Charles Pierce wouldn't suspect a thing.

CHAPTER EIGHT

On July 13, 2017, Charles opened the door to the Wine Therapist. Rachel was near the door, unloading a case of wine and inserting the bottles into the wine rack that lined the wall.

"Good afternoon, Counselor," she said.

He laughed. "I haven't been called that in a while."

"Once a lawyer, always a lawyer, right, Charles?"

"Unless you're disbarred, of course."

"Excellent point. Give me a minute and I'll pour you a glass of Renaldo."

"Take your time." He glanced around the bar. A couple was seated at the left end of the bar, and a woman sat three seats from the other end. Charles perched on top of his chair and checked his phone for emails. Rachel walked up behind him and said, "You're not going to give me a hug today?"

"Sorry. I wouldn't miss a hug for the world."

Charles and Rachel hugged. Rachel then made her way around him to go behind the bar. She paused in front of Mrs. Simon and asked, "Lynn, would you care for another glass?"

"Why not?" she replied.

Charles quickly peeked over at the woman but did not

recognize her. She was thin, with gray hair that was pulled back in a bun. Her glasses hid most of her face. He looked past her to the couple at the other end. They were having a friendly argument about which Texas pro football team would be better next season. Rachel appeared in front of the gray-haired woman and refilled her glass of chardonnay. She then walked down to Charles and pulled a clean glass from beneath the bar. "There's still enough in the bottle to give you a generous pour," she said, draining the remainder of the chardonnay into his glass.

"Thank you. I assume you have more Renaldo in the fridge?"

"Yes, Charles. I put a couple of extra bottles in to chill in anticipation of you coming in today." Rachel playfully wrinkled up her nose, which made her look like a teenage girl. She walked to the other end of the bar to check on the couple. Charles thought of attempting to talk to the woman next to him. But she was preoccupied with her phone.

Charles heard the familiar scraping of metal on metal as the front door opened. Everyone at the bar except Mrs. Simon turned around to see who was coming in. It was a blonde woman, probably in her forties.

"Megan," Rachel called out from behind the bar.

The blonde woman said, "Rachel, how are you, girlfriend?"

Rachel rushed around the bar, and the two embraced. Charles could not help but watch. Rachel's eyes darted around the bar, and she looked at Charles. She nodded in his direction. "Why don't you sit in the chair by Charles? He's a friend. That way, I can talk to you both when I have a chance."

Megan eased onto the chair next to Charles. She was wearing medical scrubs and smelled of lavender. She looked over at him and smiled. "Hi, I'm Megan."

He grinned. "I gathered that. My name is Charles."

Rachel returned with a bottle of pinot noir. She said, "Megan, you're going to love this pinot. I thought about you the first time I tasted it." Rachel poured Megan a full glass. Megan sniffed it. "A hint of cinnamon and black cherry," she said.

"Girlfriend, you know your wines."

"Can you actually smell those scents in the glass?" Charles asked. "I've tried, but I never could smell anything other than wine."

"Maybe you just need some practice." She held up her glass. "Cheers."

"You two actually have something in common," Rachel said. "Megan recently went through a divorce, and Charles lost his wife."

Charles thought, *My God, why did Rachel have to bring up my deceased wife?* Every time he heard her referenced in the past tense, he felt a profound sense of loss and sadness.

Megan looked at Charles. "I'm so sorry for your loss. How—" She stopped herself from asking how his wife had passed away.

Charles stared down at his glass of wine. "Thank you." He did not volunteer any more information. Rachel was aware that Charlotte had committed suicide. Sensing she should not have said anything, she excused herself to go check on the other customers.

Mrs. Simon was closely following the conversation. She wondered if she would get a chance to get near Charles's glass. Mrs. Simon viewed her opportunities as limited. She hoped that maybe he would go to the restroom and leave his glass unattended. She did not want to kill him yet, only to make his life miserable or cause him to have an accident. She reasoned that this would be the perfect scenario. Mrs. Simon wanted the killing to come at a later time.

Rachel interrupted Mrs. Simon's thoughts. "How are you doing on your wine, Lynn?"

Mrs. Simon looked down at her glass. It was half-full. "I'm fine. But, Rachel, where might I find the ladies' room?"

Rachel pointed at Charles. "If you go around the end of the bar where that man is seated, you will take a left down that hallway. The ladies' room is the first door on the right."

"Great, thanks." Mrs. Simon nursed her chardonnay as she listened to the conversation between Charles and Megan.

"Have you known Rachel for a long time?" Charles asked.

"About six months," Megan said. "We instantly became close friends. She helped me through some dark times when I was going through my divorce. What about you?"

"I met her about six months ago as well. This place is close to where I live. One day, I just stumbled in here and loved the ambiance. I noticed your scrubs. Are you a doctor?"

Megan tugged at her collar. "No, a physician's assistant."

"So you do all the work, and the doctor gets all the credit and money?"

Megan laughed. "No, the doctor I work for is great. I love my job. What do you do?"

"I'm retired. I used to practice law."

"Really? What type of law?"

"Litigation. I defended insurance companies when their various insureds sued them for not covering a benefit. In short, I helped the insurance company save money by screwing people who paid exorbitant insurance premiums. It was very distasteful at times. I eventually gave it up for that reason."

Mrs. Simon was seething. She could hardly contain her emotions.

Charles said, "Would you excuse me? I need to go to the restroom."

Megan said, "Of course. I must leave soon. I just came in to say hi to Rachel."

Charles got up from his seat and walked toward the restroom. Mrs. Simon peered over at Megan. She was studying her phone. Mrs. Simon pulled a vial with a small eyedropper out of her purse. She eased out of her chair and walked to the end of the bar and hesitated. Her hands were trembling as she leaned over Charles's unattended wineglass.

Before she could squeeze the dropper into Charles's glass, Rachel spotted her from across the bar. "Lynn, can I help you with something?"

Startled, Mrs. Simon grasped the eyedropper tightly in the palm of her hand so that it could not be seen. Several drops spilled out onto the bar, next to Charles's glass of wine. "Yes, do you have a tissue? I didn't want to bother you, so I thought I would look for a box of tissues behind the bar."

Rachel reached behind her and pulled several tissues out of a container. She walked over and handed them to Mrs. Simon.

Mrs. Simon dabbed her eye with the tissue. "Thank you. I think I must have gotten something in my eye. May I have my bill, please?"

"Of course." Rachel walked over to the register and brought back Mrs. Simon's bill. She handed it to Mrs. Simon. Without looking at it, Mrs. Simon gave Rachel a twenty and a five-dollar bill and headed toward the exit.

"Don't you want your change?" Mrs. Simon did not turn around but shook her head no.

Rachel removed Mrs. Simon's glass from the bar and said to no one in particular, "That was strange. What the hell was the matter with her?"

Charles returned to his seat. "Did I miss something?"

Megan said, "No, not really. That woman seated there just left for some reason."

Charles said, "I didn't get a good look at her. She kept to herself." He felt something damp on his right sleeve. "Did someone spill something on the counter?"

Rachel said, "That woman was standing near there. She said she was looking for a tissue. Perhaps she spilled something." Rachel wiped the counter clean with her rag. "Care for another glass of chardonnay?"

"No, just the check, please."

Charles took a final drink of his chardonnay, paid his bill, and said his goodbyes to Megan and Rachel.

CHAPTER NINE

Mrs. Simon read and reread her private investigator's report on Charles Pierce. She was becoming more obsessed each day and wanted another opportunity to spike Charles Pierce's drink with ketamine. Recently, she had become a member of the Nasher Sculpture Center, the Dallas Museum of Art, and the Dallas Modern Dance Society. She received an email from the Nasher Sculpture Center inviting her to a happy hour at 7:00 p.m., August 9, 2017, for members only. It would include a talk by the senior curator about a newly acquired Giacometti piece in the Hammons Exhibition Gallery, along with complimentary wine. The dress was cocktail casual. Mrs. Simon clicked on the calendar icon on her computer. She had five days to plan her next move. She wondered if Charles Pierce would be there. What should she wear to be as inconspicuous as possible? Would Charles Pierce recognize her? Should she change her hair color? Maybe a wig, or just risk going with her usual gray hair?

* * *

THE DAY BEFORE THE RECEPTION, Mrs. Simon decided to visit

the Nasher Sculpture Center to become familiar with the layout. She toured the entire facility and sculpture garden, checking for restrooms, exits, and vantage points. The Hammons Exhibition Gallery, though, was closed until the members-only happy hour the next evening.

* * *

AT 5:00 P.M. ON WEDNESDAY EVENING, she donned a brunette wig and applied her makeup. Mrs. Simon selected a short but age-appropriate black evening dress. She polished off her outfit with a new pair of smoke-tinted glasses to conceal the color of her eyes. Satisfied she was suitably attired for the evening, she located her purse and double-checked to make sure the vial of ketamine was inside.

Mrs. Simon drove to the Dallas Arts District. At the Nasher Sculpture Center, a valet opened the door of her car and helped her out. Several people were talking near the entrance. She walked past them into the Center and was greeted by an employee carrying a sheet of paper. "Welcome, ma'am, may I have your name?"

"Yes. It's Mrs. Jamie Simon."

The employer checked her sheet of paper and marked off her name. "Mrs. Simon, the happy hour is held in the Hammons Exhibition Gallery just to your left."

Without hesitation, Mrs. Simon entered the gallery. She was greeted by a white-gloved server with a tray containing champagne and white wine. "Would you care for white wine or champagne?"

"Is the white wine chardonnay?"

"No, ma'am. It's sauvignon blanc."

Mrs. Simon wrinkled her nose. "Is chardonnay available?"

"Yes. The bar over there is serving chardonnay. Would you like me to bring you a glass?"

"No, don't bother. I'll get a glass for myself." Mrs. Simon made her way over to the bar. "I was hoping to get a glass of chardonnay," she said to the bartender. "I was told you might be serving some here."

"Of course." The bartender pulled a bottle of chardonnay from the cooler behind him, poured a glass, and set it in front of Mrs. Simon. "Please enjoy."

"Thank you. By the way, why aren't the servers offering chardonnay?"

The bartender smiled. "I was told they didn't stock enough chardonnay, so they're only offering sauvignon blanc unless someone requests chardonnay."

"Really? Well, I will probably be visiting you again." *This might work out well,* she thought. If Charles Pierce wanted chardonnay, he'd have to come to the bar. That might give her an opportunity.

* * *

CHARLES PIERCE WALKED INTO THE Hammons Exhibition Gallery and was greeted by a server. "Sir, would you care for a glass of white wine or champagne?"

Charles glanced at the tray. "I'll have the white wine, please."

To his left, Mrs. Simon was watching. The server handed him a glass of wine. He took a quick sip. *This stuff is terrible, he thought. Sauvignon blanc. Way too tart. The server didn't say this was sauvignon blanc.* He started to look around for a place to lose his glass. A woman standing near a covered sculpture in the middle of the room said, "Ladies and gentlemen. If you would like to get some refreshments, please do so now. We are about to unveil our newest acquisition, and Dr. Morton, our senior curator, will say a few words about the Giacometti piece."

Mrs. Simon hustled over to within a few feet of the bar.

Charles approached a server. "Excuse me. Are you serving any chardonnay this evening?"

"I'm not," the server said, "but it's available at the bar. Would you like me to bring you a glass?"

"Do you mind? That would be great. That way, I can get a choice spot to hear about the Giacometti. Thank you."

The server walked over to the bar. Charles joined the small crowd forming a semicircle around Dr. Morton. His server waited while the bartender helped other people. Mrs. Simon got in line behind the server. She clutched her wineglass in one hand and managed to remove the vial of ketamine from her purse. Her heart was pounding, and her hand trembled. She moved forward when the server was directly in front of the bartender.

The bartender asked the server, "What do you need?"

"A glass of chardonnay."

Mrs. Simon positioned herself just to the right of the server. The bartender placed an empty glass in front of the server and removed a bottle from the cooler behind him. He held it up to the light. "Damn, this one's almost empty. Wait a second; I'll have to go get another one from the kitchen."

The bartender left to get another bottle of chardonnay. From across the room, Dr. Morton said, "I think we're ready to start, if you will kindly move in closer."

The server turned around to look at the crowd. Mrs. Simon had the opening she needed. She dropped a small dose of ketamine in the glass resting in front of the server and retreated to stand on the fringe of the crowd surrounding Dr. Morton. The bartender returned with a bottle of chardonnay.

A Nasher employee approached the side of the bar. She asked the server, "Can you please take a glass of chardonnay to that woman in the red dress over there?"

"Yes," the server said. "I have to deliver a glass to a gentleman as well." When the server turned around, he had two glasses of chardonnay on his tray.

Mrs. Simon watched the exchange between the Nasher employee and the server from a distance. She was horrified. *Two glasses,* she thought. *What if he gives the wrong one to Pierce?*

The server disappeared into the crowd with his tray. He handed a glass to the woman in the red dress and the other glass to Charles.

Dr. Morton pulled the veil off the Giacometti piece. He pointed at the sculpture, which rested on a plain white pedestal. "This is a fabulous addition to the Nasher collection. It's titled *Venice Woman IV* and was part of a series of female figures made by Giacometti for exhibition at the 1956 Venice Biennale. He produced a total of nine Venice Women in 1956, all from the same supply of clay and with the same wire armature. Characteristic of Giacometti, the Venice Women rise stiffly from their oversize feet to their diminutive heads. The aggressive modeling of the thin, attenuated forms leaves a figure that seems eroded by space. Monumental and solid despite their severe reduction, the figures also recall the ancient…"

The woman wearing the red dress fainted, and her wineglass shattered against the hardwood floor. One woman screamed. A man shouted, "Give her some room! Is anyone a doctor?"

A man next to Charles said, "I'm a doctor." The crowd parted to let him through. He knelt and placed his hand on her neck and took her pulse. A shard from the broken wineglass had sliced open her arm. A pool of blood was forming around her hand. The doctor calmly asked, "Has someone called nine-one-one?"

"Yes," a Nasher employee replied. "They're on their way!"

"Is anyone with her?" the doctor asked.

"We came together. She's my friend," a woman to the right of the doctor said.

The doctor looked up at her. "Has she had much to drink?"

"No, I picked her up at her house, and we came straight here. She just ordered a glass of wine."

The doctor placed his ear near the woman's mouth. "Her breathing is very labored."

A woman near the entrance of the Hammons Exhibition Gallery shouted, "They're here!"

Charles took a drink of his chardonnay and watched as the emergency medical technicians began to examine the woman. Within a few minutes, they had her on a stretcher and were headed out of the Nasher Sculpture Center to a waiting ambulance parked outside the entrance.

Dr. Morton said loudly, "Ladies and gentlemen. Ladies and gentlemen. May I have your attention?" The crowd silenced. "In light of this tragic turn of events, I'm not going to continue with my talk. I will, though, be available to answer anyone's questions about the new sculpture."

Most of the crowd moved slowly toward the gallery exit. Mrs. Simon was among them. She paused every few steps to look at Charles Pierce. She could see that he got the wrong glass.

A few remained to talk with Dr. Morton. The doctor who examined the woman in red said, "That's very strange. She has all the symptoms of being extremely intoxicated."

"What do you suppose is wrong with her, then?" a man asked.

"I don't know. It could be almost anything. The doctors will run tests at the hospital."

Charles walked over to the bar and set his glass on top of it. The bartender was packing up some glasses. "Thanks for the chardonnay," Charles said.

CHAPTER TEN

The next morning, Charles sat staring at his computer screen. He was searching for some kind of exotic trip that he could take. Charles was cognizant that he couldn't sit there for the rest of his life and sulk. He was still haunted by the note Charlotte was clutching in her hand and the mysterious Jamie. His wife was dead, but that didn't mean he didn't have a life left, or did it? Charles knew he couldn't spend the rest of his life just going to the Wine Therapist and attending cocktail receptions at museum functions. He thought of the novel he was reading. Surely there was some adventure or something that he could do! What would Sam Spade do? Why couldn't Charles return to the 1920s in pursuit of the Maltese Falcon? After all, Sam's partner, Miles Archer, had just been murdered in the first chapter. He could use a new partner. Dashiell Hammett could find a man of Charles's talents useful to help solve the mystery of the falcon

So far, Charles had read only a couple of pages. Regardless, he was hooked.

He closed his eyes and rested his head in his hands. Did he want to travel? Having just turned sixty-three years old, he wondered if all his adventures were in his rearview mirror. He was no longer eighteen years old and driving eighty miles an hour down Bar Harbor Avenue with his friend Mark in a death-trap of a Volkswagen Beetle with no hope of survival if someone had crossed their path. It would've been certain death—at least for Charles because he was riding shotgun. Mark was an excellent driver, but no one would have been able to avoid death on that narrow street had a car backed out of a driveway or a child suddenly decided to cross the street in front of them. Nonetheless, Mark and Charles had survived this land-speed record on a warm summer Friday night in 1973. No one else had witnessed it, thank God. If Charles were a cat, the experience would have counted for one of his nine lives. Now that was a breathtaking adventure by teenage boys who had their whole lives ahead of them.

Charles knew he needed an adventure—something to change the trajectory of his life. He dreamed of getting out of Dallas while also having the opportunity to curl up with an electronic version of *The Maltese Falcon*. Charles desired something a little less frightening than setting a speed record on a suburban street in Dallas. But what?

He thought of his travel agent. Was she still working? The last contact he'd had with her was several years ago. She was a spry woman in her early eighties who was well traveled and still had a lust for life. He started typing an email:

Hi, Donna. Are you available to help me plan a trip? This is going to sound kind of strange, but I'm not sure where I want to go or even what I want to do. I only know that I need to get out of Dallas for a while. When I say "a while," I mean more like a month. Any thoughts would be greatly appreciated.

Donna suggested a cruise or a safari for Charles's consideration. He opted for a monthlong cruise that sailed from Los Angeles to Sydney, Australia. The cruise was touted as the "Exclusive Pacific Sojourn—Hollywood in the South Pacific."

Academy Award–winning cinematographer John Keenon would lecture on the wonders of cinematography. Actor Tom Huston would give the highlights of his fifty years of experience in Hollywood. The priceless Volk Yellow Diamond worn at the Academy Awards would be on exhibit in the Sterling Boutique.

Sailing on an upscale cruise from January 22 until February 20 certainly sounded appealing to Charles.

CHAPTER ELEVEN

Mrs. Simon's obsession had reached new heights. She was depressed and began to drink heavily. Her next opportunity would be Thursday night, September 7, 2017, she thought. *That bastard better be attending that author lecture at the Dallas Museum of Art.* God, she hoped they'd be serving alcohol. She so despised author lectures.

* * *

She arrived at the Dallas Museum of Art at 7:00 p.m. The lecture was not scheduled to start until 7:30 p.m. Mrs. Simon was wearing the same brunette wig and tinted glasses that she wore to the Nasher Sculpture Center reception. This time, though, she chose to wear a gray pantsuit that perfectly matched her frames. She presented her membership card to the docent behind the reception desk.

The docent said, "Good evening, Mrs. Simon. The lecture will be in the Horchow Auditorium down the hallway on your right." She handed Mrs. Simon a ticket.

Mrs. Simon grasped the ticket. "Is any alcohol being served?"

"Yes, there's a cash bar located in the reception area just

outside the auditorium."

Mrs. Simon reached the reception area and went straight to the bar. As she waited in line, she surveyed the crowd, looking for her target. The man in front of her paid for his drink and stepped away from the bar. The bartender asked, "May I help you?"

Mrs. Simon fidgeted with her purse. "Do you have chardonnay?"

"Yes, ma'am. Would you like a glass?"

"No. Please give me a double vodka tonic."

The bartender mixed her drink. "That will be thirteen dollars."

Mrs. Simon handed him a ten and a five-dollar bill. "Keep the change." She took her drink and waited at the other end of the reception area. *You better be here, Pierce. I'm running out of patience with you.* She monitored the crowd.

* * *

CHARLES PRESENTED HIS MEMBERSHIP CARD to the docent and received his ticket. He wondered if his friend Felicia was there. She said she would meet him near the bar. Charles had known Felicia for over two decades. She was one hell of an attorney and a dear friend. He could always count on her to support him even if it meant going to an author lecture on the art minimalism movement of the 1960s. Felicia couldn't even pretend to be interested when Charles called and told her about the lecture. Finally, she acquiesced to meet him at the DMA after he promised there would be a bar. Charles had promised without being certain. Fortunately, when he entered the reception area outside the auditorium, he spotted a bar. Felicia was nursing a gin and tonic. When Charles drew near, she said, "Sorry to begin drinking without you. But I didn't think you would mind."

"The only thing I mind is that I wasn't here earlier, so I could have paid for it."

"Trust me. This won't be my last one."

Charles got in line and waited until it was his time to order.

"What would you like?" the bartender asked.

"Do you have citron vodka?"

He looked over his shoulder at his stock. "No, just plain vodka. I can add a lemon to it, though."

"OK. Perfect. I'll have a vodka and soda."

He rejoined Felicia. "How are things with you?"

She rolled her eyes. "Super busy. But I'm doing OK. What about you? Are you enjoying retirement?"

"No, not really. However, I don't miss representing insurance companies. Since Charlotte's death, I feel my life is without any direction. It seems like all I do is drink and attend art events."

"Well, I'm glad to hear you're attending art events. It gets you out of your man cave and interacting with people."

"That's true. Speaking of which, did you read about what happened to that woman a few weeks ago at the Nasher?"

Felicia took a taste of her cocktail. "I heard some woman was poisoned. I didn't hear any of the specifics. What happened?"

"I was at the Nasher that evening. The curator was midsentence, describing a newly acquired sculpture, when this woman fainted right before him. The paper reported that the toxicology reports indicated that she had ingested ketamine. Apparently, it's a drug used to help sedate animals. She had almost enough in her system to kill her. How could that happen at a cocktail reception? Isn't that bizarre?"

"How did it get into her system? Do you think someone tried to poison her?"

"The police don't have a clue. They're still investigating. We better go find some seats before the auditorium gets too crowded."

"Yes, Charles. We would hate for the auditorium to fill up and have to miss hearing all about minimalistic art."

"Hey, don't diss the lecture yet. You may end up enjoying it."

"Sorry, Charles. I seriously doubt it."

They settled into two seats at the end of the aisle, and Mrs. Simon sat behind Charles.

Felicia asked, "Are you doing any traveling, or are you only enjoying attending events where women get poisoned?"

Charles laughed. "Believe it or not, I've just booked a trip."

Mrs. Simon leaned forward in her chair so that she could hear the conversation.

Felicia said, "Seriously? Where are you going?"

"Get this: I'm taking a cruise from LA to Sydney, Australia."

"No way. You're kidding, right?"

"I'm not kidding. I told my travel agent that I needed a change of scenery and asked her to find me something that was about a month long. Anyway, she came up with this cruise."

"A month long? You'd never have been able to do that while you were still practicing law."

"No kidding."

"Who is your travel agent?"

Charles placed his cocktail on the left armrest so that he could retrieve his wallet from his coat pocket. Mrs. Simon shot a glance at his glass but did not make a move. He said, "Her name is Donna Hightower. Here's her card."

Felicia read it aloud. "Donna Hightower, Strom Travel Agency."

Mrs. Simon made a note of the name on her phone.

"Have you used her before?"

Charles picked his cocktail back up. "Yes, she handled the arrangements for all the trips that Charlotte and I used to take. She's wonderful."

"I've never used a travel agent before. Do you mind if I keep her card?"

"Be my guest. Tell her that I recommended you."

"Why? Will that give you a free trip or something?"

Charles smiled. "No. But I guess you never know."

A woman onstage stepped to the microphone. "Ladies and gentlemen, thank you for coming to our seventh and final author lecture for the year. Tonight, we're honored to welcome Dr. Barbara Dalton, art historian and professor of modern art. She will be discussing her new book, *Breaking Down the Barriers, 1960s Minimalism Revisited.*"

After they had braved the author talk, Charles asked, "Would you like another cocktail?"

Felicia gazed at the bar in the reception area. "No, I guess not. It looks like he's packing up for the evening."

He asked, "Have you had dinner?"

"No. I was trying to decide if I wanted dinner tonight."

"We could go to the Water Grill for dinner and a cocktail. It's only a block away."

Felicia looked at her watch before answering, "Sure. Why not."

A few minutes later, they arrived at the Water Grill and located two chairs at the bar. Felicia asked, "Do you come here often?"

"Yes. It's just down the street from my apartment. Among other things, they serve a phenomenal Dover sole."

A bartender took their drink orders. They both ordered a glass of chardonnay.

While they were studying the menu, Mrs. Simon sat down nearby. She was positioned on the side of the bar where it took a sharp left turn. Felicia and Charles were both in plain sight. Mrs. Simon could observe their every move.

The bartender brought their wine and took their dinner order.

Their dinners arrived fifteen minutes later.

Mrs. Simon got the attention of the bartender. She asked, "Could you please get me another glass of chardonnay and one for my friend. She should be here any minute. Also, could I please have my bill?"

The bartender poured two glasses of chardonnay and placed them in front of Mrs. Simon. He asked, "Are you finished with your first one?"

"Not quite."

The bartender walked to the other end of the bar. Mrs. Simon read the bill and left thirty dollars on the bar. She removed the vial of ketamine from her purse. She filled the eyedropper with ketamine and cast a glance around the bar to see if anyone was watching. She carefully concealed her actions with one hand while emptying the contents of the eyedropper into the two glasses of chardonnay with her other hand. Then she sat patiently and waited for the right moment. She watched as the overworked waiters scurried back and forth, delivering food and drinks. Out of the side of her eye, she spied a waiter checking on one of the tables. When the waiter walked by, Mrs. Simon tugged at his sleeve. "Excuse me, sir."

He stopped next to Mrs. Simon. She could tell by the expression on his face that he was perturbed by her intrusion. "Yes?"

"Would you please deliver these two glasses of wine to that couple over there? I saw them order them, but the bartender mistakenly put them in front of me. I was looking at my phone and didn't notice that he placed them in front of me by mistake."

The waiter gave the bartender at the end of the bar a dirty look. He said, "Yes, ma'am," and hastily snatched the two glasses of wine from the bar.

Mrs. Simon left and quickly exited the Water Grill.

The waiter placed the two glasses of chardonnay in front of Felicia and Charles. He said, "The bartender mistakenly gave your chardonnay to someone else. Sorry about that." The server left before they could respond.

Charles asked, "You didn't order another glass of chardonnay, did you?"

"No. One glass is all I wanted."

"Do you think they're on the house?"

Charles looked at one of the glasses. "This is strange." He held the glass up to the pendant light just above his seat. "There's some kind of liquid film on the side." He smelled his glass. "Smells like chardonnay, but I have the worst sense of smell."

Felicia picked up the other glass and held it to the light. "I don't see anything on mine."

The bartender approached them. "Is everything OK?"

Charles said, "A server delivered these two glasses of wine

that we supposedly ordered. He said they were delivered to someone else by mistake."

The bartender looked puzzled. "You only ordered one glass of chardonnay each. Here, let me take those." He removed them from the counter and poured the contents down the sink. "I'll be happy to get you two more on the house."

Felicia said, "Thank you, but that's not necessary. I just wanted one anyway."

"How about you, sir?"

"No. Thank you, though."

They finished their dinner and exited the Water Grill. Charles asked, "Would you like me to walk you to your car?"

"No, I'm valet parked over by the museum. Do you need a lift back to your apartment?"

"Thanks, but I think I'll enjoy the walk back. It's a nice night."

Felicia kissed Charles on the cheek. "Thank you for a completely stimulating evening. I can't remember the last time that I enjoyed hearing about the art minimalism movement so much."

He smirked. "Have you ever heard anything about art minimalism before?"

"First time tonight. Good night, Charles. Have a safe and wonderful trip. Please try to enjoy yourself."

"Thank you, Felicia. Good night, my friend."

CHAPTER TWELVE

Mrs. Simon scoured the newspapers and other media outlets for several days. She had hoped to find news of a poisoning at the Water Grill. Sorely disappointed, she plotted her next move.

"Hello, this is Donna Hightower."

"Hello, Ms. Hightower. Are you with Strom Travel Agency?"

"Yes. May I ask who's calling?"

"My name is Mrs. Simon. I was hoping you could help me plan a trip."

"I'll certainly do my best. Can you tell me how you got my name?"

"Yes, I was attending a lecture the other night and overheard a conversation on what sounded like a fabulous cruise. A gentleman said that you were the travel agent who put together a trip for him."

"I see. Were you interested in taking a cruise?"

"Yes. But not just any cruise. I want to take the same cruise that you arranged for this gentleman."

"OK. Did he happen to mention the itinerary or the cruise line?"

"I didn't catch the cruise line, but I did hear him say that he was sailing from LA to Sydney, Australia."

"Let me check my computer. Can you give me a few seconds?"

"Of course. I heard the man's name, but I can't remember it."

Donna checked her list of travel bookings. "Yes, here it is. It's a Sterling Cruise that initiates in Los Angeles on January twenty-second and ends in Sydney, Australia, February twentieth. Yes, a Mr. Pierce has booked that cruise. Please excuse me. That was a slip. I try to protect the privacy of my clients."

"Not a problem. I didn't hear you say a name anyway."

"Thank you, Mrs. Simon. Do you want me to work up the costs and itinerary and get back to you?"

"That would be wonderful. Thank you."

Mrs. Simon heard Donna tap her computer screen with a pen. "As I recall, I was able to get my other client a pretty sweet deal. Is the number you called me from the best one to reach you?"

"Yes."

"Very well. I'll be in touch soon."

"Thank you."

Mrs. Simon set her phone down on the table next to her. If she couldn't get Charles before January 22, then she would have a month aboard the ship to kill him. That would be especially dangerous. She knew she had to be patient. Surely she would have more chances to get him before the cruise. It would make life so much simpler. Maybe she could lure him from the Wine Therapist to a more discreet location. *This time, though, I'm going straight for the kill. He needs to burn in hell.*

Mrs. Simon placed a call to Frank.

"Hello, Frank Austin speaking."

"Frank, this is Jamie Simon."

"Well, hello, Mrs. Simon. How are you doing?"

"Fine, Frank. I may have some work for you. Is this a convenient time to talk?"

"Sure. Shoot."

"Frank, do you know any reliable, high-class prostitutes?"

There was a pause on the other end of the line. "Mrs. Simon, did you say prostitutes?"

"Yes. I need someone to lure the target to another location. That's why I thought of a prostitute. She needs to be very upscale, beautiful, and smart to appeal to the target."

Frank rubbed his brow. "Let me do some research. I'm sure I can find someone appropriate. Mrs. Simon, I must be honest with you. Please understand that I cannot be involved in perpetrating any crime. It would cost me my license."

"Yes, Frank. I understand. The woman you find for me will not be a party to any crime either. I can promise you that."

"When do you need this person?"

"Just as soon as possible."

"OK. I'll be in touch."

"Thanks, Frank."

"Goodbye, Mrs. Simon."

"Goodbye, Frank."

CHAPTER THIRTEEN

"Hello?"

"Is this Mrs. Simon?"

"Yes."

"This is Donna Hightower at Strom Travel."

"Hello, Donna."

"I have some excellent news for you. Do you remember that I told you I was able to get my other client a wonderful deal on the LA-to-Sydney cruise?"

"Yes."

"I did a little arm-twisting, and I was able to get you the same deal if you're interested. There's only one drawback. You need to decide very quickly and pay the entire cost this week."

"Yes. Of course. Not a problem at all."

"Wonderful. I'll email you the information and requisite forms. Please complete them and email them back to me. I'll take care of the rest."

Mrs. Simon gave Donna her email address and hung up. She thought a monthlong cruise might be nice even if she was successful in killing Charles Pierce before then. If not, she would have a whole month on board to get the task done.

She called Frank Austin.

"Good afternoon, Mrs. Simon. I was just getting ready to call you. I have someone I think might be perfect for the assignment we discussed."

"Excellent, Frank."

"Are you available to come to my office tomorrow afternoon to meet her?"

"Yes, Frank. What time?"

"How about two o'clock?"

"I'll be there."

* * *

AT 2:00 P.M. THE NEXT DAY, Mrs. Simon pulled her car up to Frank Austin's office. It was a midcentury, one-story brick building located in an industrial part of the city, surrounded on both sides by car repair shops. Frank's dad was a dentist, and he'd had his practice in this building for over thirty years before the neighborhood started to take a turn for the worse. Mrs. Simon parked her car and pressed a buzzer next to the door. A woman's voice over the intercom said, "Hello, Mrs. Simon. Please come in." A latch clicked, unlocking the door.

Mrs. Simon entered the reception area and was greeted by Vonda, Frank's secretary. "Good afternoon, Mrs. Simon. Frank is waiting for you in the conference room."

Frank ushered Mrs. Simon into the room. Seated at the table was a striking blonde woman. She was conservatively dressed in slacks, a matching jacket, and a white blouse. The woman stood up from the table when Mrs. Simon entered the room. She was almost six feet tall and towered over both Frank and Mrs. Simon. The woman resembled a slightly older version of the actress Blake Lively.

"Mrs. Simon, this is Jennifer Riverton."

Ms. Riverton extended her hand toward Mrs. Simon, who ignored the gesture. She said, "Hello, Ms. Riverton."

After they were all seated, Frank said, "I think Ms. Riverton might be perfect for the assignment you have in mind, Mrs. Simon. I don't know all the specifics, but I generally briefed her that it would involve her seducing a man and luring him to a public location. I assured her that she would not be in any danger or involved in any criminal activity. That is the extent of what I know. Ms. Riverton indicated to me that she might be interested if she is paid her hourly fee for five hours, regardless of how long it takes to accomplish her task."

Mrs. Simon stared at Ms. Riverton for a few moments. "May I ask what your hourly fee is?"

Ms. Riverton said in a firm but quiet tone, "Two thousand dollars an hour."

"So your fee would be a total of ten thousand dollars for five hours of work?"

"Yes. But I expect that I can seduce your target in less than an hour."

Mrs. Simon sneered. "You seem pretty sure of yourself."

Ms. Riverton cracked a slight smile. "Mrs. Simon, I was born to seduce. I have honed these skills to perfection. My profession demands flawlessness, and I deliver."

Frank cleared his throat. "Ms. Riverton comes highly recommended."

"I'm sure she does," Mrs. Simon replied sarcastically. "The target in this assignment is a prominent lawyer. He's sharp enough to see through a sham even if he has had too much to drink. If he suspects that you're a…" Mrs. Simon paused. "Do I make myself clear?"

"*Prostitute* is the word that I believe you intended to use. Mrs. Simon, I don't think you have a clue what I do. My clients are the one-percenters in the world. They are successful, wealthy men and women. I provide them the type of service that they deserve and expect. Your prominent attorney most likely would not even make the cut for me to consider him as a client. Do I make *myself* clear?"

Frank was uncomfortable with the direction of the conversation. "May I get either of you ladies a bottle of water or a soft drink?"

Ms. Riverton said, "I'd love a glass of champagne."

Mrs. Simon said, "Make that two."

Frank stood up. "Yes, I believe we do have some champagne in the kitchen." He walked down the hall and retrieved a bottle of Dom Perignon from the refrigerator and three glasses. He reentered the conference room. Both women were checking emails on their phones. "Not only do I have champagne, but I have Dom Perignon," he said. "I was saving it for a special occasion. This seems like as good a time as any."

He popped the cork and filled three glasses full.

"Thank you, Frank," Ms. Riverton said. "You're quite a gentleman."

Mrs. Simon focused her attention on Ms. Riverton. "Ms. Riverton, would you care to hear the details of the assignment?"

"Yes. Thank you."

"Frank has thoroughly investigated the target, Charles Pierce. He can give you all the background on him. I won't get into any of those details." She turned to Frank. "Feel free to share all of Pierce's information with Ms. Riverton. I will sign any release you require."

"Of course, Mrs. Simon."

Mrs. Simon continued. "One of Pierce's favorite haunts is a wine bar downtown called the Wine Therapist. Have you ever heard of it?"

"No. My clients tend to frequent places like the Mansion."

"Frank will give you all the details. Pierce goes to the Wine Therapist on Thursday afternoons around four o'clock. I want you to wait outside just before then. There's a small park across the street with benches, so you can sit if you have a long wait. Frank has photos of Pierce, so you'll know what he looks like. After he has been inside for about fifteen minutes, I want you to go in and sit next to him. He usually sits in the end chair on the right side of the bar as you face it from the front door."

"How do you know he'll be alone?"

"He's a loser. His wife couldn't stand to live with him. She committed suicide. He's toxic. He's distraught and depressed. No woman is going to be attracted to him."

"I think you're wrong, Mrs. Simon. I'm going to be infatuated with our Mr. Pierce."

"I'm counting on you. My plan is for you to lure Pierce back to the Adolphus Hotel. It's only a few blocks from the wine bar. Tell Pierce to meet you on the second floor in the bar. Wait for him outside the bar, and try not to be conspicuous. He will most likely take the elevator up from the lobby. It's located across from the bar. Meet him as soon as he gets off the elevator, but keep an eye on the bar in case he takes the stairs. I want you to get to him before he gets to the bar. Ask him to go get cocktails for you both, and say that you'll meet him in a cozy area right around the corner. There's a fireplace. If possible, try to have Pierce sit facing the fireplace on the small love seat directly in front of it. I'll make sure no one sits there until you arrive.

"I want you to sit on the love seat next to him. A side table is positioned on each side. Make sure he places his drink on the table next to him. Pierce will either be drinking chardonnay or vodka and soda. After you engage in some 'intimate' conversation, I want you to excuse yourself to go to the ladies' room. I won't tell you how to dress, but I want you to pretend to be an executive. A dark suit would be appropriate."

Ms. Riverton interrupted. "I have a stellar charcoal-gray Armani outfit that will be perfect. The skirt is deliberately tailored short. It exposes just the right amount of thigh. It will have him drooling."

Frank refilled the three glasses.

Mrs. Simon said, "When you stand up to leave for the ladies' room, I want you to do something to distract Pierce. Maybe lean over to pick something up. Just make sure he can't take his eyes off you."

Ms. Riverton took a drink of champagne. "I assure you, that won't be a problem."

"Instead of going to the ladies' room," Mrs. Simon continued, "I want you to walk down the hall past the restrooms. At the end of the hall is another staircase. It leads to an area outside the conference rooms. There's an exit there. Take the exit and disappear. You'll need to visit the Adolphus in advance so that you're familiar with the layout. Make sure it's early in the week so that no one will remember you. You're a stunning woman. However, on the day you scout it out, I want you to wear dark glasses and nonflattering clothing. In other words, I don't want anyone to remember you when you're there with Pierce. With any luck, no one will see you and Pierce together. Any questions so far?"

"Mrs. Simon, I have no doubt that I can pull this charade off without a hitch. But I don't want to be involved in anything illegal. What's going to happen to Pierce?"

Mrs. Simon picked up her glass of champagne and swirled it around in the glass. "Ms. Riverton, you're not going to be involved. You're merely a ghost. As far as anyone is concerned, Pierce left the Wine Therapist alone. Instead of returning to his apartment, he decided to go have a drink at the Adolphus Hotel. Perhaps he wanted to hit on women at the hotel bar. Who knows what a loser like him is up to?"

"Mrs. Simon, there's one more thing." Ms. Riverton set her glass on the table. "I require payment in cash and in advance. Is that going to be a problem?"

Mrs. Simon leaned back in her chair. "What do you think, Frank?"

Frank finished off his champagne. "I think that's pretty much standard procedure. Again, my source speaks very highly of Ms. Riverton."

Mrs. Simon said, "Very well. I will leave ten thousand dollars in a sealed envelope with Frank no later than noon next Wednesday. I assume that's OK with you, Frank?"

Frank said, "Yes, I have a safe in my office."

"Is that satisfactory to you, Ms. Riverton?" Mrs. Simon asked.

"Yes. I assume you would like me to do the assignment the next day, which is Thursday."

"Precisely."

"Perfect. I'll scout out the Adolphus Hotel this Friday afternoon and become familiar with the layout."

CHAPTER FOURTEEN

Friday afternoon at 1:00 p.m., November 10, 2017, Jennifer Riverton valet-parked at the Adolphus Hotel. She drove a black Jaguar F-Type. The valet helped her out of the car.

"Are you checking in, ma'am?"

Ms. Riverton was dressed in faded blue jeans, a white blouse, and a sport coat. A pair of tinted glasses shielded her face. Her blonde hair was pulled back in a ponytail.

"No, I'm just meeting a friend. I won't be long."

The valet said, "I'll keep her parked out front. Just let me know when you need her."

"Thank you, dear."

A doorman held the door open for Ms. Riverton. She was used to this drill. She familiarized herself with the lobby, elevator placement, and staircases. She took the main elevator to the second floor. Just as Mrs. Simon indicated, it was situated across from a bar. She walked over and peered into the bar. Two men were seated at the bar, each drinking a beer. Ms. Riverton made her way to the fireplace around the corner. *There's the love seat, perched in front of the fireplace. Poor guy is going to be so disappointed when I don't return from the ladies' room.* She backtracked, taking the course Mrs. Simon described. She passed the restrooms. At the end of the hall, she descended the staircase that led to an area outside two conference rooms. She noted a small bank of telephones that lined one of the walls next to the side exit. Satisfied that she had the layout down pat, she returned to the lobby and exited through the front door. The valet saw her and sprinted for her Jaguar.

This should be a piece of cake, Ms. Riverton said to herself.

CHAPTER FIFTEEN

Charles finished paying his last bill online. He checked the clock at the lower-right side of his computer screen. It was already almost 4:00 p.m. Charles wanted to go see Rachel. He hadn't left his apartment in two days. He felt the need to get out and be sociable. Charles slipped on a pair of jeans, a light-blue dress shirt—left over from when he used to practice law—and a tweed sport coat. It was a cool day downtown. The tall buildings shielded the streets below from the sun for much of the day. He arrived at the Wine Therapist and opened the door.

Unlike most Thursdays, there were a few people seated at the bar. They appeared to be together and were congregated at the left end. Rachel was standing in front of them, holding court. She and Charles made eye contact as he slid onto a chair at the other end. He pulled out his phone and began to scroll through his email.

Rachel said, "You're not going to get out of giving me a hug by pretending to be checking your email."

Charles laughed. "Rachel, you won't believe this, but your hug is always the highlight of my day."

They hugged. She said, "Let me get you a glass of chardonnay. I suspect that it will then be the highlight of your day."

She placed an empty glass in front of Charles and poured her usual generous amount of wine. He glanced at the label on the bottle. "I see you're still serving the Renaldo."

"Today is the last day," Rachel said. "I'm down to my last two bottles. I'll have to spring something new on you next time." She walked back and returned the bottle to the refrigerator.

Charles picked up his phone from the bar counter and resumed checking his email. The door to the Wine Therapist resonated with the usual scraping sound. He did not bother to check to see who came in.

The conversation at the other end of the bar halted. The woman who strode in wore a dark-gray Armani suit coat, a matching skirt, and a pale-yellow Armani blouse that accentuated her features and her blonde hair. She was five-ten and pure perfection. Confidently, she strolled over to the bar and placed her hand on the back of the chair next to Charles.

Ms. Riverton asked in a hushed tone, "I don't suppose anyone is sitting here?"

Charles looked up from his phone and almost fainted. *My God, she is otherworldly stunning.* He managed to say, "No. No one is sitting there." Charles could smell a hint of her perfume as she sat down. She set her purse to her left on the bar top. It partly screened her from the people at the other end of the bar. He looked over at Rachel. She slowly started to walk in their direction.

"Would you like to see a wine menu?" Rachel asked.

Ms. Riverton peeked at Charles's glass. "No. I think I'll have a glass of chardonnay—one with a hint of oak, if you have it."

Rachel cast a glance in Charles's direction and smiled. He

knew what Rachel was thinking. *Charles, you schmuck. You're already infatuated, and this poor unsuspecting woman only wants a glass of wine.* Rachel returned with the bottle of Renaldo and showed her the label. Rachel said, "This is a nice oak chardonnay. It's what the gentleman sitting next to you is drinking."

Ms. Riverton turned and looked into Charles's eyes. She smiled slightly. "Well, then, I'm sure it will be lovely."

Rachel poured her a glass and returned to the other end of the bar.

Ms. Riverton picked up her wine and turned in her chair to face Charles. "Cheers," she said.

He picked up his glass. "Cheers. How do you like it?" he asked as she sipped.

She swirled it in her mouth. "Well, it's no Rombauer, but it does have a strong oak finish." The woman set her glass on the bar top and gazed at Charles. Her blue eyes sparkled, and he noticed the outfit she was wearing. Her suit was flawless and tailored to conform to her figure. She crossed her legs, which revealed more of her right thigh.

Charles wanted to just sit there and stare at her but searched for something to say. "So you're a wine connoisseur?"

Ms. Riverton said, "In my profession, you have to wear many hats."

"May I ask what you do for a living?"

She smiled. "Let's just say I'm in executive sales. What do you do?"

Charles took a drink of chardonnay. "I'm retired."

She ran her eyes up and down Charles's body. "You look much too young to be retired."

"Well, I'm an attorney. I soured on the kind of law that

I practiced. After a trial defending an insurance company, I decided that I couldn't stomach that type of work anymore."

"I see. How did your family handle that decision?"

"My wife . . ." Charles choked up. "I'm sorry, my late wife wasn't too thrilled with my retirement. Not long after I retired, she took her own life."

Ms. Riverton rested her hand on top of his. He could feel the warmth from her smooth hand. She said, "I'm so sorry for your loss." Charles felt her caress his hand.

"You two doing OK?"

Charles was so distracted, he hadn't noticed that Rachel was now standing in front of him. "Uh, yes, just fine."

Ms. Riverton lifted her hand off his and took a drink of chardonnay. "I'm fine as well," she said.

Rachel smiled. "OK, I'll leave you two alone." She walked to the other end of the bar.

Charles said, "I'm sorry; I still have raw nerves when I mention my wife."

"There's no need for you to apologize. You're quite fortunate that you had a meaningful relationship and that you cared so dearly for your wife. I've never had such a relationship." She gestured with her left hand. He saw she was not wearing a ring.

He thought, *How could a woman this beautiful and charming have never had a meaningful relationship?*

"Are you serious? You've never been in a committed relationship?"

"Well, maybe I had some crushes as a young girl, but not in my adult life. I'm way too committed to my work. Quite frankly, I don't have the time. Besides, I only meet jerks. They think because I'm beautiful that I'm an airhead and vulnerable to their juvenile passes. I can't tell you how many guys I've had to kick in the balls."

Charles laughed. "I wouldn't want to get on your bad side. By the way, I'm Charles."

She flipped her blonde hair out of her eyes. "I'm Skylar," she said. "Pleased to meet you, Charles."

"Likewise. Are you from Dallas?"

"No. I'm in town on business. My hotel is just a few blocks away, so I thought I'd get some fresh air. When I saw this place, it seemed charming and quaint, so I decided to come in."

Charles said, "I hope you're not too disappointed with the Wine Therapist. A week would not be complete for me unless I came in here on Thursday afternoon."

Skylar looked down at her wineglass. It was almost empty. "Do they only serve wine here?"

"Yes, just wine and a limited selection of beer."

"I see. It's a little unusual for me, but I would really like a vodka and tonic right now. I don't like to drink alone in a bar because I'm constantly harassed by men. Would you have any interest in meeting me for a drink at my hotel?"

Charles thought, *Did she just ask me to go back to her hotel with her? This only happens to James Bond in the movies. It never happens to me.* "Sure. Do you want to leave now?"

"No. I'll finish my glass of wine and then go back to the Adolphus Hotel. I take it you're familiar with the place?"

"Yes. I've been there on a number of occasions."

"Great. Have another glass of wine and then meet me on the second floor outside the bar. I don't want people here to see us leaving together. They'll just think I'm a hooker. Are you OK with that?"

"Of course. I'll do exactly as you suggest."

"Excellent." Skylar finished off her glass of wine.

"I'll pay for your glass of wine. Rachel will be disappointed if I let you pay for it. She'll think I'm losing my touch."

"OK, Charles. I'll see you in a little while. Please don't tell her that you're meeting me."

"I won't. I promise."

"Goodbye, Charles." In a loud voice for everyone to overhear, she said, "It was nice visiting with you."

"Thank you. You too."

Ms. Riverton glided effortlessly toward the door. All eyes in the bar were watching her every move. Once she had exited, a guy at the other end of the bar shouted, "Hey, buddy, why did you let that one get away?"

Charles did not respond. He was no doubt the kind of jerk that Skylar mentioned usually hit on her.

Rachel came over to him. "Sorry about that guy at the end of the bar. But it did look like you were doing pretty well there."

Charles finished off his glass of wine. "No. We just had a nice visit."

"I assume the gallant Mr. Pierce volunteered to pick up her check."

"Of course. You'd be disappointed if I didn't."

"Let's just say that I would have been super surprised. What's her story, anyway? She's not our usual kind of patron."

"I'll tell you if you will get me one more glass of chardonnay."

Rachel retrieved a bottle of Renaldo from the refrigerator and refilled Charles's glass. "OK, Counselor, what's the scoop?"

"Well, she's in town on business. I don't know what kind of business. She said she was in executive sales."

"Did you get her card?"

"No. I was too infatuated. I was barely even able to speak to her."

Rachel laughed. "You seemed to be doing OK for yourself. I saw her put her hand on top of yours."

"When she did that, I almost hyperventilated."

"See, Charles. It pays sometimes to come into the Wine Therapist."

"I agree."

Rachel left to put the wine bottle back in the refrigerator.

Charles thought, *My God, should I tell Rachel that I'm meeting Skylar at the Adolphus Hotel for drinks? But I promised her that I wouldn't say anything. Besides, what good would come from it?*

Charles nursed his glass of chardonnay for another ten minutes. Rachel brought his bill and he paid it, leaving his usual 30 percent tip. He left the Wine Therapist and started walking in the direction of the Adolphus Hotel. The closer Charles got to the hotel, the more he started to doubt if Skylar was going to meet him there. He was now about half a block shy of the ornate entrance. Valets wearing red jackets were busy parking cars for guests checking in. Charles stopped in his tracks. He wondered why this woman would want to meet him for a drink. Was she just messing with him? Maybe that was how she got her kicks. What did he have to lose? The worst-case scenario was that he would have a cocktail by himself. The best-case scenario… he was not going to go there.

Charles walked up to the front door and entered the lobby. Stepping inside this historic hotel was like going back in time to another era. Although it had been updated over the years, most of the original features had been preserved for generations.

He searched for the elevators. They were to the right of the concierge desk, surrounded by elaborate carved-wood paneling. Charles pushed the brass button and waited. The door to one of the elevators slid open, and he hit the second-floor button. The doors opened and he went inside. Groaning upward, the elevator creaked to a stop on the second floor, and opened its doors. Charles stepped out. The bar was across the room. Neither Skylar nor anyone else was in the immediate area. He started across the room toward the bar.

"Charles."

Charles turned. "Skylar, you're here."

"You seem surprised. Did you think I was going to stand you up?"

"I wouldn't be telling the truth if I said that it didn't cross my mind."

She grabbed his arm, and they headed toward the bar. She stopped right before the entrance. "Charles, I discovered this cozy place around the corner next to a fireplace. Would you mind terribly if we enjoyed our cocktails there instead of in a stuffy old bar?"

"No. Fine with me."

"Would you mind ordering them in the bar and then meeting me there?"

"Sounds like a plan. Did you say earlier you wanted a vodka and tonic?"

"Yes. Please have them add a slice of lime."

"OK. I'll join you in a few minutes."

Charles walked up to the bar and allowed his eyes to adjust to the subdued lighting. One guy was sitting alone at the bar. A woman was sitting next to the wall, looking down at her phone.

There was no one tending bar, so he sat down on a stool. He thought that Skylar was going to be wondering what happened to him. Finally, a man dressed in black appeared from behind a door.

"Sorry for your wait," he said. "May I help you?"

"Yes, I'll have a citron vodka and soda and a vodka tonic with a slice of lime."

The bartender started mixing the drinks. Charles glanced at the man at the end of the bar. He was writing on a legal pad. He was probably an attorney. Who else used legal pads these days? He looked over to the woman next to the wall. She had disappeared. He paid the tab and exited the bar. Skylar had said this quaint little seating area was right around the corner. It was interesting there were so few people on the second floor. *There must be another bar in the lobby where the hordes of guests hang out after their conferences*, he thought. Charles rounded the corner and spotted Skylar's blonde hair from behind. He couldn't believe his eyes as he saw she was sitting on a love seat. He walked up behind her and said, "Madam, your cocktail has arrived."

Skylar whipped her head around. "Just the man I wanted to see. Don't you find this little area so appealing? Please sit down." She patted the seat cushion next to her.

Charles leaned over the back of the love seat and handed Skylar her cocktail. "One vodka and tonic with a slice of lime." He eased into the love seat next to her. Their hips touched in the confined space.

She took a sip of her cocktail. "Hmmm… exactly what I needed."

"Yes, much better than a glass of wine." Charles rested his

cocktail on a coaster sitting next to a stack of books on the side table. "I'm surprised that more guests don't take advantage of the peace and quiet up here." He gestured at the books. "Maybe they come up here to read in front of the fireplace."

She nodded. "I discovered this area the first day I checked in and thought it was so inviting." She crossed her legs, revealing more thigh.

Charles couldn't believe this was happening. He asked, "So how long are you staying in Dallas?"

"Just a few more days, and then I'm off to LA."

Skylar looked down at her cocktail. "I really went through that one. Would you have one more with me?"

"Sure, why not?" Charles guzzled down the rest of his drink. "Let me go get two more."

"Thank you. I promise not to get you drunk." She winked at him.

He was starting to feel the effects of two glasses of wine and the cocktail. The last thing Charles needed was another drink. He stood up from the love seat and carefully ambled back to the bar. The same guy was still sitting there, scribbling on his legal pad.

"Two more?" the bartender asked.

Charles set the empty glasses on the counter. "Yes, please."

He paid the tab and rounded the corner with two more cocktails. Skylar was checking emails on her phone. "One more vodka and tonic with a slice of lime, as you ordered."

Skylar put her phone back into her purse. "Thank you, dear."

Charles slid back onto the love seat next to her. "Did I miss anything?"

"No, it's pretty quiet. Charles, do you mind if I ask you a personal question?"

"No, I don't mind at all."

"Are you seeing anyone?"

He had to let the question register before responding. "Do you mean am I dating anyone?"

"Yes, that's what I meant."

Charles took a sip of his cocktail and placed it next to him. "No. I haven't really tried. Mentally, I'm not ready yet."

Skylar put her right hand on his left leg. "I see. I think you're closer to being ready than you know."

Charles froze.

"Would you excuse me just a few minutes while I go powder my nose in the ladies' room?"

He didn't want her to remove her hand from his leg. "Of course. I'll hold down the fort."

She stood up and straightened her skirt. As she started to step away, she dropped a tissue. They both watched it flutter a few feet in front of her. Charles almost rushed over to pick it up for her. She kneeled to retrieve it, which exposed most of her left thigh up to her buttocks. He was fixated on her. She stayed in that pose for what seemed like an eternity. She finally straightened back up. She flipped her blonde hair and said, "I'll be back in a jiffy."

Charles turned in the love seat and watched her slither away and disappear around the corner. It was already 6:00 p.m. He scrolled through his phone and checked emails and then Facebook. Ten minutes later, he had not touched his cocktail. He suspected that Skylar was not coming back. He convinced himself that she was just messing with him, but he could not fathom her motive. Did she rob him? Panicked, Charles quickly pulled his wallet out of his coat and started thumbing through his cash and credit cards. Nothing was missing.

He stood up and started walking down the hallway toward the restrooms. Twenty minutes had now elapsed since Skylar had left to go to the ladies' room. Charles paused by the restrooms and waited another ten minutes. He decided to go to the men's room. As Charles came out and rounded the corner, an elevator opened, and some people exited. He made his way over to the elevator bank and hit the brass button. As Charles waited for the elevator to arrive, he took a few more steps so that he could see where he and Skylar had been sitting.

A young man dressed in a black shirt and slacks was clearing away their cocktail glasses. He sniffed Charles's glass and took a sip. The elevator doors opened, and Charles hurried over to catch it. A few seconds later, the doors opened in the lobby area. He half expected to see Skylar seducing some other man. But she was nowhere in sight.

Charles started to walk back to his apartment. He thought, *What a strange experience.* He speculated that maybe the woman did plan to rob him, but something spooked her. An ambulance roared past with sirens blaring. Charles looked behind him and saw that it had pulled up in front of the Adolphus Hotel.

CHAPTER SIXTEEN

The next morning, Charles opened the door to his apartment. His newspaper was resting on the carpet just outside. He leafed through it in search of the sports section but stopped when he came to the local news section. A picture of the Adolphus Hotel was on the first page. The headline above the picture read "Adolphus Hotel Employee Found Dead."

Charles thought, *Really? At the Adolphus Hotel?*

The article stated:

> Johnny Ross, a twenty-one-year-old employee, was found dead on the second floor of the iconic Adolphus Hotel. The cause of death is still being investigated by police. They have not ruled out foul play. A guest notified hotel security that a man's body was lying around the corner from the second-floor bar. An emergency medical unit transported Mr. Ross to Parkland Hospital, where he was pronounced dead. An autopsy will be performed to determine the exact cause of death.

Charles instantly remembered that the guy who was clearing their cocktail glasses had taken a sip of his cocktail! Had it been meant for him? Did Skylar try to kill him? He concluded that there was no way she could have spiked his drink. There was no opportunity.

Charles contacted the police. Two hours later, his apartment's concierge called him. "A Detective White and Detective Gonzalez are here to see you."

"Thank you. Please send them up."

Charles opened the door to his apartment and waited at the entrance. The elevator chimed, and the doors rattled open. Two large men in dark suits rounded the corner. "Hello, I'm Charles Pierce. Please come in."

"I'm Detective White, and this is Detective Gonzalez." Both men gave Charles their cards.

"Would you like to sit down over there?" Charles asked, motioning toward the living room.

Detective White sat in a chair, and Detective Gonzalez sat on the couch. Detective Gonzalez began the questioning. "Let's first get a little background. What do you do for a living, Mr. Pierce?"

"I'm a retired attorney."

"What kind of law did you practice?"

"Defense litigation. I exclusively represented insurance companies."

"I see. Are you married?"

"No. My wife passed away."

"You live alone?"

"Yes."

"And you told the nine-one-one operator that you might

have some information relevant to the death that occurred at the Adolphus Hotel yesterday?"

"Correct."

"You were at the Adolphus yesterday?"

"Yes."

"What brought you there on a Thursday afternoon?"

Charles squirmed in his chair. "Well, I met this woman earlier in the afternoon at the Wine Therapist. It's a wine bar down the street. She said she was staying at the Adolphus Hotel, and after we visited for a while, she said she wanted a cocktail. She invited me to meet her at the second-floor bar at the Adolphus Hotel for a drink."

"What was this woman's name?"

"She told me her first name was Skylar, but she never mentioned her last name."

"What did this woman look like?"

"She was astoundingly beautiful. Think an older version of Blake Lively. She was tall, thin, with blonde hair."

The detectives exchanged glances.

Detective Gonzalez said, "No offense, Mr. Pierce, but why do you think she was attracted to you?"

Charles leaned back in his chair. "In retrospect, I doubt she was attracted to me. Now I think she was probably going to rob me or something."

"I take it that she didn't?"

"That's correct."

"Let's focus on what happened at the Adolphus Hotel. Tell us what happened as soon as you arrived, and go from there."

"I entered the lobby and took the elevator up to the second floor. When the doors opened, I saw the bar directly across the floor. Skylar caught up with me from behind and stopped me right before I entered the bar. She said there was a cozy seating area around the corner. Then she suggested that I get us both cocktails and join her there. I did as she suggested. Skylar was sitting on the left side of a love seat opposite the fireplace. I sat down beside her. We engaged in some idle conversation and drank our cocktails. She suggested that I go and get two more cocktails. I did and returned with them. After a few minutes, Skylar said she needed to go to the ladies' room."

Charles decided to tell them about her dropping the tissue. "Before she left, she bent over to pick up a tissue she had dropped. It exposed all of her thigh and part of her butt."

Detective White said, "She gave you an eyeful, huh?"

"Yes. What was strange is that she seemed to linger in that pose forever, although it was probably only a few seconds. I then watched her walk away until she disappeared around the corner."

"Was there anybody else in the area?"

"I saw a woman in the bar when I initially went inside; she was sitting by herself next to the wall. She was gone before I even got my drinks. There was another guy seated at the bar, writing on a legal pad. When I walked around the corner the first time, I saw a woman sitting by herself in another seating area a few feet away from where Skylar and I were sitting. It might have been the same woman. I can't say for certain. She may have been there when Skylar left to go to the restroom. I can't say that for certain. I wasn't paying attention to her."

Detective Gonzalez said, "But no one else was near where you were seated except possibly this woman?"

"Our backs were to the rest of the floor, so I don't really

know. I didn't hear anyone else."

Detective Gonzalez said, "OK. Go ahead."

"Time went by, and Skylar never came back. It finally occurred to me that I had probably been duped. I just didn't know why. Other than a glass of wine at the Wine Therapist and the two cocktails, she got nothing from me."

Detective White asked, "Mr. Pierce, how the hell does this experience relate to the man's death?"

"When I was waiting for Skylar to return, I checked my phone for emails and pretty much did everything to occupy my time except take a drink of my cocktail. This is extremely relevant. Before leaving, I decided to use the restroom first. This took no more than five minutes. Before walking over to the elevators, I peered around the corner to where Skylar and I had been sitting. A young man was clearing our cocktail glasses. He picked up my full glass and sniffed it. Then he took a drink from it. My elevator arrived, so I hurried to catch it. When I read in the newspaper this morning that an employee died on the second floor of the Adolphus Hotel, I was wondering if there might be a connection. Did Skylar or someone spike my drink with poison meant for me, and instead, this poor man was an unintended victim?"

Detective Gonzalez scratched the side of his face. "I see. Did the same bartender make your cocktail each time that you went to the bar?"

"Yes. It was the same guy both times."

"And when you set it down next to you, it was never out of your sight?"

"That's correct."

Detective Gonzalez said, "Mr. Pierce, we're not yet certain

what caused this young man's death. It might not be poisoning. We're going to investigate it as a homicide just the same unless the autopsy rules that out."

"I see."

Detective Gonzalez asked, "You don't have any plans to leave town, do you?"

"Yes, but not for well over a month away."

Detective Gonzalez looked over at Detective White and asked, "Detective, do you have any more questions for Mr. Pierce?"

"No, I think we're OK here. Let's go over to the Adolphus Hotel and question this bartender."

The two detectives stood up and started toward the door. Detective Gonzalez turned back around. "If you think of anything else that might be relevant, give one of us a call."

"Will do. Thank you, Detectives."

CHAPTER SEVENTEEN

Two days later, Charles was reliving the 1970s, listening to vinyl record albums in his apartment, when the phone rang. "Hello?"

"Is this Charles Pierce?"

"Yes."

"Mr. Pierce, this is Detective White. We need you to come down to the police headquarters as soon as possible. Do you know where the main headquarters is located on South Lamar?"

"Uh, yes. Is everything OK?"

"We'll fill you in when you get here."

"I'll be right there."

"Just ask for me or Detective Gonzalez at reception."

Charles pulled his car out on Main Street and hooked a left on South Lamar. It was a short two-mile jaunt to the Dallas Police headquarters. He parked in the area for visitors and pushed the intercom button next to the reinforced glass doors. A voice asked over the intercom, "Can I help you?"

"Yes, I'm here to see Detectives White and Gonzalez." The door buzzed open. Charles walked in, and an officer escorted him through a security metal detector. He pointed to a high counter a few feet away. "That's reception. You can check in there."

Charles stood in front of the counter for several minutes before a woman looked up from her computer screen.

"May I help you?" she asked.

"Yes. I'm here to see Detectives White and Gonzalez. They're expecting me."

"Have a seat over there. I'll let them know you're here."

Ten minutes later, the elevator opened, and Detective White walked over to where Charles was sitting.

He said, "This way; we're going to the fourth floor."

The hall was lined with closed doors. Detective White opened the door to a room marked "3" and slid the cover of a sign next to it to the side, revealing the word *Occupied*. He said, "Have a seat at the table. I'll be back in a few minutes." He shut the door behind him.

The room was painted a faded mint green that used to be so prevalent in hospitals several decades ago. The only furniture was four wooden chairs and a wooden table. Judging by the scars and scuff marks on them, they had been around for a while.

The door opened, and Detectives White and Gonzalez entered the room and closed the door behind them. Detective Gonzalez said, "Thank you, Mr. Pierce, for coming down on short notice."

"Is this an interrogation?"

"Not really. I'm going to read you your Miranda rights, though, because that is standard procedure. You have the right to remain silent. Anything you say can and will be used against you in a court of law. You have the right to have an attorney. If you cannot afford one, one will be appointed to you by the court. With these rights in mind, are you still willing to talk with us?"

Charles paused before answering, "Yes, I'm willing to talk to you."

"We're trying to track down all the information on this Ross homicide," Detective Gonzalez said.

"Homicide? So an autopsy was done?"

Detective Gonzalez ignored Charles's question. "Do you know what ketamine is?"

"Ketamine? Yes, I read about it somewhere."

"It's a drug customarily found in animal clinics. It's used to help calm animals during surgery. A form of it is also used recreationally by humans. It can have a hallucinatory effect. In large quantities, it can be fatal. This Johnny Ross had enough in his system to kill a horse."

"Do you think that was what he drank in my cocktail?"

"We don't know yet. The glass broke when he passed out. The hotel staff threw the shards away before the police arrived."

"Did you question the bartender?"

"Yes. Right now, he's still a person of interest."

"Am I?"

"Mr. Pierce, please let me ask the questions."

"OK. Sorry."

"You're a member of the Nasher Sculpture Center, aren't you?"

"Yes. But what does that have to do with this case?"

"Possibly nothing. But you remember the reception earlier this year when a woman fainted and was rushed to the hospital?"

"Yes. I was there that night."

"I know, but I wanted you to confirm it. A toxicology report revealed that the woman had ketamine in her system. It's her good fortune that it was not a lethal dose."

"That's where I heard about ketamine. I remember reading it in the article in the newspaper. Do you think these cases are related?"

Detective Gonzalez tapped the table with his fingers. "The one common element in both cases is you. We need to determine if that is coincidental or not."

Charles swallowed. "I see."

"Mr. Pierce, had you ever seen the Skylar woman you were with at the Adolphus Hotel before that afternoon?"

"No. When she walked into the Wine Therapist, that was the very first time. You can ask Rachel Wilkens. She manages the bar."

"We have. She corroborated your story. Do you think you would have remembered if this woman had attended the reception at the Nasher Sculpture Center?"

"There are always a lot of beautiful people at those kinds of events. I can assure you, though, if I had seen this woman, I sure as hell would have remembered her."

"What about the woman you mentioned seeing in the bar and then perhaps sitting close to you and the blonde? Do you think you might have seen her at the Nasher Sculpture Center?"

"I didn't get a decent look at her at the Adolphus Hotel."

"Mr. Pierce, have you got any enemies?"

"Enemies? No."

"No one has threatened you at any time over the past year?"

"No."

"The manager at the Wine Therapist told us about a young man you mentioned might be tailing you. What about him?"

"Yes. A man came into the Wine Therapist one afternoon. I recalled that I had seen him that morning in the lobby of my apartment building. When I asked him about it, he denied being there. Then he abruptly left the bar. When I was discussing this with Rachel, I suddenly remembered that I had also seen him at other places I frequent."

"Was he at the Nasher event?"

"I don't remember seeing him there."

"Why do suppose he was tailing you, then?"

"I don't have a clue."

"OK, Mr. Pierce. I think that's all the questions we have for you at this time. Oh, and to answer your question, presently, we don't consider you a person of interest."

"I guess I should be relieved. But somehow I'm not."

"One last thing, Mr. Pierce."

"Yes?"

"Watch your back. It very well could be that someone is out to kill you."

"Yes, Detective. One last question. I'm scheduled to go on a monthlong cruise in January. I assume it's OK that I still go?"

"Yes, unless your status in the investigation changes. What date are you leaving?"

"January twenty-second."

"If you don't hear from us first, give either Detective White or me a call no later than January fifteenth."

"OK, Detective."

CHAPTER EIGHTEEN

At 10:00 a.m. on January 15, 2018, Charles placed a call to Detective Gonzalez.

"Hello. Detective Gonzalez."

"Detective, this is Charles Pierce."

"Yes, Mr. Pierce."

"You asked me to call you a week before I was scheduled to leave on my cruise. Any change in the status of the investigation?"

"We have a few loose ends we're investigating. However, we've had no major breaks in the case. Anything change with you? I assume no one has threatened you since we last talked?"

"No. I've been lying low, just waiting for my trip."

"OK, Mr. Pierce. I don't see any need for you to cancel your trip. You obviously still hae my card. Would you email your contact information for while you're on your trip? I will only contact you if necessary."

"Yes, Detective. You will have it this afternoon."

"Thank you. Goodbye, Mr. Pierce."

* * *

On January 22, 2018, Charles landed in Los Angeles. He

departed the plane and followed the signs to the baggage claim. As soon as he had exited airport security, a whole host of drivers greeted him, holding up signs bearing various people's last names. Charles knew he was supposed to be met by someone from Sterling Cruise, but he assumed he didn't warrant a private driver. He collected his bag from the baggage conveyor belt and then paused to pat himself down to make sure he still had his wallet and passport handy. Charles glanced around to get his bearings. Just to his left, he noticed a woman holding a Sterling Cruise sign and a clipboard visiting with another passenger from his flight.

He walked over to her. "I believe I'm to be entrusted to your care."

"Are you Mr. Pierce?"

"Yes, ma'am, I am."

She made a note on her clipboard. "Excellent. My name is Debra. We're only waiting for one more couple, and then we can catch our transport to the cruise terminal. If you wish, you can wait over there with the rest of our group."

Charles glanced over to where the group was standing. There were ten to twelve people divided into three groups, visiting with one another. He decided to stay where he was and wait for Debra to round up the missing couple. Charles didn't particularly feel like socializing with strangers. For that matter, he didn't even feel like socializing with friends. What friends? The only friend he saw regularly was Rachel. She was a captive audience at the Wine Therapist. Hell, she was required to be nice to him. No, it was just Charles and Sam Spade against the world. He watched Debra as she walked around the baggage claim, waving her sign as passengers exited the security turnstile.

Finally, a couple approached her, pushing a cart loaded with several enormous bags.

When they came closer, Debra said, "Mr. and Mrs. Dunning, this is Mr. Pierce. He will be a fellow passenger on your cruise."

Mr. Dunning and Charles shook hands.

Charles said, "Nice to meet you, folks."

"Are you traveling alone, Mr. Pierce?"

"Most definitely. I always travel alone. It allows me to do everything I want to do and, more importantly, nothing that I don't want to do, if that makes sense."

Mr. Dunning nodded in agreement. "I hear you."

Mrs. Dunning shot him a glance to show her disapproval. They joined the group and proceeded to introduce themselves. There was only one other person who appeared to be traveling alone, a gray-haired woman wearing tinted glasses. Debra led the group to an exit marked "Ground Transportation." A bus was waiting for them a few yards away, and they all boarded it for a short drive to the ship terminal.

When Charles entered the terminal with bags in tow, a woman wearing a crisp white uniform with "Sterling Cruise" imprinted on her badge came up to meet him. She handed him a slip of paper with "9" printed on one side.

She pointed across the room. "We're boarding in groups. Please take a seat over in that section and wait for your number to be called."

The terminal was a huge, single-story building with row after row of folding chairs facing several tables centered at the front of the room. A Sterling Cruise banner was centered over the tables. Charles walked over to where the woman had instructed him to wait and settled down in a vacant row with his luggage. A few minutes passed, and then he saw a man grab a microphone from one of the tables at the front.

"Ready for group five. Please proceed to the front desk with your passports and cruise tickets."

About thirty people from the middle of the room made their way up to the front table and waited in a single-file line. Charles closed his eyes. He wondered how long this whole process was going to take. He unzipped the front pocket of his carry-on bag and pulled out his tablet. Quickly, he checked his email. Nothing there. Charles closed his email and hit the books app. Several new books surfaced, which he had added prior to his flight. They were all critically reviewed as "suspenseful" or "spellbinding." He was thankful that he had downloaded a ton of books. Charles didn't know why, though. Would he actually read them?

CHAPTER NINETEEN

An announcement from the front of the room interrupted Charles's train of thought.

"We are now ready for group eight. Please proceed to the front desk with your passports and cruise tickets. Thank you."

Charles's fingers fumbled to retrieve his number from his shirt pocket. It was nine, all right—he hadn't missed it. He looked around at his fellow passengers. They were predominantly people ranging in age from sixty to ninety. A few people could pass for younger, but that could also be attributed to having the finest cosmetic surgery that money could buy. To afford this cruise, money had to be of little concern—at least to everyone except Charles. The cost of this cruise would put a significant dent in his retirement fund.

A woman sat down in front of Charles's row and adjusted her luggage to her side. She appeared to be alone. As she turned her head, he noticed a streak of blue carefully positioned on one side of her otherwise brunette mane of hair. She was thin and probably in her midfifties. He liked her sense of style. What was her story? Why was she traveling?

Once again, the man at the front of the room picked up the

microphone. "We're now ready for group nine to come forward with your passports and cruise tickets."

Charles rose to his feet, along with the woman with the blue streak and several other people, including a woman wearing sunglasses keeping an eye on Charles. They made the short trek up to the desk at the front of the room and obediently lined up single file. Charles happened to be positioned three people back from the front and behind the woman with the blue streak. A mere few minutes later, the woman with the blue streak approached the table. She handed her passport and cruise ticket to one of the women seated at the table.

"Good afternoon, and welcome aboard."

"Thank you. I can't believe I'm going to be on a ship for over a month, though."

"I'll take your passport for safekeeping. Please make your way over to your right, and that gentleman will take your photo."

The woman with the blue streak posed for her photo and then proceeded down a corridor that led to the ship. Charles approached the woman at the table, surrendered his passport, had his photo taken, and walked down the corridor. This was his last chance to change his mind. Charles felt like he was getting ready to walk the plank. He needed a drink.

The boarding experience was a memorable event. The crew members, attired in their dress whites, made sure everyone was properly greeted. The concierge area of the ship was decorated in brightly colored balloons and fresh flowers. A string quartet was playing. Champagne was abundant and served by white-gloved attendants. The sights, sounds, and scurry of activity almost overwhelmed the senses. As soon Charles entered the concierge area, he was handed a glass of champagne by one attendant while another one took his luggage from him. The attendant with Charles's luggage in tow took him over to a desk, where he was presented with a plastic room key. Another attendant then escorted him to a stateroom and showed him all the amenities. Every action was seamlessly orchestrated. As soon as the attendant left, the doorbell rang, and a young male attendant cracked open the door.

"Mr. Pierce, I have your luggage."

"Great."

He placed both of Charles's bags on the protective covering on the bed.

"Would you like me to help you unpack?"

"No, I can handle that. Thanks."

He bowed his head. "Please let us know if you need anything at all. Just dial zero on your phone."

"Thank you. I will."

Charles spent the better part of the afternoon getting unpacked and acquainted with his surroundings. He investigated the amenities on the ship. Although he knew it was a small ship in terms of passengers, he was surprised that he didn't see more people milling about. He guessed they must still be unpacking. Charles took an elevator up to the twelfth floor at the front of the ship. As he suspected, there was a quaint lounge overlooking the bow. A handful of people were seated at various cocktail tables surrounding a dance floor. He spotted a bar at the other end of the lounge. It was empty. Perfect. He could enjoy a glass of chardonnay by himself.

As soon as Charles relaxed on a stool, a young man behind the bar approached him. "Good afternoon, sir. What may I get for you?"

"Good afternoon. Do you stock a lovely oak chardonnay?"

He retrieved a bottle from a refrigerator under the bar and poured just enough in Charles's glass for him to taste. "See if you like this one."

Charles did the obligatory sniff test, then sipped enough to swirl around his palate, emulating a true connoisseur. "This is fine. Thanks."

The young man filled the remainder of his glass. "Are you on the ship for the entire cruise to Sydney?"

Charles winced. "Yes, I'm a little concerned about all the days at sea."

"There will be lots of activities to keep you occupied. And besides, there are many onboard bars to explore."

They both laughed.

"Well, I guess I can always occupy my time drinking, if nothing else."

The young man introduced himself. "I'm Marvin Thursby, the early evening bartender."

Charles extended his hand. "I'm Charles Pierce, reluctant passenger, retired attorney, and imaginary partner of Private Detective Sam Spade."

Marvin looked at him, puzzled. "Did you say you're an imaginary partner with someone?"

Charles chuckled. "Yes, you said your last name was Thursby, correct?"

Marvin hesitated before answering. "Yes, I'm Marvin Thursby."

"Any kin to a Floyd Thursby?"

Marvin shook his head. "Not that I am aware. Why do you ask?"

With as somber a tone as Charles could muster, he said, "Well, it's possible that Floyd Thursby murdered Sam's prior partner."

Marvin seemed to hang on every one of his words. "Did you say murder?"

"Ever read *The Maltese Falcon*?"

Marvin shook his head. "No."

"Well, it's a book written by Dashiell Hammett in the 1930s about Sam Spade, a hard-boiled private detective in San Francisco. Sam and his partner, Miles Archer, are hired by a beautiful woman to tail a man named Floyd Thursby. Just a few sentences into the second chapter, Sam is notified by the police that Archer was found murdered. Thursby is the logical murder suspect because he was the man targeted to be trailed by Archer. You and Floyd share the same last name. That's why I asked if you were related to him. For all I know, Floyd Thursby may be innocent. I'm only a couple of chapters into the book."

Marvin appeared relieved by Charles's explanation. "You had me going there, asking whether one of my relatives had committed a murder."

He took a drink of his chardonnay. "I apologize. I shouldn't have kidded you. I guess you encounter all types of people on board, though, don't you?"

Marvin grinned. "It never gets boring."

Marvin went to wait on a woman who had drifted into the lounge and perched on a seat across the bar from Charles. It was the woman who had kept an eye on Charles in the terminal. She was confident that Charles would not recognize her. Afterall, it had been a long time since he cross examined her at the trial involving her husband's denied insurance claim. Charles watched as Marvin made her a vodka and tonic. While Marvin talked with the woman, he finished his glass of chardonnay. Before he could move from his stool, Marvin glanced back at him.

"Charles, would you like another glass?"

Charles stood up. "No thanks. I've caused you enough trouble for one day. But I will keep you posted on whether or not this Thursby fellow is the culprit."

Marvin saluted Charles as he walked away from the bar. Mrs. Simon watched out of the corner of her eye. Marvin turned back around to face his only patron. "Did you just board?"

"Yes. My butler is unpacking my clothes, so I decided to do a little exploring of the ship."

"Butler? You must be in one of the penthouse suites?"

"Yes. I decided to splurge."

"I can assure you that you will be well cared for. By the way, my name is Marvin."

"Hello, Marvin." Mrs. Simon was careful not to tell Marvin her name. "Tell me, Marvin, what was that gentleman drinking?"

Marvin walked over to the refrigerator and removed a bottle of chardonnay and brought it to where Mrs. Simon was seated. "This is a very oak-driven chardonnay."

"What kind is it? I don't have my reading glasses."

"It's a 2016 Markham Chardonnay from Napa Valley."

"I see. Is this type of chardonnay served throughout the ship? In other words, if I asked my butler to stock my refrigerator, would he automatically bring the Markham?"

"No, ma'am. We stock all types of wine and replenish the stock each time we are docked in port. Excuse me."

Marvin left Mrs. Simon to wait on a couple who had arrived

at the bar.

I must find a way to get to Pierce's wineglass or bottle without raising suspicion, Mrs. Simon thought. She finished off her drink and left the Panorama Lounge. *Where's your stateroom, Pierce?*

* * *

THE FIRST NIGHT ON BOARD was uneventful. Charles decided to dine alone on the pool deck, which featured casual food. It was a brisk night—the ship was sailing out of Los Angeles in January. Fortunately, he had packed a pullover sweater at the last minute. Because the ship was sailing to the South Pacific, Charles assumed he would be wearing nothing but shorts and T-shirts during the day. He downed a tasty dinner consisting of spaghetti Bolognese and two glasses of zinfandel. One of the many perks of an all-inclusive cruise was that all the food and drink was free. When you were finished with dinner, you simply stood up and left. Charles set his napkin down on the table, rose, and walked away. When he reached his stateroom, there was an envelope in the mail slot just to the left of his door. He entered his room, closed the door, and opened the envelope. A simple but elegantly embossed card read:

> Dear Mr. Pierce,
> You are cordially invited to join fellow single guests aboard for cocktails tomorrow at 5 p.m. in the Panorama Lounge, 12th floor.

Charles hadn't been on board a day yet, and he had already been outed as a single loser.

He got ready for bed and read several more chapters of *The Maltese Falcon*.

Charles set down his tablet and closed his eyes. The gentle rocking of the ship sailing through calm waters was extremely therapeutic. He quickly fell asleep.

CHAPTER TWENTY

Charles slipped a charcoal-gray tie over a crisp white dress shirt and began the process of tying a knot. He couldn't remember the last time he had worn a tie. Probably to some funeral. He smirked at his reflection. It was not perfect, but it looked OK. He glanced down at his phone. It was already 5:10 p.m.

Charles left his room on the ninth floor and walked down the narrow passageway to the closest exit, which led to a bank of elevators and a staircase. He decided to use the stairs. It would take him longer to get to the reception on the twelfth floor and slightly postpone the agony of the inevitable. When he reached the twelfth floor, he could feel his heart pounding from the minor physical exertion it took to climb the three flights.

The sound of a string quartet wafted through the air. When Charles entered, he was greeted by the ship's social director, dressed in her formal white uniform. She welcomed him, and then a young staff person carrying a tray full of champagne glasses offered him one. He thanked her and took one off her tray. Charles tried to get his bearings. How would Sam Spade handle this reception? He no doubt would be dangling a freshly rolled Bull Durham cigarette from his lips, scoping out the scene.

There were approximately twenty people in attendance, evenly divided between men and women. Charles noticed, though, when he got closer to the group, that all the men except him were wearing Sterling Cruise name tags. When he approached the group, he made eye contact with a blonde woman in her late fifties.

She said, "Well, you must be a *real* single guy." Charles must have had a befuddled look on his face. "You're not wearing a name tag," she clarified.

Unsure as to how to respond, he just stared down at the empty lapel on his suit coat. One of the gentlemen came to his rescue. "All the men here are employees of Sterling. One of our many duties on board is to serve as dancing partners for any single women—or women whose spouses are incapable of dancing. Sir, you appear to be the only single man on board who is not an employee of Sterling. You're going to enjoy your cruise!"

Startled by this conversation, Charles took a huge swig of his champagne.

The blonde woman tugged at his sleeve. "I'm Ann. Don't worry; I don't bite. I'm just having a little fun."

He recovered a bit. "Nice to meet you. I'm Charles Pierce." He had identified what he thought was an Australian accent. "Are you from Australia?"

She sneered. "No, I'm from New Zealand."

Charles countered by smiling. "Well, close enough. Down Under. That sort of thing." Sam Spade would approve of his smart-aleck response.

Ann said, "Excuse me," and turned her back to Charles to

speak to a woman behind her. He thought she was probably warning her not to speak to him. Ann was wearing a white evening gown with a plunging back that revealed a tattoo consisting of four stars. *Isn't that part of the New Zealand flag? Why would anyone get part of a flag tattooed on their back?* he wondered.

When Ann turned back around, Charles said, "I like your tattoo." That was a lie. He generally hated tattoos.

"Oh, my precious stars! They are lovely and only revealed with certain clothing—or when I am nude, of course." She smiled at her own statement.

"Are they intended to represent the stars on the New Zealand flag?"

"You're very observant."

"No, not really. I would have guessed the Australian flag if I didn't already know you were from New Zealand."

Ann looked displeased. "What do you do for a living?"

"I used to practice law."

She quickly shot back, "Criminal law?"

"Far from it. These days, though, I'm Sam Spade's imaginary partner." Charles had no idea why he repeated that inane business about his imaginary partnership. Ann stared at him, thinking he was either a lunatic or an ass.

"Good evening, Mr. Pierce," she said.

She abruptly turned and walked away. He watched as her stars jiggled with every step she took. Charles thought that he must have really offended her for her to address him by his last name. He'd always had such a suave way with women. He was the antithesis of Sam Spade—in that regard, anyway. It would be a close call in a drinking contest, though.

Charles gazed around at the crowd. Some people were already leaving the lounge. He also noticed that Marvin Thursby was tending bar.

Charles joined Marvin at the bar. "Good evening, Sir Charles. A glass of chardonnay?"

Charles laughed at the way Marvin addressed him. "Sir, huh? I like that. And I like that you used my first name. To your question, though. No, I want something a little stronger. How about a citron vodka and soda?"

He watched as Marvin meticulously mixed his drink. A woman also watched. She wanted to see what type of drink that Charles had ordered. Marvin set his cocktail on a napkin in front of him and asked, "How's your evening going?"

"Except for offending my fellow passengers, it's going great. How about you?"

"Every day at sea is wonderful!"

Charles took a sip of his cocktail. "I suspect you answer that question the same way every time."

Marvin nodded.

"Well, Marvin, I've got some good news and some bad news for you." The smile suddenly left his face. "Your namesake, Thursby, from *The Maltese Falcon*, probably is not a suspect for the murder of Sam's partner." Marvin listened politely. "Let's put it this way. Whether or not he was a suspect, the point is kind of moot now. You see, Floyd Thursby ended up dead himself."

Marvin grinned. "Well, I'm sorry my 'relative' only made a cameo appearance in your book. So who is the murderer, then?"

Charles took another taste of his cocktail. "Not sure yet. Too early in the book. I suspect the beautiful woman must be involved in some way, though. She's too mysterious."

"Mysterious in what way?"

He took one last drink from his now-empty glass and set it down on the bar counter. "I can't put my finger on it. But mysterious."

Marvin grabbed Charles's glass. "Well, maybe she's the murderer. Or perhaps a relative of hers is the murderer—similar to how Thursby is a relative of mine. Care for a refill?"

Charles shook his head. "No, thanks. I need to go to dinner. I'll keep you posted as the plot thickens." He rose from his stool.

"Good night, Sir Charles."

He playfully saluted Marvin the way he had saluted him the night before. "Good night, Mr. Thursby."

A server approached Mrs. Simon's table. "Would you care for another glass of chardonnay?"

Mrs. Simon said, "No. I want to be adventuresome. Tell you what. I just saw a gentleman leave the bar. Would you ask the bartender to make me the same cocktail he was drinking?"

"Yes, ma'am."

The server took another order before returning to the bar. She said, "Marvin, I have a strange order request."

"Let me guess. Someone wants a tequila sunrise?"

"No. Stranger than that. She wants whatever you served a man who was sitting at the bar earlier."

"Really? I guess she means the guy who just left. I made him a citron vodka and soda."

Mrs. Simon had her back to the bar. She pretended to be applying makeup but was observing the exchange between Marvin and the server through her compact mirror.

The server brought Mrs. Simon her cocktail and placed it on a napkin before her.

"Thank you, dear. What kind of cocktail am I getting ready to enjoy?"

"It's a citron vodka and soda. The same cocktail that Marvin made earlier for the gentleman."

Mrs. Simon sniffed her drink. *So Pierce still drinks vodka,* she thought. *Not much of a smell, though. I wonder if he could smell ketamine in it?*

CHAPTER TWENTY-ONE

Charles's dinner reservation was for 7:00 p.m. He checked his phone for the time. It was 6:45 p.m. When he arrived, there were hordes of couples in all shapes and sizes waiting in front of the maître d' station. He was already regretting his decision to dine there. Much to his surprise, the staff hurriedly and efficiently seated everyone in front of him. When Charles approached the station, the maître d', dressed in a black tuxedo, addressed him. "You must be Mr. Pierce."

"Yes, I am," he replied, slightly startled.

Without hesitation, he motioned to one of the female staff members. "Please escort Mr. Pierce to table 911."

They walked the length of the enormous dining room. He felt like a show pony. Everyone seemed to be staring at him. When they reached a table set for two, his escort said in what he believed to be an Eastern European accent, "This is your table, Mr. Pierce." She pulled out a chair for him.

Charles sat down. "Is this referred to as table nine-eleven, or table nine-one-one?" She stared at him with a puzzled look. "I'm sorry. I was attempting to make a joke. Nine-one-one is the number you call in the States when there's an emergency."

She did not understand his attempt at humor. "Your server

will be right with you," she replied, then walked away. *Well, that was an inauspicious start to dinner*, he thought.

The waiter arrived with a menu, and the sommelier showed up with a bottle of Chablis and a bottle of pinot noir. Without even perusing the menu, Charles selected the Chablis. When the waiter returned, he ordered, then leaned back in his chair and surveyed the dining room. From his vantage point, he could see at least half of it. At first, he did not recognize any familiar faces, either from his boarding experience or from the reception for single passengers that he had attended.

Then Charles spotted Ann walking alongside another woman. He watched as a staff member seated them at a table for six. Judging by their body language, they did not appear to know the folks who were already seated. During his dinner, he continually studied his fellow diners. Although most were his age or older, all ages from about the midforties up were represented. There sure were a lot of obese people, though. That was probably the norm for these cruises. *I'll likely be obese myself by the time I arrive in Sydney. Not only a functional alcoholic, but an obese functional alcoholic.*

While Charles was lost in thought about people's shapes and sizes, his waiter returned to the table. "Care for any dessert this evening?"

How timely! "No. I'll pass tonight, thank you."

He rose from his chair and cast a glance over at Ann's table. Ann was talking with the man seated next to her. He exited the dining room and started toward the elevators to return to his room. Then Charles changed his mind and decided to explore a new bar on the ship. Marvin said there were several. He walked over to a diagram of the ship's layout, listing all the features, that he remembered seeing on his way to the dining room. He reviewed the assorted options. *Let's see. There's one called the Saloon on the seventh deck. That should do nicely.*

Charles took the elevator to the seventh deck, and after a few wrong turns, he came across a dark, cozy, wooden bar. The swinging doors to the bar were a twenty-first-century interpretation of the saloon doors seen in old western movies. He pushed his way through the doors and headed to an empty stool at the bar. A man dressed in a tuxedo was playing the piano on the other side of the room. Small clusters of people were seated at tables surrounding the piano.

He was surprised there were not more people. They were most likely attending the performance in the Stars Lounge. He remembered reading in the ship's daily newspaper that the Sterling Cruise Orchestra was performing show tunes. Yet another reason to be in a bar instead. Charles ordered a citron vodka and soda and proceeded to check the email on his phone. The internet service out on the ocean was almost nonexistent. He stared at his phone screen for several minutes, trying to will it to retrieve his email. Frustrated, he gave up and slipped it back into his jacket pocket.

While Charles was occupied with his phone, he had not noticed that several people had joined him at the bar. Almost all the seats were now full. A rotund bald man, who appeared to be in his thirties was the center of attention. He was wearing a black suit appropriate for formal nights on a cruise. But he was also clad in a dark-red shirt, which accentuated his round physique. One woman to his left said, "Hey, Jasper, do that trick for everyone where you make all the suits of cards disappear.,"

Jasper took a sip from his cocktail and asked, "Does everyone want to see the vanishing-cards trick?"

He was greeted with a unanimous chorus of yeses from those within earshot. All eyes at the bar were glued on Jasper. He pulled a deck of cards out of his coat pocket. He held out the deck in the palm of his hand. "Could I ask someone to please examine the deck to make sure it's a complete deck of fifty-two cards?"

A man leaned forward and took the cards from Jasper's hand. He turned them over and inspected each one. Once he was satisfied, he placed the cards on the bar and shuffled them. He then handed the deck back to Jasper. "They look legitimate to me."

"Thank you, sir." Jasper set them down on the counter and took another sip from his drink.

Charles kept his eyes fixed on the deck. From his position, he had a decent vantage point to watch all the man's movements. When Jasper set down his drink on the bar, he rested his right hand on top of the deck of cards. "Who would like to pick a card?" he asked, gesturing wildly with both hands. "And please do not show it to me or tell me what it is."

A woman from the other side of the bar called out, "May I please pick?"

Jasper smiled. "Why, of course you may pick."

The woman made her way over to where Jasper was sitting with his right hand outstretched, gripping the cards. It was Ann, Charles's nemesis from New Zealand. She reached into the upper third of the deck and grabbed a card. She cupped it tight to her breast so that no one could see it.

"It's OK to show it to others, just not me."

Ann then turned her back to Jasper and waved the card in front of the rest of the group. It was the nine of clubs. Jasper shifted his weight on his stool. "OK, now please slide it back into the deck anywhere you like."

Ann slid the card into the middle of the deck.

Jasper said, "Magic makes me thirsty." He set the deck down on the bar, rested his right hand on top of it, and took a sip of his cocktail with his left hand. A few in the crowd chuckled. Charles's eyes never left the man's right hand resting on the deck. If he was doing something with the cards, Charles sure didn't see it.

Jasper picked up the deck. "Tell me a suit of cards that is different from the card you selected," he said to Ann.

Ann cried, "Hearts!"

Jasper said, "Let's lose the hearts, then."

The deck in Jasper's hand began to appear smaller, as if he were losing a quarter of the cards. "OK, now tell me another suit that is different from the card you selected."

"Diamonds."

The deck in Jasper's hand again appeared to grow thinner. He then said smartly, "Your card is not a spade, either, is it?"

"No."

Jasper extended his right hand, holding the now thin deck of cards toward Ann. "I possess the suit of clubs in my hand. Which means that I still possess thirteen cards, correct?"

Ann was puzzled by the question.

Jasper said, "Trust me—there are always thirteen clubs in a deck of fifty-two cards. This gentleman examined the deck to make sure it was a normal deck."

Ann regained her composure. "Yes, of course."

Jasper nodded. "Please select one of the remaining thirteen cards."

Ann touched several cards before selecting one. She finally withdrew one from the remaining deck.

"Is your card the nine of clubs?" Jasper asked.

Ann flipped over the nine of clubs.

The crowd broke into applause. He knew his stuff. Jasper placed the cards back on top of the bar and then slipped them into his coat pocket. With a slight slur in her speech, another woman asked, "Would you do another trick?"

Jasper shook his head. "No, I must save some tricks for my performance later in the cruise."

Ann asked, "So you're a professional?"

"Yes, I'm a graduate of the legendary Magic Castle in LA. I'm on board courtesy of Sterling Cruise."

Enough magic and cocktails for one evening, Charles decided. Enough magic, anyway. He walked by Jasper on his way to the exit. He was visiting with several people, including Ann. Charles leaned in and lightly tapped his shoulder. When Jasper looked in his direction, Charles said, "Excuse me for interrupting. Wonderful trick. I look forward to seeing your full performance." They shook hands.

"Thank you. My name is Jasper Gutman."

"Mine is Charles Pierce. Nice to meet you."

As Charles started to leave, he made eye contact with Ann. She gave him this incredulous look, as if to say, "How dare you interrupt us."

CHAPTER TWENTY-TWO

This was day five at sea. Charles spent time sitting on his veranda, staring at the churning white water created by the ship's propulsion through the Pacific Ocean. It was kind of amazing being on this opulent island of a boat, cruising seamlessly for thousands of miles without seeing land. The time at sea, though, regenerated his love of reading. Charles had quickly polished off *The Maltese Falcon*.

This stretch of sailing would end tomorrow when they sailed into Honolulu. He was looking forward to seeing Hawaii again. It had been so long since he last visited. Mai Tais and beautiful sunsets! This evening, though, Charles needed to pay Marvin a visit on the mysteries uncovered by Sam Spade. He was sure Marvin would be thrilled. At 5:00 p.m., Charles slipped on his sport coat and headed to the Panorama Lounge. As usual, there were just a few customers. He saw only one other person sitting at the bar. Marvin was busy assembling bottles of alcohol and otherwise prepping the bar. Charles sat down on the same barstool that he had occupied a few nights earlier. Marvin peered up from studying a label on a bottle as Charles made himself comfortable.

"Sir Charles. I have not seen you in a few days."

"Yes, I've been checking out your competition on board."

"So, Sir Charles, is it going to be chardonnay or vodka tonight?"

"I'll go with vodka."

Marvin mixed Charles's cocktail and placed it on a napkin in front of him. He said, "By the way, you have a secret admirer."

"What do you mean?"

"Do you remember your last time in here when you ordered a vodka and soda?"

"Of course."

"Well, after you left, a woman requested to have the same drink as the man who just left the bar. She was referring to you."

"How strange. What did she look like?"

Marvin scratched his head. "I don't know. The woman placed her order with Cynthia. She's one of the servers. Apparently, she asked Cynthia to bring her the same drink that you had."

"Interesting. God, I hope it was the woman with the blue streak."

"Sir Charles, are you falling for a fellow passenger?"

Charles smiled. "Perhaps. I have to occupy my time doing something on a monthlong cruise."

"This is the most beautiful time to be in the Panorama Lounge." He pointed behind Charles. "I enjoy a beautiful sunset almost every night."

Charles twisted around on his stool. "Yes. It's without a doubt the best view on the ship most evenings. Marvin, before I forget, I have some news for you." Charles could tell by his expression that he knew he was going to discuss *The Maltese Falcon*.

"As we suspected, the beautiful woman was involved.

However, she didn't kill your namesake Thursby, as we thought. A punk killed him. The woman, though, killed Miles Archer, Sam's partner. There were a lot of shady characters. The falcon everyone was after turned out to be fake."

"Seriously, a fake?"

"Yes, a Russian had a duplicate fake made and kept the original. I suppose it's possible there never was an original Maltese falcon. It was a fun book."

"I must get it and read about the perilous plight of my 'relative,' Floyd Thursby."

Marvin left to wait on the other individual at the bar. He made him a cocktail and talked with him. Charles nursed his vodka and enjoyed watching the tail end of the sunset. The view was stunning as the sun slipped below the waterline, highlighting the clouds above. Before he could finish his drink, Marvin rejoined him.

"Would you like another one?"

Charles always wanted another one.

"No, I'll have a glass of chardonnay instead, and then I'll head to dinner."

Marvin found the same type of chardonnay that he had served him a few evenings ago and poured a glass.

"Thanks, Marvin. You're the best."

"My pleasure."

"So, Marvin, I know you didn't see my secret admirer, but I mentioned the woman with the blue streak. Any chance you've seen her?"

"I've seen a lot of women in the bar with dark hair. But I can't remember any with a streak."

"The dark-haired woman is a mystery," Charles said. "But I

doubt she's a murderer. Did we discuss Ann? She's the one with the stars tattooed on her back."

Marvin raised his eyebrows. "Sir Charles, how do you know she has stars tattooed on her back?"

Charles laughed. "No, it's not what you think. She was wearing an evening gown with a plunging back that exposed her tattoo."

"Is that the woman you told me you insulted at the cocktail party?"

He took a drink of chardonnay. "Precisely. I think she's suspicious. I can't yet say why."

"Sir Charles, you're Sam's new partner. Why don't you investigate?"

"I think I will. With all the days at sea, I'll have ample time. I can't just read all the time."

"Sir Charles, may I ask you a personal question?"

"Sure, Marvin, shoot."

"Why are you traveling alone on such a long cruise?"

"Well, Marvin, I have experienced a life-changing loss in my life. My wife…" He paused to compose himself. "My wife of thirty years committed suicide. We didn't always get along, but I never thought she was that unhappy and depressed." Charles took a drink of the chardonnay.

"I am so sorry. I didn't mean to upset you."

"No, it's OK. One night I came home late after meeting a law school buddy for drinks. All the way home, I kept anticipating what kind of argument I would get into with Charlotte. That was her name. I found her in the den of our house. She had hung herself with a sheet from a beam." Charles felt tears fill his eyes. "Besides being devastated, I felt so ashamed. What could I have done differently to prevent her from taking this dreadful action? Why did I always have to be an insensitive jerk? After her death, I sold the house and did little more than get drunk and mope around my apartment. I had to do something exciting or different in my life. So I booked this cruise. Then, believe it or not, I almost didn't get to go on the cruise." He hesitated. "Sorry, Marvin. Probably more than what you wanted to hear."

"No, Sir Charles. I'm glad you chose this cruise. I'm always here if you want to talk."

"I appreciate it, Marvin. I have all kinds of bizarre stories to share with you in the future. You're a good man and an excellent bartender."

Marvin gestured to Charles's drink. "May I pour you another glass?"

Charles looked at his almost-empty glass. "No, but could you do me a favor? If Ann comes in the bar, will you let me know if you observe anything peculiar about her? I know you need to be careful because you're a crew member. So don't do anything you're not comfortable doing."

"I think I'm capable of doing my duties and a little detective work on the side."

Marvin and Charles shook hands. Charles rose from his stool. "Remember, Ann is blonde, attractive, and in her mid- to late fifties, and she has a New Zealand accent and the unusual tattoo on her back, although you probably won't see it unless there's another formal night."

"I got it. Good evening, Sir Charles."

CHAPTER TWENTY-THREE

When Charles woke the next morning, the ship was docked in Hawaii. It was comforting to see land again. He showered, had breakfast, and returned to his room. In the mail slot near his door was the ship's daily newspaper that had been delivered the prior evening, the *Sterling Cruise Reflections*. It provided all the information concerning excursions and onboard activities, as well as a brief history of the port they were visiting.

Charles sat on the veranda with a cup of coffee and perused the paper. He always checked the evening's entertainment and any available lectures first. Although he was not so enthralled by the performances on board, he was impressed by the diversity and quality of the lectures so far.

One day, guests were treated to a PowerPoint presentation on current-day dictatorships by an excellent professional from Cape Town. Another day, an Academy Award–winning cinematographer shared the nuances of cinematography, using movie clips to help illustrate his points. Charles's eyes were drawn to the bold print describing tomorrow's lecture:

Hold On to Your Wallets: The Art of the Steal
Tom Elliott, Professional Pickpocket Lectures
4:00 p.m.

That should be interesting, he thought. At the least, it would break up the monotony of his day.

He spent a day in Honolulu, touring all the major tourist sites, such as Diamond Head, the USS *Arizona* memorial, and different vantage points overlooking the beautiful island of Oahu. It was comforting to walk on land again. Charles spent the late afternoon reading. At 5:00 p.m., it was time to visit Marvin in the Panorama Lounge. Again, the lounge was sparsely occupied. He made a beeline to the bar and his usual stool. There was only one couple sitting at the bar, each drinking a glass of wine. There was no bartender.

A minute later, he felt a tap on his shoulder. "Hello, Sir Charles. Vodka and soda?" Marvin unlatched a section of the bar that permitted bartenders to enter the inner sanctum from where the guests sit. He latched it behind him.

"Yes, that would be great. Thanks. Marvin, you had me worried. I thought you had abandoned ship in Honolulu."

"No, I'm here, as always." He set Charles's cocktail down in front of him. "How was your day, Sir Charles?"

The couple at the bar was staring at Charles. They were likely trying to figure out why Marvin was referring to him as Sir Charles. "OK. I took in some of the sights today. Were you able to get off the ship?"

Marvin shook his head. "No, I'll get off at the next port, if I'm permitted. By the way, I have some news for you."

"You mean about the blonde?"

Marvin glanced over at the other couple. "Would you care for another glass of wine?"

The man said, "No, we're all done here."

Marvin took their glasses from the bar and said, "Enjoy your evening, folks." He set the glasses on a tray under the bar and returned to where Charles was sitting. "Yes, I think she was here late last night. I was working a double shift. The whole bar was full. I noticed this woman with a glass of champagne in her hand. Do you know how bees pollinate when they move from one flower to another flower?"

Charles took a sip of vodka. "Sure. Go on."

"Well, that's what she resembled. She would approach a man or a couple and visit for a few minutes. Then, as if she were bored, she'd move to the next person."

Charles glanced over Marvin's shoulder as another couple approached the bar.

Marvin spun around. "Good evening Mr. and Mrs. Higgins. How are you this evening?"

The woman said, "Excellent, Marvin, and you?"

"Wonderful. Thank you."

Marvin obviously knew these people well. He started mixing them cocktails without inquiring what they wanted. He gently set the drinks down in front of them and stepped back over to Charles.

"So did you hear any of her conversations or speak to her?"

Marvin frowned. "I could hear only bits and pieces. She had a New Zealand or Australian accent."

Charles rubbed his head. "Nothing, huh?"

"No. Nothing, really. Just small talk. The usual things you hear on a cruise ship."

Charles finished his cocktail and set it down on the counter. "Thank you, Marvin."

"Another one?"

Charles stood up. "No. Only one tonight. So far, anyway. Thanks, Marvin, for your report. You'll be rewarded handsomely someday."

Marvin was now accustomed to his dry sense of humor. "You're very welcome, Sir Charles. See you soon. Good luck with your investigation."

Charles gave a slight wave. "I'm always on the job. Even if my job is make-believe. Thanks, Marvin."

Charles dined on a margherita pizza in the casual dining area on the pool deck. The pizza, paired with an earthy zinfandel, was a wonderful culinary experience. It was a beautiful evening outside. The ship was far enough south in the Pacific that evenings were now balmy and comfortable. He decided to go down to the seventh deck and take a walk. It was the only deck on the ship that allowed the passengers to walk the entire perimeter of the ship. During the day, it was full of joggers and others out for some exercise.

Charles took the stairs and exited on the seventh deck. He opened the door and walked outside, checking both right and left so as not to impede some nightly jogger. Except for him, the deck was deserted. He decided to make the entire lap of the ship at least once and take in the stars. When he reached the stern, he could hear some voices below, on the sixth deck. Charles walked to the rail. It was dark, but he could make out the figures of two men talking and gesturing with something in their hands. Someone opened the door that led to the deck below, and the men were briefly illuminated. He could then see that the men were holding golf putters. *Oh yeah, the golf area on the ship.* They probably met for a nightly drunken putting competition. Time to move on. He continued his walk.

It was very quiet except for the noise created by the movement of the ship sailing the Pacific. Through the parted clouds, Charles could see stars that he had never seen before—he had never been in this part of the world. He was surprised more people weren't taking advantage of this experience. Charles lapped the ship twice and then decided to have one more drink before retiring to his stateroom. He decided to visit the Cove Bar on the fifth deck. Why not?

Charles took the stairs down from the seventh deck. The bar was almost completely full, but he spotted a couple of stools. He hurried over to one situated between two women. They were facing in opposite directions and not together.

The bartender waited for Charles to get settled before approaching. "Good evening, sir. What may I bring you?"

For some reason, he scanned the bar to see what other people were drinking. To his surprise, he said, "A White Russian."

Charles wondered why he ordered a White Russian. Did he think the bartender had a Russian accent? He had not had a White Russian since he last saw the movie *The Big Lebowski*. This cruise was starting to mess with him.

The bartender placed his cocktail on a napkin in front of him. "Thank you. I have not had one of these in several years."

The bartender did not respond.

Soon, the crowd started to thin out. The bartender noticed that Charles had yet to touch his drink. "Is everything OK with your cocktail?"

"Yes, I'm just savoring it. By the way, may I ask where you

are from?"

She came closer. "Belarus."

He took his first taste of the White Russian and set the glass down. "Belarus? I have only met one other person from there. She was a beautiful woman. It must be a national requirement."

Charles hoped she didn't think that he was trying to hit on her. He was only trying to get over the awkwardness of drinking a White Russian. The bartender was gracious. "Thank you. My name is Darya. It is a country of many things. Some good, and some quite bad."

"I suspect that is true for most countries. I'm Charles."

"Pleased to meet you." She then left to wait on a man who took a seat a couple of stools down to Charles's right. She made him a cocktail and then left the bar, presumably to take a break. Charles watched as the man took two quick gulps from his glass. *He must need a drink bad.*

The man said, "I love this part of the inclusive cruise fare. Don't you?" He toasted Charles with his cocktail.

Charles smiled. "There are certainly perks."

The man took another taste of his cocktail. He pointed at Charles. "You cruise often?"

Charles shook his head. "No, not often. What about you?"

He beamed. "Oh yeah. Being on the sea is second nature for me. I've been on the water more than land for most of my life. I started off working on my dad's fishing boat as a small boy. I learned everything there was to know about boats and sailing. My dad even taught me how to pay the devil."

"Pay the devil?"

The man blinked his eyes as if reliving his past. "Yes. The devil is a wooden ship's longest seam in the hull. Caulking the seams between the boards of the hull was done with 'pay' or pitch—a kind of tar. The task of 'paying the devil'—caulking the longest seam of the hull—was despised by everyone. Most people don't realize the cliché 'there'll be the devil to pay' is actually an old nautical term. Nowadays, it just means performing any unpleasant task."

"I never heard that. I've learned something new tonight."

The man ignored his comment. "I was able to turn my passion for ships and sailing into a profitable shipping business based out of Boston. It's a hell of a lot more fun now when my wife and I cruise. I get to be on the water and not worry about business. My only worry on board is what I'm going to drink next." He paused to laugh at his own comment.

"It sounds like you've had an interesting life."

He set his cocktail down. "I can't complain." He stood up and extended his hand to Charles and said, "Nice to talk to you."

They shook hands. "Likewise, thank you."

The man walked past Charles. "My wife is going to wonder what happened to me."

Charles took a sip from his White Russian. He pulled his phone out of his coat pocket to check the time. It was 10:15 p.m. Darya was mixing cocktails for two couples across from him.

"Care for another one?" Darya was standing in front of him, staring at his empty glass.

"Yes, please." Charles purposely did not say *White Russian* out loud. While Darya was mixing his drink, he felt the presence of someone sitting down next to him. When Charles glanced over, the first thing he saw was a blue streak in an otherwise dark-brunette head of hair. He thought, *Oh my God, it's her. The mystery woman.*

Darya set the White Russian in front of him. The woman and Charles made eye contact. Then she lowered her gaze down to his White Russian.

"What are you drinking?"

"It's a White Russian," Charles whispered, feeling a little embarrassed.

Darya asked the woman, "May I bring you a drink?"

"Just a glass of champagne."

"Have you ever seen the movie *The Big Lebowski*?"

The woman looked puzzled. "Perhaps. It sounds familiar."

"Well, it's kind of a cult classic, and the lead character always drank White Russians. I thought it'd be fun to order one tonight. I can't remember the last time I had one."

The woman smiled. "I see."

"I know. It's kind of silly."

The woman leaned a bit closer. "I don't think it's silly at all. Actually, I think it's kind of cute."

Charles felt a little more emboldened. "Well, this is my second one tonight, and I'm pretty sure the last one for another decade."

"What do you normally drink, then?"

Charles cleared his throat. "Chardonnay or vodka and soda."

She took another sip of her champagne. "Well, sometimes you have to live dangerously."

"I have to admit, I never thought drinking a White Russian was what you would call living dangerously. But tonight, I'll accept it."

They raised their glasses for a toast. "So how do you live

dangerously, Ms. …?"

"Vicky LeBlanc." She extended her hand toward Charles.

It felt soft and delicate as he shook it. "I'm Charles Pierce. Pleased to meet you, Vicky."

"Pleased to meet you, Charles. So you want to know how I live dangerously?"

Charles nodded.

"Well, to be honest, I try not to live dangerously. But sometimes life and circumstances place you in that position. You can always choose to take the safe, predictable course in your life, but even then, something dangerous will most likely happen to you at some point. Through no fault of your own, you might be involved in a car accident or a shipwreck. These are inherently dangerous things." Vicky took a sip of champagne. "So if danger is an inevitable part of living, why not be willing to take some chances pursuing a particular passion, even though it may prove to be dangerous?"

Charles tasted his drink and let the last statement sink in. "Is it too personal to ask what type of passion you're pursuing?"

Vicky's eyes darted around the bar. She motioned him to come in closer. She whispered in his ear, "You're not to mention this to anyone. Do you understand?"

"Of course. I'm traveling alone. I don't know anybody on the ship, anyway."

Sensing a lack of sincerity on his part, Vicky frowned. "I'm very serious. You're not to mention this to any guest, bartender, or anyone."

Charles nodded somberly. "I understand. I promise not to mention it to anyone."

"I'm meeting someone at our last port, in Sydney," she said

in a very hushed tone. She stopped speaking and again surveyed the immediate vicinity around them. "This man is married."

Charles took a final drink of his cocktail. "Not married to you, I take it."

Vicky peered down at her empty champagne glass. A boisterous group approached the bar to Vicky's left. Charles said, "The performance just let out."

Vicky rose from her stool, leaned over, and whispered in his ear, "Let's continue this conversation later." She touched his shoulder. "Good night, Charles."

"Good night. Take care!"

Charles waited a couple of minutes after Vicky left the bar before leaving himself. He took the elevator to the ninth deck, where his stateroom was located. The *Sterling Cruise Reflections* was in the mail slot next to the door. He grabbed it, entered his room, and sat down on the bed. *What exciting activities are in store for me tomorrow? Oh yeah, the pickpocket guy will lecture tomorrow afternoon.* Charles wanted to make sure he saw that performance. He searched the *Sterling Cruise Reflections* for anything mildly interesting. In bold print was a teaser for the next few days events:

**The Priceless Volk Yellow Diamond worn
at the Academy Awards will be unveiled in the
Sterling Boutique.
Please join expert gemologist Able Vitroil
as he discusses the Volk Yellow Diamond
and other jewelry for sale in the
Sterling Boutique, Sixth Deck.**

What a perfect marketing opportunity, he thought. *You get a bunch of wealthy people confined on a ship for several weeks and dangle expensive jewelry in front of them. Brilliant!* He decided he would attend that event as well.

After a quick shower, he hopped into bed to read before going to sleep. He pulled his tablet off the nightstand and opened his book. Before he had even completed a page, he closed it and set it back down. Charles turned the light off and closed his eyes. His thoughts drifted to the events of the evening. The whole experience with Vicky was nothing short of bizarre. They started out talking about White Russians and ended up talking about her living dangerously by meeting some married man in Sydney. Why was that so dangerous? Why did she confide in him? The only beautiful and interesting woman he'd met on board was having an affair with a married man. Sam would be laughing his ass off at his predicament. Charles fell asleep and started dreaming.

Vicky! I want to help you, but you must tell me what you are afraid of. No, no, no—put the gun down. Don't even think about such a thing. That won't solve anything. I will help you through it all. No, please don't leave. Wait! Please don't go.

Charles woke up in a cold sweat. He sat up in bed and switched on the reading light. He whispered, "Vicky!" No one was there.

This whole trip was getting under his skin. He was dreaming about some woman he had just met like she was the most important thing in his life. On the other hand, but for his dreams, his life was rudderless. Great, now he was using nautical terms to think about his life. He imagined that Sam would kick his butt.

CHAPTER TWENTY-FOUR

Charles arrived early for the performance of Tom Elliott, the professional pickpocket. The theater was about half-full. He selected a seat on the left aisle, about fifteen rows from the stage. A spotlight bathed the stage in white. People filed down both aisles. Charles saw Ann walking down the right aisle with a couple of men. They all took a seat about four rows back. He then saw Vicky walking down the right aisle by herself. She found a seat on the aisle next to a couple.

At 4:00 p.m., a booming, baritone voice came over the PA system. "Hold on to your watches, wallets, and wives. Ladies and gentlemen, please give a warm round of applause to Tom Elliott, professional pickpocket!"

The spotlight hit Tom Elliott as he made his way down the right aisle of the theater. He stopped occasionally to shake hands and otherwise interact with the audience on his way to the stage. As soon as Tom stepped onto the stage, he held both arms up in the air over his head. Attached to each arm were several wristwatches.

Tom examined the first one closely and asked, "Anyone missing a Rolex?" He then went on to the next. "How about a Montblanc?" Tom continued until he had returned all the watches to the proper owners in the audience. Throughout his performance, he would invite people onstage and remove some item from them without their knowledge. Sometimes his hands would move so quickly that no one in the audience could tell what he was removing. At other times, he slowed down so that the audience could just catch a glimpse of him removing a wallet or other item from the volunteer on the stage.

Tom ended his show by inviting one last volunteer to join him. The volunteer was a short, rotund man who appeared to be in his sixties. Tom positioned the man alongside him and then turned to address the audience. "You choose. What item should I remove from this gentleman?"

One person called out, "Remove his underwear!" Another, "Take his socks!"

Tom waved his hands, feigning frustration. "You're a tough crowd. I was hoping you'd just say his wristwatch. By the way, I've already taken it."

He handed the watch to the man, who proceeded to slip it back on his wrist. Tom then asked the man, "Feeling a little breezy?" The man seemed a bit confused at the question. Without hesitating, Tom produced a pair of boxer shorts from behind the man's back. "These look familiar?" The man was totally astonished. Tom handed the boxer shorts to the man and directed him off the stage.

"Thank you, ladies and gentlemen," Tom said, wrapping up the show. "If there are any questions that I can answer without giving away all my secrets, I will be here at the right side of the stage for a few minutes."

With music blaring over the speakers, the audience rose and gave Tom a standing ovation. Charles started walking to the back of the theater and stopped to glance over his shoulder. He saw Ann standing with a small group visiting with Tom. *She must have a thing for magicians and pickpockets.* Charles didn't recall seeing her at the lecture on current dictatorships in the world. She would probably have a thing for an actual dictator, though. She seemed the type. Why the hell was he thinking of Ann being attracted to dictators? My God, he hadn't had an intelligent thought in what seemed like forever.

Charles pulled his phone out of his coat pocket and checked the time. It was 5:15 p.m. He decided to pay Marvin a visit. When Charles entered the Panorama Lounge, he walked to the other side of the bar and slid easily onto a favorite stool. Marvin had already placed a cocktail napkin on the counter and was busy fishing for something under the counter. He then straightened up with a bottle of chardonnay in one hand and a bottle of citron vodka in the other.

"May I guess which one?"

"Of course."

He placed the chardonnay back under the bar counter. "Vodka and soda?"

"You guessed it!"

Marvin made Charles's cocktail and set it on the napkin in front of him. "So, Sir Charles, how was your day?"

"Well, it was another day at sea. Although I did see an interesting performance a few minutes ago."

"The professional pickpocket?"

"Yes."

"I heard he was great."

Charles picked up his cocktail and stared at it for a moment. "I agree. Has he been on the ship before?"

"No, I think this is his first time performing on a cruise ship. He usually performs in Las Vegas."

Marvin left to wait on a couple. Charles wanted to tell Marvin about the conversation with Vicky. It was not because she told him anything significant, other than that she was meeting a married man in Sydney. She seemed concerned about something she wanted to share. He promised her that he would not reveal to anyone what she told him. Marvin returned.

"Any sightings yet of the brunette woman with the blue streak in her hair?" Charles asked.

"No. I have seen a lot of gray-haired women, though."

Charles laughed. "I bet you have. What about Ann? You know, the blonde?"

"Yes. She was here last night." He pointed at an empty table near the bar.

"Was she doing anything of interest?"

Marvin mopped the counter with his rag. "No, she and a man seemed to be engaged in deep conversation, though."

"Why do you say that?"

"Because they were here for a long time, and I don't think either one of them touched their drinks. It was as if they didn't want to be bothered by the server—or anyone else, for that matter."

"What did this guy look like?"

Marvin winked at Charles. "You're taking this detective work pretty seriously, aren't you?"

Charles spun his cocktail glass around and smiled. "I guess I am. I still have a hunch something is up with that woman."

"But to your question. He was a younger guy. At least, he was younger than her. He looked like one of those guys who spends half his life in the gym."

"Similar to me?"

Marvin laughed. "No, Sir Charles. He was perhaps a little more muscled up than you."

"I see. Anything else remarkable about him?"

Marvin thought a moment. "Well, he was like you in one respect. He also had a shaved head."

"Interesting. I don't think I've seen this guy. But with almost a thousand guests on board, it's possible you may not see everybody."

Charles finished his cocktail. "Good evening, Marvin. I'm off to dinner."

CHAPTER TWENTY-FIVE

At 2:00 p.m. the next day, Charles reached the Sterling Boutique on the sixth deck. There were already around twenty guests present. One of the boutique workers, dressed in black with a Sterling Cruise name tag, greeted people as they arrived. "Please take a seat. There is room for only a few more guests."

When the chairs were full, the boutique worker blocked the door. "We apologize. There are no more chairs. The diamond will be on exhibit for the duration of the cruise. You can peer through the window or listen through the door if you wish."

A man dressed in a neatly pressed black suit stood next to a small table covered with a white cloth. An attaché case was resting on top. With a cue from one of the boutique workers, he began.

"Good afternoon, ladies and gentlemen. Welcome to the Sterling Boutique and its exquisite collection of jewelry. I am Dr. Able Vitroil, a senior gemologist. I am so happy Sterling Cruise has invited me to help present the priceless Volk Yellow Diamond that has graced the red carpet at the Academy Awards. Dating back to the 1800s, the Volk Yellow Diamond is deemed one of the world's largest and finest yellow diamonds. Only two women have ever worn the diamond. Actress Mary D. Pritchett wore it in a necklace to the 1957 Academy Awards, and Audrey Hepburn wore it in 1961. But it is here for the duration of the cruise."

Dr. Vitroil put on a pair of white gloves and unlocked his attaché case. He then removed a purple velvet purse from the attaché case and pulled open the drawstrings. With precision, he emptied the contents onto the table in front of him. A yellow diamond rolled to a stop right in the middle of the table. Dr. Vitroil reached inside his coat pocket and pulled out a loupe, a handheld magnifying glass. He held the diamond up to the light while he examined it through his loupe. A smile crossed his face. "It's brilliant! Would you like to hold it?"

A boutique worker made the rounds, handing out white gloves to everyone. She said, "Please come up one at a time if you are interested in holding the diamond and looking at it through the magnifying glass."

One by one, most of the crowd within the boutique, including Charles, handled the diamond under the watchful eye of Dr. Vitroil and a Sterling Cruise security man. One man joked, "You better not let Tom Elliott anywhere near this diamond." Another man said, "He'd clean the entire boutique out in five minutes."

After Charles had held the diamond in his gloved hands, he turned to leave. Waiting in line just outside the boutique was Ann. Charles purposely did not make eye contact with her. She ignored him as well. As soon as the original group inside the boutique had viewed the diamond, people were let into the boutique in small groups. Charles walked across to the other side of the atrium and pulled his phone out of his pocket to check the time. It was 2:45 p.m. He snuck one more look over at the boutique. Vicky was standing at the end of the line to view the diamond. Very interesting. Should he wait for her outside the boutique so that they could continue their conversation? What would Sam do? Probably roll a cigarette. He decided to go to his room.

That evening, Charles dined at his usual table, 911. The dining room did not seem to be as crowded as usual. After dinner, he took his now customary walk around the ship on the seventh deck. It was balmy, comfortable, and clear. He took his coat off and held it in his arms and sat down on one of the benches on the deck to enjoy the feel of the light breeze on his face. Charles's eyes closed. He heard the pounding of footsteps in the distance. They were getting louder. When he opened his eyes, he saw a woman jog by. He rose to his feet and walked the perimeter of the ship twice before reentering the ship's interior. *Decision time. Should I go to the Panorama Lounge, the Cove Bar, or the Saloon for a cocktail?* He decided to try the Saloon again. After all, it was just down the hall on this deck. It seemed all he thought about was where he was going to get his next drink. Kind of pathetic.

Charles entered the Saloon and checked out the bar. There was a group of three unoccupied stools. He walked straight to them and sat down on the one farthest to the right. The bartender was busy at the opposite end of the bar. There was a cluster of occupied tables surrounding the stage, where the same pianist from the other night was again playing the piano. He had quite a following. Charles surveyed his fellow patrons at the bar. There was one group of two couples. One of the men was pretending to swing a golf club for the other man's amusement.

The two women were having their own conversation but would turn to smile occasionally at their significant others.

The bartender finally noticed his presence. "Sorry about that. I got several orders at once. May I get you a drink?"

"Sure. How about a citron vodka and soda?"

Without acknowledging Charles's order, he placed a white cocktail napkin in front of him and hurried off to mix his cocktail. After placing it on Charles's napkin, he stepped to the other side of the bar. Charles took his phone out of his pocket and set it on the counter in front of him. Charles started to check his email and then hesitated. He knew he would only be frustrated by the slow speed and end up staring at a small blue screen for ten minutes.

He was startled by a tap on his shoulder. Vicky was standing there, dressed in a stylish black dress. Her eyes were darting around the bar.

Charles asked, "Hey, how are you?" Vicky perched on the edge of the stool next to Charles.

"I'm OK. How are you?"

"I'm fine. Are you sure you're OK?"

She looked at him and smiled. "Yes. All is fine. I'm just a little on edge."

The bartender moved toward them. "Care for a drink?" he asked, addressing Vicky.

She shook her head. "No, thank you."

Charles took a sip of his cocktail. Vicky rested a hand on his wrist. "I need to talk," she said.

"Of course."

She glanced around the bar. "Not here, though. It's too crowded. She or someone with her might overhear us."

"Who is 'she'?"

Vicky put her finger to her lips. "Shhh." She again checked out the area surrounding the bar. "Do you mind coming to my stateroom?"

Charles thought, *Did she just ask me to come to her room?* How would Sam respond? For that matter, how should he respond? He faked an air of coolness and took another sip of his drink. "Sure. Just say when."

She was studying his face. "On second thought, that might not be wise. Someone may be watching."

Someone may be watching? Was she serious? Charles asked, "Would you be comfortable coming to my stateroom, then?"

Vicky lifted her hand from his wrist. "Yes, that would be better. You sure you don't mind?"

"Is now an appropriate time?"

She stood up. "We shouldn't leave together. I'll meet you there in thirty minutes. Give me your stateroom number and order another drink after I leave the bar."

Another drink was exactly what he needed! "You've piqued my interest with all this mystery. My stateroom is 9068."

Vicky looked down at her phone. "It's now ten fifteen. I'll be there at ten forty-five."

Charles cracked a smile. "I'll be waiting for you."

Vicky turned and walked toward the door. Her head shifted from side to side, scrutinizing the crowd. He watched until she had disappeared from view. This was strange. Was she for real? She was acting like she was in danger. How could anyone be in danger on a cruise? That seemed unbelievable. It was certainly possible she had some ulterior motive. With his luck, she'd be psychotic or a murderer. Or both. Lost in thought, Charles did not hear the bartender.

"Sir? Sir? Would you like another drink?"

"Yes, please."

He nursed his cocktail and occasionally checked the time on his watch. There was plenty of time. It was a short walk and an elevator ride to the ninth deck and his stateroom. What had he gotten himself into?

Charles reached his stateroom at 10:40 p.m. He grabbed the daily *Sterling Cruise Reflections* from the mail slot. Before unlocking the door, he looked both right and left. A woman down the hallway was letting herself into a stateroom. Other than her, there was no one around. Charles was getting as paranoid as Vicky. He unlocked the door, tossed the *Sterling Cruise Reflections* on the desk, slid the door to the veranda open, and went outside. The only visible light was reflected from the ship onto the surface of the ocean. He checked the time on his phone. It was 10:46 p.m. Charles wondered if Vicky was really coming. Maybe she had changed her mind or misheard his stateroom number and gone to some other guy's stateroom. He left the door to his veranda open but went back inside and grabbed the *Sterling Cruise Reflections* from the top of the desk. The headline read "Yes, Another Exciting Day at Sea."

Charles heard a tapping at his door. When he peered through the peephole, he could see Vicky standing there, staring straight ahead.

Charles swung open the door. "Hello. Fancy meeting you here. Please come in."

Vicky entered, and Charles closed and locked the door behind her. When he turned around to face her, she tightly embraced him. After a few seconds, she gently released her grip on him so that she could see his face. "Thank you for letting me come here."

"Of course. A glass of wine?"

She dabbed her eye with her finger to wipe away a tear. "That'd be lovely. Thank you."

Charles walked over to the mini refrigerator in his stateroom and retrieved an unopened bottle of chardonnay. "There is a choice of chardonnay or chardonnay. Sorry, I don't have any red wine."

Vicky crossed the room and stood near him. "Chardonnay is fine."

He opened the bottle, poured two glasses, and handed her one. They toasted one another with a slight clink of their glasses. "Would you care to go out on the veranda?"

"Yes."

Charles followed her through the open door onto the veranda. Neither one of them spoke for a while. He finally broke the silence. "It's quite overcast tonight. The only light you see is generated by the ship." Charles was sure Sam Spade would have had something clever to say. He hoped she didn't respond with, "Yes, but we aren't here to talk about the weather, are we?"

Vicky took a sip from her glass. "Yes. It's quiet too."

"Are you comfortable out here, or would you prefer to go back inside?"

"Please, let's go inside. I need to talk, and we can't do it out here. Someone may overhear us."

Charles followed Vicky back inside and closed the door to the veranda. Vicky sat down on the small sofa. To give her some space, he pulled up the chair from the desk and sat down across from her. Charles smiled. "OK, we're now in my soundproof stateroom. Are you comfortable talking now?"

Vicky took a drink of chardonnay, so he did the same. "Do you remember I said I was meeting a married man in Sydney?"

"Yes. Then you were interrupted by the boisterous group at the bar."

Vicky continued. "His wife was in the States, visiting some friends. Well, I got a text from him after we set sail from LA that she'd decided to take a cruise to Sydney. I'm worried she might be on this cruise. According to Miles—that's the man's name— she's been diagnosed with a dependent personality disorder. She's emotionally unstable and capable of violent outbursts."

"Surely she told Miles what cruise she was taking," Charles said.

Vicky set her glass down. "No, they hardly speak."

"Do you know what she looks like?"

Vicky shook her head. "No. When I first met Miles, I didn't want to know what she looked like."

"So you never saw a picture of her?"

Vicky teared up. "No. But I texted Miles from Hawaii when I had strong internet service and asked him to send me a photograph of her. However, he never responded. I tried to call him, and it just goes to his voice mail. I'm worried that something has happened to him."

Charles got up and opened the refrigerator and grabbed the bottle of chardonnay. "Would you care for a refill?"

Vicky extended her empty glass toward him. He refilled her glass and then his. "Well, even if she's on this ship, she doesn't know about you, does she?"

"You mean that I'm the other woman?"

"Yes. Has she seen a photo of you?"

Vicky wiped her eyes with her finger. "She knows there is another woman. In fact, she put Miles in the hospital when she learned about me. She hit him over the head several times with a wine bottle."

"Ouch. I see that she can be violent."

Vicky's lips tightened. "Miles was in a haze after she hit him over the head. He thought he recalled her taking his phone. He couldn't find it when he was released from the hospital. He eventually got a new one."

Charles took a drink of chardonnay and set his glass down. "Any photos of you on Miles's old phone?"

Vicky started to sob. "Yes, several selfies of the two of us."

He groaned. "Do you know this woman's name?"

"I think it's Anita. But she and Miles have different last names, and I don't know hers."

"I see. If you knew her last name, you could inquire about her at the front desk."

Vicky did not respond.

"Let me ask you this: Has any woman or man threatened you since you've been on board?"

Vicky shook her head. "No, not directly anyway. I'm picking up some bad vibes from several people, though." She took another drink of chardonnay. "What should I do?"

Charles smiled. "Enjoy the cruise."

Vicky stared at him in disbelief.

"What I mean is that there is nothing you can do about this woman unless she threatens you. That is, assuming she's even on this ship. So act as if she's not on the ship and enjoy all the ship has to offer—with one caveat. Do what you're already doing, and that is being aware of those around you. Don't let your guard down. Even if this woman is as unhinged as you think she is, I doubt she would risk doing something foolish aboard a small cruise ship."

Vicky smiled for the first time that night. She set her glass of chardonnay down and stood up, then leaned over and kissed Charles on the lips. He thought, *See, Sam, I still got some life in me.* He stood up, and they continued to kiss. Vicky then pulled away. "I better leave."

"I understand. Would you like me to walk you to your stateroom?"

"No thank you. I'm only one deck down. I'll be fine."

He followed her to the door. "By the way, I saw you the other day at the unveiling of the yellow diamond."

She twirled around. "You were there?"

"I was across the atrium from you. I did get a chance to hold and examine it early on, though."

Vicky turned back and cracked open the door. "I was the last person to hold it before it was locked safely into its display case. Oh, by the way, may I ask why you are traveling alone?"

"My wife recently passed away. I needed to get away and have a change in my life."

"I'm so sorry."

"Thank you."

"Good night, Charles. And thank you again. I may be needing more moral support before this cruise is over."

"You know where to find me."

Vicky laughed. "Yes, I can find you here—or in one of the bars on board. Good night."

After Vicky left, Charles got ready for bed. *My God, another day at sea!* He found the *Sterling Cruise Reflections*, switched on his reading light, and got into bed. In bold print on the second page was tomorrow afternoon's entertainment:

> **From the Famed Magic Castle**
> **Sterling Cruise Proudly Presents**
> **The Master of Illusion, Jasper Gutman**
> **4:00 p.m. Sterling Lounge**

Charles wanted to see this guy. He was quite a showman. He set the paper down, picked up his tablet, and attempted to check his email. Frustrated, Charles clicked on the book icon and read a few pages from a novel with a World War II theme. It held his attention for only a few minutes. He set the tablet down, switched off the reading light, and went to sleep.

CHAPTER TWENTY-SIX

At 3:50 p.m. the next day, Charles was sitting in the Sterling Lounge, halfway down the auditorium, in an aisle seat on the left row. He watched as the auditorium started to fill up. Magic shows must be popular, he thought. Any entertainment or distraction was welcome when "lost" at sea. He looked around to see if he could spot Vicky, but she was nowhere in sight. Behind him, Charles could hear a woman speaking in a New Zealand accent. He recognized the voice of Ann. He watched as she and a diverse group of individuals passed him on their way down the aisle. They took a seat in the center section. Vicky must not be interested in magic. On the other hand, she still might be concerned about that guy's wife and was lying low in her stateroom. *Such a bizarre story.*

His train of thought was suddenly interrupted by an announcement.

"Ladies and gentlemen, please give a warm welcome to master illusionist and Magic Castle alumnus Jasper Gutman."

The curtain opened, and Jasper Gutman walked to the center of the stage dressed in a dark suit and what appeared to be the same dark-red shirt he had worn the other night in the Saloon. There was a table covered with a cloth, and other props were positioned onstage.

Jasper performed various tricks for about forty minutes. They were of the type you would see on any variety show. Charles watched Ann and her group throughout the performance. She was very animated.

For his grand finale, Jasper spent a great deal of time explaining how complicated it was to perform his next trick. He asked for a female volunteer from the audience. Ann was enthusiastically waving her arms, but she failed to catch Jasper's attention, which was focused on the other side of the auditorium. A slim woman rose from her seat and made her way up to the stage. Charles wondered if she was a plant. She resembled Vicky in stature, age, and beauty, although she was a blonde. He was too far back from the stage to see her features distinctly.

Jasper shook her hand and asked, "What is your name?"

The woman said in a hushed tone, "Janet Wonderly."

"Ms. Wonderly, have we ever met before?"

"No."

Jasper then addressed the audience. "Ladies and gentlemen, I am going to perform the ultimate illusion. You may have seen something similar performed before, in which a magician is locked in confinement by his beautiful assistant. With a few tugs of a magic cape, the illusionist suddenly trades places with the beautiful assistant. She is now locked in a confined place, and he is not. However, you have never seen the illusion I am about to perform—and perform with a perfect stranger."

A young woman rolled a large storage trunk onto the stage. Jasper instructed the young woman, "Please show the audience that this is a solid trunk."

She picked up a strategically placed hammer and proceeded

to hit every side of the trunk. She then whirled it around and hit each side of the trunk again. The young woman then exited the stage. Jasper grabbed a cape from behind the table and demonstrated to Ms. Wonderly how he wanted her to shake it. After a few attempts, Jasper was satisfied that she could perform the task.

"After I get into the storage trunk," he instructed Ms. Wonderly, "you lock the latches and use this step stool to climb on top of the trunk. Once you're on top, shake the cape three times, exactly as you have just learned."

Jasper pulled out a pair of handcuffs and had Janet slip them on his wrists. He then labored to get his rotund body into the trunk. Ms. Wonderly followed his instructions, locking the trunk and climbing up on its top with the cape. She hesitated a few moments before she began to shake the cape. Each time she shook it, her body was concealed for a few seconds.

After the third shake, the cape was lowered, and Jasper was suddenly the one holding the cape. Ms. Wonderly was nowhere in sight. Jasper unlocked the trunk, and up out of the trunk emerged the young assistant wearing the same handcuffs that Jasper had been wearing earlier. There was a smattering of applause.

One man called out, "Where is Ms. Wonderly?"

Jasper faced the audience, pretending to be surprised, and held up his hands. He walked over to the trunk and looked in. Again, he feigned being dumbfounded. He shouted, "Ms. Wonderly?"

From the other side of the auditorium, a faint voice answered, "Yes."

Jasper asked, "Can you hit the house lights?" On cue, the

house lights came on. Ms. Wonderly was sitting in the same seat in the auditorium she had occupied prior to the trick. She waved. The audience broke into applause.

At the end of the performance, Charles decided to check out the yellow diamond. He wanted to see how they were exhibiting it. The Sterling Lounge was on the same deck as the Sterling Boutique, so he walked down the passageway to the shop. There was the yellow diamond, sitting inside a Plexiglas display case. Next to the case was an old photograph of Audrey Hepburn wearing a necklace containing the diamond.

It was time to pay Marvin a visit. Charles took the stairs up to the Panorama Lounge. He followed his customary routine of walking the length of the lounge back to the bar. Although there were a few people lounging at the bar, "his" stool was unoccupied, so he made a beeline for it. A young, muscular bald man was sitting three stools to his left.

Marvin saw Charles and came over. "Sir Charles. Citron vodka and soda?"

"That would be wonderful. Thanks."

Marvin made Charles a cocktail and set it down on a napkin. He asked, "How was your day?"

"Another day at sea. I read this morning and watched a magician this afternoon."

Marvin rested his hands on the counter. "Well, tomorrow we're in Samoa."

Charles took a sip of his cocktail. "You're right. I so look forward to seeing land again."

The muscular young man left the bar and sat by himself at one of the tables near the wall. Marvin nodded in his direction. "You remember me telling you about the muscular guy who was with the woman you think is suspicious?"

Charles snuck a glimpse at the man. "Is that him?"

"Yes! And don't look now, but the blonde is joining him."

Charles continued to look at Marvin. "Are they looking this way?"

Marvin checked the bar area to make sure his services were not needed. "No, they're looking at one another."

Charles stole a glance at the couple. "That's Ann for sure. I saw her at the magician's performance with a different group of people."

Marvin left to wait on a couple who had arrived at the bar. Charles continued to work on his vodka and soda and intermittently checked out Ann. A waiter served them two cocktails. Ann and the man clicked glasses, and each took a drink.

"Sir Charles, would you like another?"

He gazed down at his glass. It was almost empty. "Sure. Why not?" Marvin fixed another cocktail and slid it onto the napkin in front of him. "Tell me, Marvin. Any sighting of the brunette with the blue streak in her hair yet?"

"The other mystery woman, right? No, I don't believe I've seen her."

"I would have assumed that everyone on board had come up here to enjoy one of Marvin Thursby's cocktails."

"Well, if she has, I didn't recognize her. So do you find this brunette suspicious like the blonde over there?"

Charles couldn't tell him Vicky's concerns about the possibility that a dangerous woman could be on board. He shook his head. "No, she's a mystery, but she's not suspicious—if that makes sense."

Marvin had a puzzled expression on his face. "What's the

difference between the brunette and the blonde, that one is suspicious and the other a mystery?"

A man neared the bar to Charles's right side. "Hey, Marvin, how is my favorite bartender doing tonight?"

Marvin went over and shook hands with the man. Charles watched as they visited for a few minutes before Marvin went to mix him a drink. When Marvin circled back around to where Charles was seated, he asked, "Are you doing OK on your cocktail?"

"I'm fine, thanks. I'm just pondering the question you posed to me about the difference between a mysterious woman and a suspicious woman."

Marvin straightened the stack of napkins on the bar near him. "Well, did you come to some profound conclusion?"

He took a final drink from his cocktail and set it on the counter. "Let's put it this way: I have empirical evidence that the woman with the blue streak is mysterious. As for Ann over there, I only…" Charles paused. "For lack of a better word, I have a suspicion that she is suspicious." He snickered at his inept explanation.

Marvin smiled. "Sir Charles, you're quite the detective. Keep me posted on the results of your investigation."

"I will, Marvin. I'm going to break the rules and order another cocktail."

"My pleasure. Sticking with the citron vodka and soda?"

"Why not?"

Marvin set Charles's third cocktail of the evening in front of him.

"Marvin, do you remember a few nights ago when I told you that I almost was not able to go on this cruise?"

"Yes."

"Well, it was the police that almost prevented me from taking this trip."

Marvin studied Charles's face to determine if he was kidding. "Are you serious?"

"Very serious. I was the one common element in two apparent crimes."

"What does a common element mean?"

"I was at the same place when both crimes were committed. The first time, I was attending an art reception at one of the museums in Dallas. The police think a woman at the reception was intentionally poisoned by someone in attendance. The second occurrence took place at a hotel. I was having drinks with a woman I had not met before that afternoon." Charles stopped speaking to pick up his cocktail glass.

"You were having drinks at a hotel with a woman you'd just met?"

"Yes. I'd met her earlier at a local wine bar. She invited me to meet her back at the bar in her hotel. Marvin, you should have seen her. She was tall, blonde, and gorgeous. That alone should have been a clue she was up to no good. Anyway, I did meet her for a drink. I left to go and get us a second cocktail. Right after I returned, she went to the restroom. I never saw her again. Fortunately, I never took a drink of my second cocktail."

"Did she try to poison you?"

"She or someone. It's an ongoing investigation. A poor guy cleaning up our glasses took a drink of my cocktail. I guess he didn't want an unfinished cocktail to go to waste. It was spiked. He died from ketamine poisoning."

"What's ketamine?"

"Not sure. The detective said it's used by veterinarians to tranquilize animals."

"Sir Charles, what a horrific story."

"Yes, it is. The detective warned me to watch my back. He thinks someone may be trying to kill me."

"My God!"

"At least that is one thing I don't have to worry about on this cruise. No, all I have to worry about is a mysterious brunette and a suspicious blonde."

Charles stood up. "Marvin, have a good evening."

"Good evening, Sir Charles, and watch your back."

"Will do."

As Charles was walking out of the Panorama Lounge, he peeked over at Ann. She and the muscular guy were still talking. Marvin had to think he was a little nuts with his suspicious and mysterious women. Possibly he was right. Charles suspected Ann of being suspicious for no real reason. The two of them obviously didn't hit it off. But that didn't mean she was evil. Well, Vicky was mysterious. What a strange story she had about her lover's borderline-personality wife possibly being on board and stalking her. He could really pick them.

Charles went back to his room and perused the room-service menu. He ordered a petite filet of beef tenderloin and a bottle of zinfandel. Twenty minutes later, Charles heard a knock at the door. A young man in a white coat entered and arranged his dinner on the table. He opened the bottle of zinfandel and poured Charles a glass. Charles thanked him and then cracked open the door to his veranda to enjoy the sound of the ship cruising through the Pacific Ocean.

As soon as he finished dinner, he poured another glass of

wine and took it and the wine bottle outside and sat down in the lounger on the veranda. Charles took a sip and set the glass down on the side table. His eyes closed. *Vicky, are you really in trouble, or are you just having fun with me? What would Sam do?* He went to sleep and started dreaming.

Vicky, please come here! I can help! You must trust me, though. I can't help you if you keep staying out of sight all the time. We need to talk!

Charles woke up suddenly. Was that someone knocking at his door? He reentered his stateroom and walked over to the door. Before Charles reached it, he heard two more knocks. He leaned forward to look through the peephole and saw Vicky standing there, dressed in black from head to toe. Without hesitation, he cracked open the door. Vicky took a step forward so that she was halfway into the stateroom. She asked, "I'm so sorry to bother you at this late hour, but may I please come in?"

"Of course. Is everything OK?"

She lowered her head and started sobbing. Charles walked over and hugged her.

She looked up at him. "I'm sorry. I'll be OK soon."

"Would you like to sit down?"

"Please." Vicky sat on the edge of the bed and slipped off her shoes. Charles sat next to her on her right side.

"Did something happen?"

She ran her hand through her hair. He was mesmerized by how the light played off the blue streak on the right side of her head. She said, "No. Nothing, really. I'm getting so stressed out constantly having to keep my guard up, wondering if that woman is on board."

"But no one has threatened you, though?"

"No, I just don't know how long I can keep this up. I only wanted to have a restful cruise to Sydney." She placed her right hand on Charles's left leg. He countered by putting his left arm around her. Vicky then gently started to rub his leg. Charles could feel her gentle touch as she worked her way up his leg to his crotch. She leaned and softly kissed Charles on the cheek. With her left hand, she began slowly unbuttoning his shirt.

Charles thought, *Is this actually happening?*

They sat in silence as she began massaging his bare chest. Vicky looked up at Charles and smiled. He leaned over toward her and kissed her on the lips. They embraced tightly for a few minutes. Vicky whispered, "You will protect me, won't you, Charles?"

Before he could respond, she stood up in front of him. Charles watched as she slipped off her blouse, followed by her bra, slacks, and panties. Vicky stood before him completely nude. She moved in closer. He could smell her subtle perfume as she pressed her firm stomach against his face.

She said, "Care to join me?" Charles did not respond but stood up and removed all his clothing. Vicky pulled him back to the bed. They made passionate love.

Exhausted, Charles and Vicky were lying side by side on their backs, staring at the ceiling. Vicky said, "I better go."

"Why?"

"Because it's the right thing to do." She eased out of bed and slipped her clothes back on. Charles got out of bed and dressed. He asked, "Would you like to get together for lunch or dinner tomorrow?"

"Let's see what tomorrow brings."

What a curious response. What does that mean? "OK. Are you

OK to go back to your stateroom?"

"I'm fine." Vicky walked over to Charles and gave him a quick kiss on the cheek. She said, "Good night, Charles. I'm sure you'll sleep well."

"Good night, Vicky." Charles followed her to the door. She opened the door and looked both ways before exiting the stateroom. He watched her walk down the hallway until she disappeared into the foyer that led to the bank of stairs and elevators.

He locked his stateroom. What a night! He needed a glass of wine. Charles walked out on the veranda and emptied the remainder of the wine into his glass. It was a beautiful, balmy night. He took a drink of wine and set the glass on the side table. The warm breeze felt very soothing on his face. Charles couldn't remember the last time he had made love. He eased into the lounger and closed his eyes.

CHAPTER TWENTY-SEVEN

Charles woke up, startled by the morning light reflecting off the water onto his face. He was still in the lounger on the veranda. Charles heard the sounds of machinery and truck engines. *My God, I passed out!* He couldn't believe that he had been out there all night. Charles stood up from the chair and retrieved his empty wineglass from the side table. His back was sore from sleeping in an awkward position all night, and his head was pounding.

The ship had docked in the port of Pago Pago, US Samoa. Charles entered his stateroom and checked the alarm clock by his bed. The time was 7:00 a.m. Within fifteen minutes, he was showered, shaved, and on his way to the dining room. A server seated him at a table for two by a window on the port side of the ship. Charles brought along the *Sterling Cruise Reflections* to read during breakfast. More diverse entertainment on board. This afternoon's lecturer was an intimate expert on cannibalism. He recalled reading that cannibalism had once been practiced in Samoa. He sneered. *A cannibal could feast for quite a while on a few of these obese passengers.*

While eating, Charles heard the ship's announcement that passengers were now permitted to go ashore. It was 8:00 a.m., thirty minutes before his scheduled tour. He drank his coffee and watched as the first trickle of people disembarked the ship, which also happened to include Tom Elliott, the professional pickpocket. He was pulling two suitcases behind him. Charles saw a man wave from behind a chain-link security fence. Tom nodded his head to acknowledge he had seen the man. When Tom exited the gate of the security fence, the man grabbed both suitcases and rolled them over to a black Mercedes-Benz limousine. Tom traveled in style. Charles wondered how much this cruise gig paid him.

Charles met his tour group on the shore. There were thirty of them assembled to explore the cultural highlights of US Samoa. They boarded a bus accompanied by a local tour guide, who told them about the major industries, the political system, and the island's history. One of the stops on the tour was a cultural history museum. On display were tools and weapons used by Samoan cannibals. After the three-hour tour, they were returned to the safe and opulent confines of the cruise ship. After boarding, Charles hurried to his stateroom to change into some comfortable clothing suitable for lounging by the pool.

He wondered where Vicky was. She was so elusive in her response to his suggestion of having lunch or dinner together. Maybe it was for the best. Why get involved with someone who was meeting her boyfriend in Sydney?

After grabbing a quick bite for lunch, Charles found a lounge chair in the shade where he could nestle in with his tablet for some concentrated reading. He had barely gotten settled when a server approached him.

"Would you care for something to drink?"

Charles peered up from his tablet. "I think I'd like a glass of chardonnay. Thank you."

The server left to take a few more orders before returning to the bar. What would Sam think of this lifestyle? Charles's detective work was much different from Sam's work back in the 1920s. He doubted that Sam would even touch chardonnay. Charles opened his book app and began reading.

After about twenty pages, he laid his tablet on the table next to his half-empty glass of chardonnay. It was time for a little snooze by the pool. He closed his eyes and fell asleep.

* * *

MRS. SIMON WAS SITTING TEN YARDS away in a lounger, shaded by an umbrella. She waited a few minutes before standing up. She collected her paperback from the armrest and pulled a vial of ketamine out of her purse. She snapped her head back and forth. All the passengers seemed to be reading or napping. She emptied the vial into Charles's glass of chardonnay. She shielded her actions with her cover-up. *Don't screw this up, Pierce! I'm almost out of ketamine!* Mrs. Simon slipped the empty vial into her purse. She only had one left. Casually, she sauntered toward the nearest entrance to the ship.

* * *

WHEN CHARLES AWOKE, HE LOOKED around to regain his bearings. In the far corner of the pool area, he saw Ann talking to some woman whose back was to him. Ann had one hand on her hip, and the other hand was shaking in the direction of the woman's head. What was that all about? Charles stood up to try to get a better viewing angle. *My God, it's Vicky with Ann!* After a few minutes, Vicky started to walk away. Ann grabbed her by the arm. Vicky abruptly pulled her arm out of Ann's grasp and hurried off. Ann followed her. This wasn't good. He needed to find out what was going on.

Charles walked briskly to where he had seen the two women exit the pool area. A few seconds later, he swung open the door that led from the pool deck to the interior of the ship. No one was in sight. Charles turned a sharp corner and hurried down the narrow corridor of staterooms. He saw a man coming toward him. "Did you happen to see two women?" he asked him. The man continued walking toward him. Charles repeated, "Did you happen to see two women?"

He seemed perplexed. "Two women?"

Charles came closer to him. "Yes, two women who were arguing?"

He studied Charles closely. "No, I can't say that I have."

Charles walked past him. "OK, thanks."

Where could they be? He walked the length of the passageway until he came to a staircase and a bank of elevators. Still no sign of either woman. This was futile.

Charles took the stairs to the ninth deck and walked to his stateroom. Should he tell security about Vicky and Ann? It might not be anything, though. He thought he should try to get a message to Vicky, so he decided to check with the reception desk. After a quick shower, he changed into his clothes for the evening and headed down toward the fifth deck. When he reached the landing on the sixth deck, a large group of people had congregated, waiting for an elevator. Charles hesitated. He asked a woman standing near him, "What's going on?"

She said, "The whole section around the boutique is sealed

off. We were asked to evacuate the sixth deck."

"Really? Why?"

"Something about a breach in the security with the diamond."

Charles shook his head. "Oh my. Just a little more excitement on board, I guess."

The woman did not respond. Charles made his way through the crowd and walked down the stairs to the fifth deck. When he arrived at the atrium, he witnessed a lot of activity. Ship personnel scurried back and forth. Charles walked over to the reception desk, but no one was behind the counter. He waited at the desk for several minutes. Finally, a woman emerged from behind a door. "I apologize for keeping you waiting. We had a minor problem we had to address."

"It appears so—you had to seal off part of the sixth deck."

"Were you there?"

Charles grinned. "No, I was walking down the stairs from my stateroom, and a woman on the sixth deck told me that the boutique was sealed because of a security breach involving the diamond."

The woman sighed. "Is there something I can do for you?"

"Yes. I need to get in touch with a fellow passenger. I know her name but not her stateroom number."

The woman behind the counter placed her hands on her keyboard. "Of course. We can deliver your message. Although to protect the privacy of our passengers, we cannot disclose any stateroom numbers."

"I understand. Her name is Vicky LeBlanc." Charles watched as the woman typed in the name. "Is that Vicky with a y?"

"Yes. I think so." The woman looked at him over the screen of her computer. "We do not have either a Vicky with a y or a Vicki with an i. For that matter, we do not have anyone on board with the last name of LeBlanc."

"Can you try other ways to spell her last name?"

The woman started to type and then stopped. "I'm sorry, sir. We do not have anyone with a name remotely close to a Vicky LeBlanc on board. Do you suppose you misunderstood her when she told you her last name?"

Charles stared blankly at the woman. "I'm positive that she told me her name was Vicky LeBlanc. Nevertheless, I must be mistaken. I'm so sorry to have troubled you."

The woman smiled. "No problem at all. You'll likely run into her soon, and then the mystery will be solved."

Charles turned around and headed back to the staircase. Bizarre. Truly bizarre. He was certain that Vicky told him that her last name was LeBlanc. He checked his phone for the time. It was 4:45 p.m. The Cove Bar was down the hall on this deck. Charles needed a drink. When he reached the Cove, he recognized the bartender from an earlier evening. There was only one other man at the bar. At least Charles wouldn't be the only one drinking before 5:00 p.m. When he settled on a stool, the bartender approached.

"Good afternoon. What can I get you?"

"You're Darya from Belarus, right?"

The bartender nodded, her face expressionless. "Yes. My name is Darya. May I get you something?"

"Yes, a glass of chardonnay."

She poured Charles's glass of wine and set it on the napkin without uttering a word.

"Thank you."

Darya stepped to the other side of the bar and began removing glasses from a dishwasher. He took a sip and peered around. There were a few people milling about the atrium just outside of the Cove. An announcement came over the PA system:

"Good afternoon. This is Captain Jacobi. Please be advised that the section around the Sterling Boutique on the sixth deck has been temporarily cordoned off. We experienced a security issue with the boutique. Dr. Vitroil has informed Sterling Cruise Security that the display case that held the Volk Yellow Diamond has been breached. We do not know the specific time this breach occurred. However, a perpetrator removed the diamond and replaced it with a fake one. As a result, we are on a *Code Red*, which is the highest security level under international maritime law. What this means is that while the Code Red is in effect, you may be limited in where you are allowed to go throughout the ship. In addition, Sterling Cruise Security and Sterling Cruise officers may question you. Although we respect the privacy of our guests, we may have to search your staterooms. No one will be allowed to leave the ship while a Code Red is in effect. We apologize for this inconvenience. If you have any questions, please feel free to contact Security on the fifth deck. I will keep you updated when there is more information to share."

By the time the captain had concluded his announcement, Charles had finished off the glass of chardonnay. Darya approached him. "Would you care for another glass of wine?"

"Please."

A woman sat down at the bar a couple of seats to Charles's

left and ordered a vodka tonic. Darya mixed her cocktail and set it in front of her. She glanced over at him and asked, "Can you believe this Code Red business?"

"All kinds of excitement on board."

He thought, *Not only did a diamond go missing, but so did Vicky—or whatever her name is.*

"Do you think one of the passengers stole the diamond?" the woman asked.

Charles shrugged. "You'd think if it was indeed stolen, the crew would have more access to the diamond than the passengers. Of course, during its unveiling, several passengers got to hold and examine it."

The woman lifted her cocktail and studied it, as if it might contain the diamond. She asked, "Did you hold it?"

"Yes, just for a moment."

"I didn't attend that event. However, I heard the gemologist just discovered this morning that the diamond on display was a fake. You would have thought he would have constantly checked on it."

"I'd assume they had security cameras in the boutique. Anyone removing the real diamond would be seen or recorded."

The woman said, "One of the security guys told me and others that there are cameras in the boutique and throughout the ship."

Charles gripped his glass of chardonnay. "Well, if that's the case, then hopefully this Code Red will be short-lived. Not a lot of places one can hide on a ship."

"I hope you're right. We're supposed to be in Fiji the day after tomorrow. I wonder what happens if we're still on a Code Red when we arrive."

He fiddled with the edge of his cocktail napkin. "My guess is if the Code Red is still in effect, then no one will be allowed to disembark. I'm sure the crew will be working overtime to try to locate that diamond and whoever took it."

Darya came over, eyeing his empty glass. "Would you care for another glass of chardonnay?"

"No, thank you. But may I ask you a question?"

Darya nodded.

"Do you remember a few nights back when I was here?"

She was staring at him. "Yes, you were sitting there."

Darya pointed at a stool two down from him.

"Yes, exactly! Do you remember the woman I was visiting with, sitting on my left?"

Darya froze, as if she were trying to remember. "No, I don't recall you talking to any woman."

"You remember the precise stool where I was sitting but not the woman sitting next to me?"

Darya took a few steps back. "No, I'm sorry. I remember, though, what you ordered."

Charles sighed. "What did I order?"

"A White Russian. I don't get a lot of requests for that drink, so I remembered that."

Charles noticed that the other woman at the bar was watching their exchange. He took a deep breath to calm down. "Darya, don't you remember the attractive woman? She was a brunette with a blue streak in her hair. Surely you must have seen her."

Darya forced a smile. "Sorry, sir. I just don't recall seeing her. Excuse me." Darya retreated to the other side of the bar to wait on a couple.

"I think you frightened our bartender," the woman said. "Is everything OK?"

Charles wondered if he should tell this woman about his experiences with Vicky. No, he didn't think that was a promising idea. As far as the Sterling crew was concerned, Vicky LeBlanc didn't exist. Maybe she was only a dream or something he conjured up in a drunken stupor.

Charles stood up from his stool. "Everything is fine, thank you. I'm sorry if I caused anyone to be uncomfortable."

The woman took a final drink from her cocktail. "This Code Red has everyone on edge."

"Perhaps you're right. Good evening." As Charles was walking away, he paused a step and said, "I'm off to catch a diamond thief."

"I hope you're successful."

Charles took the stairs from the fifth deck up to the ninth. When he rounded the corner by his stateroom, he saw a group of men huddled outside. Oh my God. What was going on here? As he got closer, he could see that the door to his stateroom was open.

Charles passed two of the men and headed into the room. A man stepped in front of him, blocking his way. "Sir, is this your stateroom?"

Stunned, Charles replied, "Yes, it is."

"I'm Deputy Security Officer Dundy. We're conducting random stateroom searches pursuant to our Code Red procedure. Your stateroom and three others were selected from this deck."

Charles peered around the officer and could see that his room was in shambles. All the dresser drawers were sticking out, and the bedcovers were pulled off. Two men were inside searching through clothes, towels, and even his empty suitcases.

Dundy continued, "We should be done soon. You can save us all some time if you'll give me the code to your safe."

Charles swallowed. "Uh, sure. It's 5215. I have some cash inside, though."

"Please follow me so that you can see what I am doing."

Dundy entered Charles's room and reached in through the open closet door to where the room safe was situated. Charles followed behind him. Dundy entered the code, and the safe door swung open. Nestled in the back of the safe was a wad of twenty-dollar bills. He pulled the bills out and searched with his other hand in the interior of the safe.

"Here's your money. You can change your code when you return to your stateroom later this evening and put your cash back in the safe if you desire."

Charles stuck the bills in his wallet. "Should I leave now?"

"Yes, please. Housekeeping will put everything back in order as soon as we're finished. I apologize for the inconvenience."

Charles exited the room. He took the stairs and walked down to the eighth deck, where the staterooms were located on the port side of the ship. As Charles entered the passageway, he could see a cluster of men surrounding one of the rooms about midship. *So I'm not the only one whose stateroom is being searched. The Fourth Amendment must not apply to ships at sea.* Charles sure as hell didn't know.

Charles entered the dining room and waited as usual while the maître d' orchestrated the seating of the people in line before him. When Charles approached, he looked up from studying the seating chart. "Still choosing to dine alone, Mr. Pierce?"

Charles frowned. "After the day that I have had, most definitely."

"Let's give you a change of scenery, then." The maître d' motioned to one of the servers. "Take Mr. Pierce to table 771."

Charles followed the server as he escorted him to a different part of the dining room. As they walked, he scanned the other tables for a possible Vicky sighting.

CHAPTER TWENTY-EIGHT

After finishing dinner, Charles wondered if the ship's security was finished ransacking his room under the auspices of Code Red. He was going to go to the Saloon and get a cocktail first before checking on it. The Saloon was about two-thirds full, the after-dinner crowd. Charles found an unoccupied stool at the bar and slid in. A bartender approached, and he ordered a citron vodka and soda.

Charles could overhear multiple conversations. Code Red was the subject everyone was angrily discussing. A man to his right said, "The bars on board are going to be as popular as this Code Red thing is unpopular."

"At least they haven't restricted access to them yet," Charles commented.

The man waved his cocktail in the air. "Excellent point. I can tell you one thing: Sterling will have a mutiny on its hands if they restrict us from the bars."

As the man was speaking, Charles watched over his shoulder as Ann entered the Saloon. She was accompanied by the muscular young guy and another man. They located some standing room next to the bar a few feet away from him. Charles could hear Ann's shrill voice over the noise of the many conversations going on in the bar. They ordered drinks. One of the bar patrons near them got up and left the Saloon. Ann quickly sat down on the now unoccupied stool. The two men huddled around her.

The man on Charles's right continued the conversation. "I hear they've even started searching some of the staterooms."

"I can personally attest to that. My room was being searched earlier this evening. They were making quite a mess."

The man set his drink down hard on the bar. "You think they're going to leave it like that?"

Charles shrugged. "The security officer said housekeeping would straighten it up after they were through. I'll find out later tonight."

Charles watched Ann's group. The muscular young man took Ann's empty glass from her hand and set it on the bar, out of her reach. She hollered, "Mr. Bartender!" She got the attention of not just the bartender but everyone else at the bar. "I need another drink."

The muscular young man grabbed her shoulder and firmly said, "Anita! Not now."

The two men helped Ann to her feet, and they left the Saloon. The man to Charles's right said, "I guess she's not having another drink, after all."

Charles glanced down at his empty glass. Should he have another one? The bartender read his thoughts, and Charles pushed the glass in his direction. Charles watched as the bartender mixed his cocktail. Had he heard that correctly? Did that guy call Ann *Anita*? Charles looked over at the man sitting to his right. He was staring straight ahead. Charles asked him, "Did you hear what that guy said to the woman before they escorted her out of the bar?"

He considered the question. "I think he said, 'Anita, not now.'"

"So you heard him say *Anita* as well?"

He asked, "Do you know her?"

"Not really. I met her once, and I thought she told me her name was Ann. Maybe she did. I guess Ann may be short for Anita."

Charles thought, *Wait a minute! Didn't Vicky tell me that Anita was the name of the wife of the man she was meeting in Sydney?* He was sure of it. She was frightened the wife might be on the ship. *So Ann is Anita, the borderline-personality-disorder wife who has a violent streak.* Had she been threatening Vicky earlier by the pool? That made perfect sense. He needed some fresh air.

Charles finished off his cocktail and took the elevator to the seventh deck so that he could get outside to the exterior deck. It was a dark, cloudy night. He couldn't see any stars. No one else was in sight. He started walking along the deck. There was no sound except for the ship breaking waves. Charles walked two laps around the perimeter of the ship and paused at the stern to study the currents trailing behind the ship. While leaning on the railing, he could just make out the white churning water illuminated by a small, exterior light mounted on the stern. Charles heard some muffled voices from the lower deck where the golf area was situated.

He heard a man shout, "There she is! Get her!"

There was a scuffling sound. Charles leaned and peered over the railing as far as physically possible. All he could see were several shadows of what appeared to be men struggling with something. There was a splash, and he saw a glimmer of color flash past the slightly illuminated churning water. Did someone go overboard? What should he do? Before Charles could move, he saw a flash of light below where someone had opened the door that led onto the lower deck. For a split second, he caught a glimpse of a blonde woman before the door closed, casting the deck back into darkness.

Charles sprinted to the nearest door leading to the interior of the ship and raced down to the deck below. It took him at least five minutes to reach the golf area. He quickly opened the door and raced outside. There was no sign of anyone. He looked around at the neatly stacked golf equipment. Charles approached the railing and looked over at the precise spot where he had seen the glimmer of color. There was nothing visible. But he felt compelled to report this to the ship's security. Charles's day kept getting stranger.

He found the elevators and pressed the button for the fifth deck. His mind was racing. *Could the blonde have been Ann or Anita, whoever she was? Was that Vicky they threw overboard? Oh my God!* Charles couldn't believe this was happening. As soon as the elevator opened, he hurried over to the reception desk. *Great! A different woman is working now. Glad it's not the same woman I asked about Vicky being a guest on board.*

"Excuse me. I think I may have an emergency to report."

That got the woman's attention. She was startled. "Yes. Please go ahead." Some people neared the desk.

Attempting to be discreet, Charles leaned in a bit toward the woman. "This sounds crazy, but I think I may have witnessed someone being pushed overboard."

"What is your name, sir?"

"Charles Pierce."

"Go over to that door. I'll need to alert Security, and then I'll let you in."

She picked up a phone, and Charles walked over to the door. Seconds later, the woman opened it. "Please go in and wait in one of those chairs over there."

As soon as Charles sat down, a woman in a white uniform with multiple stripes on her shoulders came into the room. She walked over to him.

"Mr. Pierce, I am Chief Security Officer Polhaus." Charles started to stand up. "Please keep your seat." Polhaus pulled up a chair and sat down across from him. "Tell me exactly what you saw."

If a woman had been pushed overboard, shouldn't she be in more of a hurry to attempt to find her? Charles felt his face flush with anger. "Shouldn't you turn the ship around? We might be able to save her!"

"Mr. Pierce, this ship was renovated last year," Polhaus said calmly. "It was equipped with the latest in radar, motion detection, and thermal-imaging systems. Absolutely nothing goes overboard without one of the systems being triggered. These systems are so sophisticated that when an object goes overboard, we can even determine its weight, and a distinct image of it is often recorded."

"If that's true, did these systems detect anything going overboard about fifteen minutes ago?"

"As a matter of fact, we were alerted about an object going overboard."

Why wasn't she more animated?

"What we detected appeared to be a bag of golf clubs thrown overboard from the sixth deck."

Charles scowled. "Golf clubs? You can't be serious!"

"Please calm down, Mr. Pierce. You can best help us by telling me everything that you saw and heard."

Charles put his head in his hands. "May I have a bottle of water?"

Polhaus left the room and returned with a bottle of water and handed it to him.

"Thank you. I went to the seventh deck to get some fresh air and—"

"Where were you coming from?"

Charles took a drink of water. "I was coming from the Saloon."

"How many drinks did you have?"

How many? "Two, I believe. How is the state of my sobriety relevant to anything?"

"Alcohol can play tricks on your brain. I must ask these questions to conduct a thorough investigation. Please continue with your story."

Charles took another drink of water. "After I got to the seventh deck, I noticed how overcast and dark it was outside. I then decided to walk a couple of laps around the ship to get some exercise." He paused.

"What happened next?"

"Well, I stopped at the stern of the ship to watch the white currents it made while sailing.It was very dark, but there was enough light to make them out. While I was leaning on the railing, I heard some voices and commotion below in the golf area."

"Did you hear anything specifically?"

"I'm paraphrasing, but I believe I heard a man shout,

'There's the woman. Get her!' I then leaned over the railing as far as I could to try to see what was going on below. Most of my view was obstructed, but I heard what I thought was a splash. Then someone below opened the door that leads to the interior of the ship from the deck. There was a flash of light from the door, and I thought I caught a glimpse of the back of a blonde woman's head."

"What happened next?"

Charles picked up his water bottle and squeezed it. "I ran down the stairs to the sixth deck. When I located the door to the golf area, I went out onto the deck. No one was there. I reentered the ship and came straight here to report what I witnessed."

"Mr. Pierce, the whole time that you were on the seventh or sixth deck, was anyone else on either deck while you were there?"

"I didn't see anyone."

"You said that you saw a blonde woman. But the voice you heard was clearly a man, correct?"

"Yes, correct. I couldn't see people, but I saw the shadows of what seemed to be three people."

"So there was the blonde, the man who shouted, and maybe one or two other people?"

"Perhaps. I think there were only three people, counting the blonde woman."

"But you actually just saw the blonde and only briefly from behind, correct?"

"Yes." Charles thought, *Should I tell her about Ann or Anita?* Vicky had asked him not to say anything. But then again, he didn't know if Vicky even existed.

Polhaus was studying his face. "Anything else you want to tell me?"

Charles took another drink of water. "Yes, there is something else I think you should know. But may I ask a question first?"

"Go ahead."

"Is it possible for me to see the image you captured of the golf bag that was thrown overboard?"

"No. It's evidence in an ongoing investigation. Intentionally and without authorization, disposing of any object overboard is a criminal offense under international maritime law."

"So are you saying that you know a golf bag was thrown overboard, but you don't know the culprit?"

Polhaus nudged Charles. "Maybe it was you, huh?"

Charles recoiled in his chair. "You aren't serious, are you?"

"Mr. Pierce, you are the only witness I have so far who may have been in that location at that time. I suspect everyone until I know who is responsible."

"So you have the technology to know what goes overboard but no video of how or why it goes overboard?"

"There are video cameras throughout the ship, but they don't cover every square inch of the ship. In this case, we didn't capture anything on our security cameras."

"I suspect that if the yellow diamond was thrown overboard, you would have captured the culprit on video in that case."

"Not certain. In fact, there are three cameras hidden in various locations within the boutique, yet . . ." She paused.

"Are you saying you didn't get a video of anyone switching out the yellow diamond for the fake one?"

"No. All I'm willing to say is that there's a reason that we are in Code Red. However, you said you had something else to tell me."

"Yes, I guess this is my moment to pay the devil."

Polhaus furrowed her eyebrows. "What do you mean?"

"A fellow passenger told me that the *devil* is the wooden ship's longest seam in the hull. The task of 'paying the devil'—caulking the longest seam of the hull—was despised by everyone. Of course, the phrase now means to perform an unpleasant task. I have the unpleasant task of telling you about Vicky, Ann, and Anita."

Polhaus looked at her watch and frowned. "It's almost ten-thirty. Is this story of yours really important to the security of the passengers on this ship?"

"Yes, I believe it is a security issue."

"Excuse me for just a few minutes. I have a small task to do, and then I'll be back."

"I'm going to go use the restroom, then."

When Charles returned to the office, Polhaus was not there. He sat down in the same chair as before and stared at his empty water bottle. The woman who was behind the desk earlier opened the door. "Chief Security Officer Polhaus will be with you in a moment. She got delayed."

"OK, thank you." Charles checked the time on his phone. It was now almost 11:00 p.m. Polhaus opened the door and came inside. "Sorry to keep you waiting."

"Please tell me you caught the diamond thief."

She grumbled, "No, it was just a small matter."

Charles could not resist. "Well, did you catch the culprit who threw the golf bag overboard?" She did not respond but gave him a stern look. "Shall I begin my story then?"

"Please."

"I met this woman on board. She told me her name was Vicky LeBlanc. After some small talk—"

"Where did you meet her?"

"At the Cove Bar."

"Of course, you were at a bar. Go on."

"May I have another bottle of water?"

Polhaus stared at Charles's empty bottle, stood up, and left the room. She returned a few seconds later with a bottle of water and handed it to him.

"Thank you." He unscrewed the cap, took a drink of water, and rescrewed the cap. "I was at the Cove Bar, enjoying a cocktail, when a woman sat down beside me. She was an attractive woman in her midfifties. Although I had never spoken with her before then, I had seen her earlier several times. In fact, she boarded the ship just before me. She has this one unusual aspect of her appearance. Almost every time that I saw her, I noticed this blue streak in her otherwise dark-brunette hair. We engaged in conversation for a few minutes about meaningless things—like my cocktail of choice that evening. Before you ask, it was a White Russian."

Polhaus cleared her throat. "OK, go on."

"Believe it or not, that is significant to my story. I made the comment to Vicky that I usually drink chardonnay or vodka and soda. In response, she said that sometimes you must live dangerously. That prompted me to ask her how she lived dangerously. I was just flirting."

"Obviously. Go on with your story."

"Vicky then started talking about how danger is an inevitable part of living. There's no avoiding it. If so, she said, then why not be willing to take some chances pursuing a passion even though it may prove to be dangerous? Emboldened, I asked if it was too personal to ask what type of passion she was pursuing. She swore me to secrecy; I promised not to tell anyone on board. I thought that should be an easy promise to keep—I don't know anybody here and pretty much keep to myself—so I agreed."

"So what was her secret passion?"

Charles took a drink of water. "She said she was going to Sydney to meet a married man. This man is not her husband. She said there was something more she wanted to tell me, but a crowd approached the bar, so she couldn't continue her story. She excused herself and left."

Polhaus stared at him. She then threw her empty water bottle across the room into a trash can. "That's it? This woman is having an affair. So what? It happens every day. This is your story?"

"I'm not finished. There's more. A few evenings later, I'm having a cocktail."

"At the Cove Bar?" Polhaus interjected.

"No, this was at the Saloon. I was sitting at the bar, staring at my phone, when I felt a tug on my shoulder. When I looked up, Vicky was standing next to me, but her eyes were darting around the bar. She seemed nervous or upset and told me that she needed to talk to me. But she was not comfortable talking at the bar. She feared that someone could be watching. At first, she asked if I would mind meeting her at her stateroom. Then she changed her mind and asked if it was OK if we met in my stateroom."

"I'm sure you were just fine with that proposal."

"Yes and no. I didn't know what I was getting myself into.

Anyway, I met her at my stateroom about thirty minutes later. We had a couple of glasses of wine."

"Just two glasses?"

"Yes. Vicky said she had received a text from Miles—that was the name of the man she was meeting in Sydney—that his wife was visiting friends in the States. Rather than fly directly home, she had opted to take a cruise back to Sydney. Then she told me that she thought the married guy's wife might be on this cruise."

Polhaus held up her hand. "Stop right there. So Vicky is worried that she's going to run into her boyfriend's wife while on board? Is that what you consider a security issue?"

Charles then repeated the story that Vicky had told him about how her boyfriend's wife had psychological issues and how she might pose a threat to her.

"Does this wife have a name?"

"Vicky told me her last name was different than her husband's last name. Unfortunately, she doesn't know the wife's last name. Her first name, though, is Anita."

"Anything else happen?"

"We kissed."

"No doubt. It appears to me that you are smitten by this Vicky. Is that the end of the story?"

Charles shook his head. "There's more. I keep seeing this Ann person on board. She seems to be everywhere. We were introduced at a singles' cocktail reception. She took an immediate disliking to me. I couldn't put my finger on it, but I had an intuition that she was up to no good."

"This is related to Vicky, correct?"

Charles described to Polhaus the apparent confrontation between Ann and Vicky that he observed on the pool deck and how he had inquired at the reception desk about Vicky, only to learn that no one with her name was registered as a guest.

Polhaus asked, "Mr. Pierce, do you think this Vicky is perhaps a figment of your imagination?"

Charles buried his head in his hands. He then raised his head and stared at Polhaus. "No."

"OK. You don't seem one hundred percent convinced. May I ask a question?"

"Yes."

"Why are you traveling alone? You're a decent-enough-looking guy and must be somewhat successful. Why would you take this type of cruise by yourself?"

Charles rubbed his eyes, which had teared up from either emotion or being tired from a very long day. "Well, I'm getting over the death of my wife, and my travel agent and I thought this might be a fun trip for me to take."

"I see. Do you think it's possible that the stress you experienced—or perhaps even alcohol—has clouded your perception of things? By that, I mean you're alone on this ship, where you're one of just a handful of single travelers. This Vicky relationship could be your way of escaping loneliness."

"You're the head security officer. Don't you think it's possible or perhaps even plausible that Vicky didn't trust me enough to give me her real name? She mentioned needing someone to lean on and watch her back. Maybe I was in the right place at the right time. Or, as it turns out, perhaps I was in the right place at the wrong time."

Polhaus looked at her watch. "It's awfully late. You almost done?"

Charles then told Polhaus of hearing Ann being referred

to as Anita at the bar and how she might be the unhinged wife Vicky feared, concluding with his worry that maybe she and some men had thrown Vicky overboard.

Polhaus said, "I'll be honest with you. I'm not sure this Vicky person even exists. However, I will give you the benefit of the doubt. I'll open an investigation into the matter. As you can imagine, most of my resources are dedicated to finding the culprit who took that damn diamond and the jerk who threw his golf bag overboard. So I want you to do some informal detective work yourself. If you see Vicky again on board, you bring her to Security immediately. Do you understand?"

Now was probably not the time for Charles to tell Polhaus that he was Sam Spade's imaginary detective partner. "Yes, of course. What about Anita?"

Polhaus stood up. "You stay away from her. She may very well be dangerous. If you see her, just let one of my staff know so that we can identify her. Do we understand one another?"

Charles stood up. "Yes. Thank you."

Polhaus said, "I think it's time we both get some sleep."

"Agreed. But one last thing. Don't you think Tom Elliott should be a prime suspect in the diamond theft? After all, he's a professional pickpocket. I watched him get off the ship this morning and drive off in a limo."

Polhaus feigned a smile. "Do you think we haven't thought of that possibility? He's being investigated by the Samoan authorities."

Charles left the office and entered the atrium on the fifth deck. It was eerily quiet. He took the elevator to the ninth deck. He was anxious to see if his room was still in shambles. Charles grabbed the ship's newspaper from the mail slot, unlocked the door to his stateroom, and entered. The only light in the room was the bedside reading lamp. His room was immaculate. Everything had been put back into place. He stripped down to his boxers and got into bed. He grabbed the *Sterling Cruise Reflections* from the nightstand. The headline of the newspaper read:

One Day at Sea until Historic Fiji

If they didn't locate the missing diamond, no one would be getting off the ship in Fiji. He set the newspaper down and went to sleep.

CHAPTER TWENTY-NINE

The next morning, Charles awoke to voices in the passageway outside his room. He slipped on a T-shirt and shorts, opened the door, and peered outside. Deputy Security Officer Dundy and a group of men were searching the stateroom next to his. Charles walked over to where Dundy was standing. "Are you doing more random searches?"

"No, the random searches didn't turn up anything, so we have to search every stateroom."

"Are you going to search my stateroom again?"

"No, we're done with you."

Charles did not respond and returned to his stateroom. He ordered room service and sat down on his veranda with the ship's newspaper to find out what was happening on board today. A destination lecture on Fiji. It seemed a tad sadistic to have a destination lecture about a place when you wouldn't be allowed to visit it. All these Code Red restrictions seemed overly oppressive. Charles couldn't just hunker down in his room all day, though. After lunch, he decided to check out all the public areas on every deck of the ship. That would give him an opportunity to get some exercise and possibly find Vicky—or even Anita, for that matter.

What if Polhaus was mistaken about the golf bag? Who would throw a golf bag overboard? That was ridiculous. A golf bag? Really? For all Charles knew, it was Vicky. Maybe Anita and her cronies had stuffed Vicky in a golf bag and threw her overboard. He had to stop this type of thinking. It was driving him crazy. Charles couldn't stop dreaming about Vicky. She seemed so real. Maybe Polhaus was right about stress affecting his mental state. If he could find Vicky, that would answer a lot of questions.

Charles had a lunch of spaghetti bolognese and a glass of zinfandel on the deck near the pool. From the table, he could see the entire dining room. Everything appeared to be business as usual in this part of the ship. Before he could finish his glass of wine, though, he watched as one of the ship's security officers moved toward the small outside bar. The officers walked behind the bar and started stacking all the bottles of alcohol on top of the bar. Charles's waiter came over to the table and said, "The bar is temporarily closed, so I cannot serve any more wine."

"No problem. I wasn't going to order another. What's going on?"

"Security is searching the bar."

Since Charles was already on the twelfth deck, he decided to explore more of the ship. He checked out the pool area. Most of the loungers were occupied by people reading or sunbathing. He passed through and walked the length of the ship to the Panorama Lounge. The bar was closed. Charles covered the entire space and checked every nook and cranny of the public areas. No sign of Vicky or Anita. He then walked through the corridors of decks eleven through seven. Dundy and other ship security personnel were on several of the decks, conducting stateroom searches.

Charles lingered on the eighth deck for a while. Hadn't Vicky told him that her stateroom was on the deck just below his? There was nothing of note, other than people entering or exiting their staterooms. He then moved down to the sixth deck. The casino, boutiques, Saloon, and the Sterling Lounge occupied the entire level. There was no one in the Saloon, and the doors to the Sterling Lounge were closed. Charles could hear music on the other side of the door. *They must be rehearsing for a performance.* As he neared the casino, the clanging noise generated by various slot machines grew louder. It was comfortably crowded, with a spirited group surrounding the roulette wheel. Still no sign of either woman.

The fifth deck contained the last areas open to passengers that he hadn't yet checked. Charles entered the atrium and saw a woman and a man working behind the reception desk. He walked down the hallway that led to the Cove Bar. There were a few people sitting at the bar, enjoying cocktails. Other than getting a little exercise, his tour of the ship had not been successful. Charles wondered if he should attend the destination lecture at 4:00 p.m. Hell, even if he wasn't able to get off the ship in Fiji, maybe he would at least learn something.

Charles reached the Sterling Lounge at 3:50 p.m. and found an aisle seat on the left. People slowly trickled into the auditorium. By 4:00 p.m., it was half-full. He periodically looked around to check the auditorium behind him. No Vicky or Anita in sight. A few minutes later, instead of the lecturer taking the stage, an announcement came over the public address system:

"Good afternoon, ladies and gentlemen, this is Captain Jacoby. I wanted to update you on our Code Red status. As you know, Sterling Cruise Security has been conducting a search of every stateroom on board. All staterooms have now been searched, according to Code Red guidelines. We sincerely apologize for any inconvenience this has caused you. We have not found the missing Volk Yellow Diamond. As a result, we will remain on Code Red. I do, though, have some good news. All passengers who wish to go ashore at the port in Fiji tomorrow may do so. However, you will be required to submit to Sterling Cruise Security screening both when disembarking and when coming back on board. We appreciate your continued cooperation. Thank you for your attention."

The crowd in the Sterling Lounge erupted into applause. The lecturer, Dr. Joel Cairo, walked to the podium on the side of the stage. "I am pleased to learn that my destination lecture on Fiji will not be strictly for academic purposes. You might now actually get to see some of the points of interest that I will discuss today."

Charles listened as Dr. Cairo gave his PowerPoint presentation on the history and highlights of Fiji. After the lecture, Charles took the stairs up to the twelfth deck and the Panorama Lounge. He walked through the lounge to the bar.

Some woman was sitting on *his* barstool. Marvin was visiting with her. No one else was at the bar. Charles settled onto a stool on the opposite side. After a few minutes, Marvin turned around and noticed him. He excused himself from the woman and made his way over to Charles.

"Sir Charles, how are you this evening?"

"Marvin, how could you let someone sit on my stool?"

Marvin smiled. "Would you like a vodka and soda?"

"Perfect. Thank you!"

He made Charles a cocktail and set it in front of him.

"So, Marvin, how have you been?"

"I'm getting so tired of this Code Red. But other than that, I'm doing fine."

"Did Security search all the crew's rooms as well?"

"Yes, they searched every inch."

"Who do you think took the diamond?"

Marvin glanced around to make sure no one other than Charles could hear. "I think it was the gemologist who brought it on board. He's the only one who had access to it after it was locked in the case. The security cameras did not detect anyone else near it."

Charles leaned in toward Marvin. "Excellent point. Since he's still on board, though, it's hard to imagine how he thinks he can get away with it. As for me, I think it was the pick-pocket. He's phenomenal at his craft. I watched as he disembarked in Samoa the other day. He was greeted by a guy driving a Mercedes limousine."

Marvin excused himself to wait on another person at the bar. A man had joined the woman sitting on Charles's stool. Charles nursed his cocktail and stared at the horizon through the window. It was a beautiful, calm day at sea.

Marvin returned to his side of the bar. Charles considered telling Marvin his experiences yesterday and the visit with the chief of security. "Marvin, I don't suppose you've seen my mysterious woman?"

"The woman with the blue streak, correct?"

"Yes. You remember—she's the mysterious woman, and the blonde is the suspicious woman."

"Oh yes, I remember your subtle distinctions. I'm afraid I haven't seen either one of them." Marvin noticed Charles's empty glass. "Care for another one?"

"Sure, why not?"

Marvin made Charles a cocktail and set it in front of him. He then went to the other side of the bar to wait on the couple. Charles took the opportunity to survey the lounge behind him. Several more people had arrived and were primarily occupying the tables near the windows on either side of the ship for a view of the ocean. From a distance, he could hear that New Zealand accent. He was certain it was Anita's voice, and it was getting louder.

Charles peeked over to his left. Anita and the same two men who were with her at the Saloon the other night sat down at the bar. As soon as Marvin finished waiting on the couple, he approached Anita's group. Marvin made cocktails for all three and shot a glance in Charles's direction. Instead of coming directly over to him, Marvin moved along the interior perimeter of the bar, checking on everyone. He finally arrived across from Charles.

"I gather you saw her?"

"Yes. Tell me, is there anyone from Sterling Security in the Panorama Lounge?"

Marvin looked startled. "You mean right now?"

Charles rested his elbows on the bar to get closer to him. "Yes. Is there anyone?"

Marvin's eyes darted around. "No. Is there something wrong?"

"I can't share the specifics, but Chief Security Officer Polhaus told me to keep an eye out for her." Charles motioned his head in Anita's direction.

Marvin was studying his expression to see if Charles was

kidding him. "You spoke to the chief security officer?"

"Yes, I reported an incident to her yesterday. Did you hear anything about something being thrown overboard last night?"

"Yes. Some nut threw a bag of golf clubs overboard."

Charles nodded. "Well, I witnessed something being thrown over. I was on the seventh deck, and whatever went overboard was right below me. Unfortunately, it was dark, and I couldn't see who threw what. But I heard voices and commotion, followed by a splash."

Marvin stole a glance over at Anita. "Are you saying that group is responsible for doing it?"

"All I can say is that Chief Polhaus asked me to alert Security if I saw her. Can you call them from the bar?"

Marvin's face turned pale. "Yes, give me a moment."

Marvin picked up a phone behind the counter. Charles watched as he punched a few buttons and whispered into the receiver. He set the phone down and nodded to him.

Charles sat on his stool and stared at the horizon out the window. How was this going to play out? Within five minutes, Charles saw Marvin making eye contact with someone approaching from behind him. Marvin subtly nodded his head in Charles's direction. Deputy Security Officer Dundy, in his white uniform, stepped up to the bar beside him.

"Good evening, Mr. Pierce. Could you please follow me outside?"

Charles set his cocktail on the bar and stood up. Trying to be discreet, he snuck a glance over at Anita. She was staring at him as he left with Dundy. As soon as they exited the Panorama Lounge, Dundy stopped and scanned the floor around them. No one was there. "Chief Polhaus has briefed me on this matter.

Is that blonde woman at the bar with the two men Anita?"

"Yes, that's her."

"Take the elevator back to your stateroom. I don't want her to know who reported this incident. She doesn't need to know. Besides, if she's dangerous, it could put you in harm's way. I'll give you a few minutes to clear out of here before I go back in."

Charles followed Dundy's instructions and took the elevators down to the ninth deck, heading back to his stateroom. He wondered what kind of investigation they would do for Anita. Hell, he wished she hadn't seen him leave with Dundy. She might suspect that he was the one who caused her to be investigated. Charles thought, *This is awful. My God, she already dislikes me.* He decided not to go back out tonight. He picked up the phone and ordered room service. After dinner, he spent most of the evening sitting on the veranda, reading and drinking wine.

CHAPTER THIRTY

Charles woke up early the next morning with a headache. *Why did I drink all that wine?* At least he had made it back to his bed before passing out. Charles looked out his window. The ship was docked in Suva, Fiji.

Should he get off the ship this morning? He couldn't stay in his room forever. When Vicky had told him that she was in danger, he had advised her to be careful but enjoy all the cruise had to offer. *Look how that turned out.* Assuming Vicky even existed, of course, outside his wine-impaired mind. Charles knew that he needed to heed his own advice. So he was going to explore Fiji, but he would be very careful.

Charles waited for the ship's announcement that it had cleared customs and that passengers were free to disembark. Passengers interested in going ashore were instructed to meet in the Sterling Lounge. Due to the heightened security under Code Red, only twenty passengers could wait in line at a time. When Charles reached the Sterling Lounge, he was given a disembarkation number. He found a seat at the rear with his back against the wall so that he could see the entire lounge area. No sign of Anita or Vicky.

Ten minutes later, Charles's number was called, and he

proceeded down to the gangway. Deputy Security Officer Dundy was overseeing the screening process as passengers waited to disembark. They were making damn sure no one possessing a certain yellow diamond was getting off this ship. Charles passed through security without incident and found his tour bus. As he boarded the bus, he studied the faces of everyone on board while walking down the aisle. Thank God, neither Anita nor her henchmen were on this bus. As a precaution, Charles took the last seat on the bus, even though it was not close to being full. The bus pulled out of the parking lot, and the tour was underway. He breathed a sigh of relief. But why was he so paranoid? *Nothing is going to happen to me here.*

* * *

AT THE END OF THE TOUR, Charles followed the group as they made their way up the narrow gangplank back onto the ship. Several passengers congregated at the top of the steps, waiting for them to pass before heading down. When Charles arrived at the top, he saw there was a small line in front of him waiting to go back through security before entering the ship. One of the passengers waiting to go down the gangplank leaned over to him and whispered, "You bastard!"

Stunned, Charles glanced over and saw Anita's contorted face. Her eyes were like slits as she stared at him. She suddenly turned her back to him and descended the gangplank. *Crap!* So much for Dundy's plan to make sure that Anita didn't know it was him who reported her. Perhaps she didn't know and just hated him anyway.

Charles cleared security and went to his stateroom. A glass

of wine or something would sure be tasty. He opened the refrigerator, but it was empty except for a few bottles of water. Marvin probably wasn't yet on duty in the Panorama Lounge. Charles decided to go to the Cove.

Several people were sitting at the bar when he arrived. There were some familiar faces but no one he had visited with before. Charles found an empty stool, and Darya approached him from the interior of the bar. She smiled. "Good afternoon, Mr. Pierce. What may I bring you?"

He was surprised by her pleasant attitude. "Hello, Darya. A light pale beer, please. Any will do, thanks."

Darya poured his beer from a tap and placed it on a napkin in front of him. "Please see if you like this one. If not, there are several others you can sample."

Charles took a sip of beer. "It's fine, thank you."

"Please let me know if I can get you anything else."

Instead of walking away as she had done before after serving him a drink, she remained in front of him.

"How has your day been?" Charles asked.

Darya smiled. "Not quite as busy as usual. How is your day going?"

He took a drink of beer. "OK. I got off the ship for a while and took a brief tour of Fiji. It was kind of interesting."

She arranged the napkins next to her on the bar and asked, "Nothing unusual happened to you today?"

"No. Why would you ask?"

"No reason, really. I was just wondering if maybe you found your lady friend."

"You mean the woman who was visiting with me when I ordered a White Russian?"

Darya's lips tightened. "I don't remember seeing any woman visiting with you that night. But I know you were very upset and intent on finding her the next time you came into the Cove."

Charles took another drink of beer. "I talked with Sterling Cruise Security about her. Believe it or not, I think she was in danger, and in fact, something bad might have happened to her."

Darya's face softened. "Yes, I know. Chief Polhaus questioned me because you mentioned being in the Cove with your friend."

"May I ask what you told her?"

"I told her exactly what I told you," Darya replied in a calm, soothing voice.

"I assume you told her, then, that you never saw me with a dark-haired woman with a blue streak in her hair. Is that correct?"

"Yes. Correct."

"What was Chief Polhaus's response?"

"I'm not sure that I am permitted to discuss my conversation with her. I will say, though, that she told me to be kind and friendly to you."

Charles finished off his glass of beer and set it gently on the bar. "So Chief Polhaus thinks this woman is a figment of my imagination. That's why she told you to treat me with care, so I wouldn't get agitated—or something worse. I don't know; maybe she's right."

Darya was listening attentively. Charles stood up. "Thank you for your kindness. I apologize for going off on a rant of sorts."

"Not a problem," she replied. "Enjoy the rest of your day."

CHAPTER THIRTY-ONE

Charles was convinced that everyone on the ship's crew thought he had mental issues or was just an imaginative drunk who made up stories to bring attention to himself. Perhaps they were right. He might as well not add paranoia to his list of problems. He needed to get out of his room.

Charles waited in the short line in the dining room by the maître d' station. Without looking up from studying his seating chart, the maître d' motioned to one of the staff on his left. "Take Mr. Pierce to table 383."

A waiter neared him. "Good evening. Please follow me."

Charles wondered why he no longer warranted table 911. Table 383 was a table set for two, positioned in the center of the dining room and surrounded by large-group dining tables. As soon as he was seated, the waiter removed the other place setting from the table. Another waiter brought him water and a menu. The dining room was about half-full. His chair was facing the entrance to the dining room.

"Care for some wine?"

"Yes, a chardonnay."

"Of course."

Charles glanced at the entrance and noticed Chief Polhaus

talking to the maître d'. The maître d' turned around and pointed to him. He could see Chief Polhaus's eyes scanning the room. When her eyes fixed on him, she started toward his table. The waiter returned with a glass of chardonnay and placed it on the table.

"Would you like to order?"

Charles gestured toward Chief Polhaus. "I think I'm about to have a visitor, so maybe not just yet."

Chief Polhaus approached Charles's table. "Mind if I join you for a few minutes?"

Without getting up, Charles motioned to the chair across from him. "Make yourself at home."

Chief Polhaus sat down and put her elbows on the table. "I apologize for interrupting your dinner. I tried to call you in your stateroom, but it seems you had already left to come here."

Charles pointed to his glass of wine. "Would you care for something to drink?"

Chief Polhaus looked at his glass of wine. "I'd love a glass of straight bourbon, but unfortunately, I'm working."

The waiter appeared at the table. "Chief, may I get you anything?"

"Could you bring me a cup of coffee and some cream, please?"

"Right away."

"I assume you have some news for me."

The waiter poured a cup of coffee and set it and a small pitcher of cream in front of Chief Polhaus. She emptied part of the cream into her coffee and began to stir it.

"Yes, I have some news for you. But most likely not the news you wanted to hear. As you know, we questioned this Anita that you identified. To make a long story short, she is not the same Anita as the Anita that allegedly threatened this Vicky of yours. True, her first name is Anita, but I independently confirmed that she is not married. Incidentally, she hates to be called Anita and prefers Ann. She claims to have never seen or had contact with anyone fitting the description of Vicky while on board."

"Not even the encounter by the swimming pool?"

Chief Polhaus took a drink of coffee. "No, Ann says she has spent a lot of time in the pool area and has met a number of fellow passengers there. However, she has not had an argument with anyone. In fact, she says she was thoroughly enjoying this cruise until we brought her in for questioning."

"So is that it?"

Chief Polhaus took another drink of coffee. "Do you mean is that the end of the investigation into this missing Vicky person? If so, then yes, you're correct. The investigation is closed." Chief Polhaus stood up. "There's one more thing. Ann knows that you were the one who caused her to be investigated. She spotted you following Dundy out of the Panorama Lounge. She put two and two together and concluded it was you. Also, Ann says you've been very rude to her on several occasions."

Charles scowled. "That's not true."

Chief Polhaus started to walk away and then turned around and returned to the table. "Mr. Pierce, Sterling has an excellent physician on this ship. Although she's not a psychiatrist, she still might be able to help you—or at a minimum, refer you to someone in Sydney or even back in the States. We only have one more port until we get to Sydney. Just think about it."

"Sure. Thank you, Chief."

Charles couldn't believe that Ann didn't recall her confrontation with Vicky. But then, perhaps that was the problem. He was relying on a faulty perception of reality. Was his drinking causing him to hallucinate and dream? On the other hand, Ann could have lied. But Chief Polhaus said she had verified that Ann was not married. That blew a gaping hole in the theory that Vicky was threatened by a jealous wife—or for that matter, that Vicky even existed. Maybe there was another Anita on board, and he had misidentified Ann just because he simply didn't like her. Who was he kidding? He had gotten himself into enough trouble. It was past time for him to keep his theories to himself.

Charles finished dinner and headed up to the seventh deck for some fresh air. It was partly cloudy and balmy, with a slight breeze. He could make out some dim stars overhead. A few other people had the same idea. One couple wearing jogging outfits was power-walking the perimeter of the ship. Another couple was leaning on the railing, enjoying glasses of champagne. Charles started walking along the deck toward the stern. He stopped at the same location where he had witnessed the commotion below on the sixth deck a couple of nights ago. It was brighter tonight. He could see much more.

Charles heard voices below in the golf area. A man asked, "How about two out of three?"

Another man asked, "You think you can afford it?"

There was laughter. Charles checked his phone for the time. It was 9:00 p.m. The last thing he needed was a drink, which was exactly why he found himself en route to the Saloon to have a final cocktail before retiring to his stateroom.

The Saloon was crowded. Charles could not see an unoccupied seat at the bar, so he located a vacant table positioned next to the wall near the entrance. A server came by, and he ordered a citron vodka and soda. Mrs. Simon was watching Charles from the bar. She had just ordered a vodka and soda. Discreetly, she emptied the remaining ketamine from the last vial into her drink. Charles's server returned to the bar to place his order with the bartender. Mrs. Simon walked over to his server and whispered in her ear, "Will you take this cocktail to my husband? He's the one sitting next to the wall by himself."

The server looked confused. "Ma'am, he just ordered a drink from me."

"I know. But I had this specially made for him. I guess he didn't see me sitting at the bar. I thought it would be fun to send a cocktail over to him."

"Yes, ma'am. Set it here. I have to place a couple of orders, and then I will take it to him."

"Thank you. I'm going to go powder my nose."

Several minutes later, the server placed a cocktail on the table. She said, "Your wife sent this over for you." Charles looked puzzled but did not say anything. He thought, *My wife? What does that mean?* He glanced around the bar but did not recognize anyone. Charles pulled his phone out of his pocket and tapped on the internet application. He sensed some movement across from him. When Charles looked up, he saw Ann sitting right across the table, staring at him.

She said, "Don't worry—I won't be staying long. I just had to ask: Why?"

Charles pretended that he didn't know what she was talking about. He said, "Care to elaborate a bit?"

Ann twisted her face. He could see that it was flushed red even in the dim lighting of the bar. She hissed, "Why the hell did you tell Security to investigate me? What have I done to you?"

The server approached the table. "May I bring you something?" Ann waved the server off without looking at her. "No!"

In a very calm tone, Charles said, "Well, I made a mistake. I thought you were someone else. I apologize—"

Before he could continue, Ann interrupted. "What's wrong with you? I have had minimal contact with you, and yet you suspected me of being some crazed, dangerous wife! You knew I was single. Why the hell would I have been invited to that singles' cocktail reception if I were married?"

"You make an excellent point."

Ann slammed her fist on the table, spilling his cocktail. She erupted out of her chair and shouted, "This is not the end of it, you bastard!"

Ann stormed out of the Saloon. Charles stared down at his spilled cocktail, dripping off the top of the table and onto the floor. The server came over with a towel and began mopping up the mess.

Charles stood up. "I'm very sorry. Apparently, I said something to upset that woman."

Charles headed to the exit. Everyone in the immediate vicinity of the Saloon was watching him as he left. When he got back to his stateroom, he immediately opened the small refrigerator. He was grateful that his housekeeper had remembered to restock his chardonnay. He opened a bottle and filled a wineglass to the brim. He found the TV remote, plopped down on the small sofa, and clicked on the TV. Methodically, he clicked through the limited number of channels available at sea. Finally, he settled on CNN International. Charles watched for about fifteen minutes and then got up and refilled his glass. When he sat back down on the sofa, he propped his feet up on the small coffee table. He balanced his wineglass on his stomach, fell asleep, and started dreaming.

Vicky, you're here. You're so beautiful tonight. Where have you been? I'm trying to protect you. Why are your clothes all wet?

Charles suddenly felt his shirt becoming drenched. *What the hell?* He jerked into an upright position. His empty wineglass fell to the floor and broke. Crap! He had fallen asleep! *Vicky was here!* Was he dreaming? He bent over and picked up the shards of broken glass and deposited them in the wastebasket. *Was she really here?* It seemed so real. He took off his wine-drenched clothes and threw them in a heap. Stumbling, Charles made his way back over to the sofa, found the TV remote, and switched it off. He fell into bed without turning off the overhead lights.

CHAPTER THIRTY-TWO

Charles slept in late the next morning and awoke to an announcement on the PA system:

"Good morning, ladies and gentlemen, this is Captain Jacoby. I wanted to update you again on our status. Unfortunately, we are still on Code Red. We are anchored one nautical mile from Mystery Island. This is our final port before we reach Sydney, Australia. All passengers who wish to go ashore must take one of our tenders. Tenders will be operating continuously throughout the day, transporting from the ship to Mystery Island and from Mystery Island to the ship. Like Fiji, you will be required to submit to Sterling Cruise Security screening both when disembarking and when returning on board. We appreciate your continued cooperation. Thank you for your attention."

Charles decided to have breakfast in the dining room. When he arrived, a waiter escorted him to a window table with a phenomenal view of Mystery Island; it resembled a movie-set depiction of paradise. Mystery Island was just a tiny speck of land surrounded by crystal clear blue water. He watched as the tenders ferried passengers back and forth from the ship.

After breakfast, Charles walked to the Sterling Lounge to

get a disembarkation number. He waited until his number was called and then walked to the gangway, passing through the screening under the watchful eye of Deputy Security Officer Dundy. The crew helped Charles's group board the tender. The small vessel set off for Mystery Island with about fifty passengers. Fifteen minutes later, they were docked at Mystery Island.

Charles could feel the intense heat from the sun on his neck as he walked the short distance from the pier to the land. It was not an illusion: Mystery Island resembled paradise up close as well as from a distance. He stepped off the pier onto a white-sand beach, leading down to the calm, warm water of the South Pacific in one direction and to lush tropical foliage in the other.

Charles followed several passengers up a trail through the foliage that led to a series of primitively constructed huts. The island was uninhabited. Residents of nearby islands came to Mystery Island every time a cruise ship anchored nearby to peddle their various wares to the ship's passengers. He walked through the row of huts, examining the items for sale. At the end of the row of huts was a huge fake pot with a sign in English that read "Fresh Cannibal Soup."

Two young men were dressed in costume, complete with spears. They were posing with anyone willing to fork over five dollars to stand in the pot with them and pretend to be an ingredient in the cannibal soup. Several people were lined up to get their pictures taken with the young men. Nearby was a hut set up as a crude bar. Several passengers were crowded around it, drinking beer. As Charles walked past, he heard Ann's unmistakably shrill voice. He shot a glance in her direction. She was with several men. Fortunately, she had her back to him. Charles picked a path and started walking. Each step that he took, he could feel the sand shift below his feet. It was like walking on the beach but surrounded by dense greenery. He walked for about twenty minutes, stopping from time to time to snap photos. Occasionally, he could hear voices from people in and near the ocean on his left.

Charles came to a clearing and saw a beach just beyond some rocks. He left the trail and started walking toward the beach. Hidden by the vegetation was a steep, narrow crevasse. Charles paused to survey the best way to maneuver past it. Suddenly, he heard a piercing sound from his left and a thud as an object ricocheted off a tree, followed quickly by the crackling of bushes behind him. He whipped his head around to look around.p As he did, he lost his balance. Charles's right foot lodged in the crevasse. He felt his body twist, and he blacked out.

When Charles awoke, he was lying awkwardly on his back. All of his body except his head was resting on firm green foliage. His head was unsupported, and there was a sharp pain in his neck that felt like whiplash. Charles sat upright and looked around for several moments. *What happened? Did someone throw a rock at me? Did I just black out?* He got on his knees and slowly stood up. His neck throbbed, and he was light-headed. Slowly, he trudged back up to the path. When Charles reached the trail, he stopped and pulled his phone out of his pocket. Thankfully, it was not broken. He checked the time. It was 1:00 p.m. He had been out for about an hour.

Charles retreated down the trail, heading back toward the huts. Except for the pain in his neck, he started to feel better. After ten minutes of walking, he saw a clearing that led to the huts and the pier. Several people were congregated around where the tenders docked, and a tender was nearing the pier. Charles picked up his pace to catch it. Suddenly, Ann appeared in his path, with the muscular young man at her side. She sneered, "You don't look so well."

"I think someone tried to hit me in the head with a rock!"

"Really? Who would do a thing like that?"

Charles didn't want a confrontation. He said, "Not sure. I didn't see anyone."

"Well, it's dangerous to go walking through the jungle by yourself. You never can tell what might happen."

Charles rubbed his neck and said, "I need to get to the ship for medical treatment."

As Charles walked past, Ann grabbed his arm and said, "You better not change your story." He pulled his arm free of her grasp and started walking toward the deck where the passengers were boarding tenders. He was concerned they were going to follow him.

As Charles neared the deck, he glanced back over his shoulder and saw Ann and the muscular young man still watching him. A crew member waved at him to board. He had just made it and got one of the last remaining seats. As they sailed over the small waves back to the ship, his neck felt each jolt. He wondered if he should report what had happened to Security. Had Ann or someone deliberately thrown a rock at him? Why would they run off afterward, if it were an accident? No, he was certain that Polhaus wouldn't believe him. She'd write it off as another symptom of his mental problems. Before the tender reached the ship, his head started to pound as well. After clearing security, he went straight to his stateroom. He decided he would see a doctor and dialed the operator, who immediately connected him to the onboard clinic.

Within a matter of minutes, Charles was in a small reception room, waiting for the physician. An assistant opened the door.

"Please come in and take a seat on the edge of the examination table. Dr. Perrine will be right in."

The examination room was compact, but it had all the accouterments you would expect to see in a physician's office. The door opened again, and a tall, lean woman wearing a white coat came in.

"I'm Dr. Perrine."

"Good afternoon. I'm Charles Pierce."

"What brings you to the clinic, Mr. Pierce?"

"I fell while walking around Mystery Island this afternoon. I think I hurt my neck."

"Let me examine it." She put both hands on his head and started rotating it. "Tell me if it hurts." When she moved his head from front to back, he winced in pain. She continued rotating it. "Did you hit your head on anything, or do you have any other pain?"

"No, I don't think that I struck my head. However, when I checked my phone for the time, I realized I had been out for a while."

Dr. Perrine examined his head. "I don't see any bruising. Do you have a headache?"

"Yes, but it's not as bad as it was thirty minutes ago."

"I suspect that you had a minor concussion."

"Can you get a concussion without hitting your head on anything?"

"Yes, any violent jolt to the brain can cause a concussion. The fact that your neck hurts would suggest that is exactly what occurred. I can give you some Tylenol for the pain. But do not take any aspirin for a week because that could make the bruising or bleeding worse. If you experience any dizziness or other symptoms that are unusual while on the cruise, please contact me. I can also give you a referral to a physician in Sydney, should you need one. It's not uncommon for symptoms to appear a week later."

"OK. Thank you."

"Any other problems?"

Charles shifted his weight on the table. "As a matter of fact, can you also give me a recommendation for a psychiatrist?"

Dr. Perrine studied his face to assess if he was joking. "Why do you think you need to see a psychiatrist?"

He frowned. "Truthfully, I am not certain that I do need to see one. Chief Polhaus thinks differently, though."

Dr. Perrine seemed confused. "Did you say the chief security officer thinks you need to see a psychiatrist? Why on earth would you say that?"

"Are you sure you want to hear this story?"

"Well, if I'm going to refer you to a psychiatrist, I need to know some symptoms."

Charles stood up from the table. "Do you mind if we sit down somewhere?"

"Let's go into my office."

He followed her into a small, windowless office next door. When they were inside, Dr. Perrine motioned to the chair opposite her desk. "Have a seat."

He sat down. "You want symptoms. Let's see now. I'll have to give you a little background."

"Please."

Charles told Dr. Perrine of all his experiences after meeting Vicky and Ann and of being informed by Sterling Reception that there was no one on board named Vicky LeBlanc.

He paused, and Dr. Perrine asked, "Why do you suppose this Vicky chose you to confide in?"

He shrugged. "I'm not sure."

"I see. What did you do after Reception informed you that no one named Vicky was on board?"

"I went to have a drink at the Cove Bar. The same bartender was working who had served Vicky and me a few nights earlier. She remembered where I sat and what I ordered to drink, but she did not recall seeing any woman with me."

"Mr. Pierce, what do you do for a living?"

"I'm retired, but I used to practice law. Why do you ask?"

"Wouldn't you agree that no matter whether you're a doctor, an attorney, or a bartender, you learn certain things that are pertinent to being successful at your profession?"

"Yes, I agree."

Dr. Perrine continued, "Bartenders are very adept at remembering their customers' preferences for cocktails, where they like to sit at the bar, and so forth. But it's a cardinal rule that you never remember who is drinking with whom unless the two customers want you to remember. Professional bartenders are better about protecting the confidentiality of their customers than probably most doctors or attorneys. If you had engaged the bartender in a conversation and referred to Vicky as your wife, then the bartender would remember and know that you were a couple. Otherwise, then likely not. By now, you're probably wondering why I know so much about bartending. Well, I put myself through medical school tending bar."

"So the fact that Darya—that's the name of the bartender—doesn't remember me being with Vicky at the bar shouldn't be a concern?"

"Not by itself. Is this when you brought Sterling Security into this?"

Charles shook his head. "No, that was later. A few nights ago, I was in the Saloon having a cocktail."

Dr. Perrine laughed.

"Why are you laughing?"

"You spend a lot of time in our bars, don't you?"

"I guess I do. That's what Chief Polhaus said, as well. Anyway, I saw Ann come in with a couple of guys. She appeared to be inebriated. When she tried to order a second drink, one of the men said, 'No, Anita' or something to that effect. If you remember, Vicky said Anita was the name of the man's wife. Later that night, I was walking on the seventh deck and stopped at the stern of the ship. Below, I heard a commotion and then a splash. It was very dark, and my view was slightly obstructed, so I couldn't see much. But when someone opened the door to the interior of the ship below, I got a glimpse of the back of a woman's head. She was blonde, like Anita. I got down to the sixth deck as fast as I could, but no one was there. That's when I went down to report to Security that I thought Vicky was in danger—or worse yet, thrown overboard."

"What happened next?"

"I was surprised that Chief Polhaus wasn't more concerned that someone might have gone overboard. She informed me that the ship's sensors had detected an object going overboard and that they even had an image of it. Chief Polhaus said that it was a golf bag and not a person."

Dr. Perrine smiled. "Some frustrated golfer."

"I'm not convinced. Some frustrated golfer or prankster throwing a golf bag overboard is not consistent with what I saw and heard one deck below me."

Dr. Perrine scratched her head. "Did you tell Chief Polhaus about there being no one registered under the name of Vicky LeBlanc?"

"Yes. I shared the whole story with her. The only thing that I didn't share with Chief Polhaus is that I also have been dreaming about Vicky. I must confess that they are more than just dreams. They are very vivid. It is as if she is there."

"Go on."

"The chief reluctantly agreed to open an investigation. She told me if I saw Anita on board to alert Security. One evening, I was having a cocktail and visiting with Marvin, the bartender in the Panorama—"

"Another bar experience?"

"Yes. I heard Anita's voice and then saw her sit down at the bar with a couple of men. I asked Marvin to call Security. Deputy Dundy arrived a few minutes later. I believe it was the next day that Chief Polhaus came over to my table in the dining room. She informed me that Anita was not the hostile wife that Vicky feared. However, she did say that Anita—or Ann, as she prefers to be called—was highly agitated and knew that I was the one who had her investigated. The chief told me the investigation was closed and that I should consider seeing if you could either help with my mental issues or refer me to someone."

Dr. Perrine stared at Charles for a few seconds before speaking. "Mr. Pierce, are you planning on staying a few days in Sydney, or are you flying immediately back to the States?"

"I'll be staying three full days."

"I cannot determine whether or not you need to see a psychiatrist. The only thing that I can say with certainty is that you are a horrible detective and that you drink too much. But I think at least one psychiatric consultation would be worth it. Then you and your doctor can mutually decide if more treatment is appropriate. I can refer you to one in Sydney and arrange to get you an appointment. It's one of the perks of traveling with Sterling Cruise. We have influence. What do you think?"

Charles stood up. "Thank you, Doctor. Let's do it."

Dr. Perrine stood up as well. "I'll be in touch."

As Charles was walking out of her office, Dr. Perrine said, "Also, let me know if you experience any symptoms related to your concussion."

"Thank you. I will do that."

CHAPTER THIRTY-THREE

The ship stopped at a small Australian port en route to Sydney to pick up three immigration officers. At 10:00 a.m. the day before the ship was scheduled to arrive in Sydney Harbour, an announcement came over the public address system:

"Good morning, ladies and gentlemen, this is Captain Jacoby. We are scheduled to arrive in Sydney Harbour at 10:30 a.m. tomorrow. In preparation for our entry into Australia, three Australian immigration officers are on board. Pursuant to Australian law, all passengers are required to present their passports to one of the officers for inspection. This inspection will be conducted in the Panorama Lounge beginning this afternoon at 1:00 p.m. You may collect your passport at the entry to the lounge. To proceed in an orderly fashion, we will be calling passengers to the Panorama Lounge by the deck where your stateroom is located. The first deck called will be the portside eleventh deck, followed by the starboard-side eleventh deck. Please listen carefully for when your deck is announced and promptly proceed to the Panorama Lounge. Thank you."

Charles's stateroom was located on the ninth deck, so he likely wouldn't be called until 1:30 or even 2:00 p.m. He decided to hang out around the pool and do a little reading. A handful of people sat in various loungers surrounding the pool. He opened his tablet and began reading.

A server approached him. "Sir, may I get you something to drink?"

Do I want a glass of chardonnay? Of course I do. Charles smiled. "You guys are always on duty."

The server chuckled. "We'll be serving cocktails until you step off this ship."

"That has been a problem for me. I think I'll pass on ordering anything right now."

The server bowed his head. "Just let me know if you change your mind."

Charles went back to reading his book. At 1:00 p.m., the immigration inspection started with the portside eleventh deck. After twenty minutes, the immigration officers were ready for the tenth deck. He waited fifteen minutes and decided to head to the Panorama Lounge. Twenty or thirty people congregated outside the lounge. The announcement came for the portside ninth deck, and the doors to the lounge opened. Several temporary desks were set up with boxes containing passports arranged in alphabetical order. Charles found the line for P and waited for his turn. Once he collected his passport, he was directed to another line in the center of the room to wait to go before one of the officers. Shortly, an officer motioned for Charles to come forward. "May I see your passport?"

Charles handed him his passport. The officer studied his photograph and looked up at him. "Are you Mr. Pierce?"

"Yes."

"What brings you to Sydney?" He stamped the passport

before Charles could answer.

"Just vacationing."

The officer handed it back to him. "Enjoy your visit."

Charles wondered if he should have told him that he might see a psychiatrist in Sydney. He exited the Panorama Lounge and started back to his stateroom. He had a thought: Vicky had told him that her stateroom was on the eighth deck. If there was really a Vicky, and she was telling him the truth about her stateroom, then her deck would be next to go through the immigration inspection. Charles decided to hang around. If he didn't see her, then he had to assume that either she only existed in his imagination or she had lied about being on the eighth deck.

Charles located a chair about ten yards away from the entrance to the Panorama Lounge. The announcement came for the portside eighth deck. He opened his tablet and pretended to be reading. No one could go into the lounge without him seeing them. He watched as passenger after passenger entered the Panorama Lounge. No blue streak among them, and only a couple of women with dark hair. And neither one of them even remotely resembled Vicky. The announcement came for the starboard-side eighth deck. This was do or die. If she wasn't in this group, he'd have exhausted his best chance of finding her.

Charles went through the same routine of pretending to read his tablet as the passengers arrived in front of the Panorama Lounge. He didn't see Vicky, but there was the magician, Gutman, with some blonde. Charles was not sure exactly why, but he thought there was something funny about a magician waiting in line with his passport to go through an immigration inspection. Charles patiently watched until the last passenger from the eighth deck entered the Panorama Lounge. No one resembling Vicky was among them.

Charles guessed that was it for his detective work. It was a prudent thing that he was going to see a psychiatrist. He took the stairs down to his stateroom. There was a sealed envelope in the mail slot next to his door. He unlocked the door and slid open the envelope. There was a brief note inside:

> *Mr. Pierce, I have made you an appointment with Dr. John Taylor at 2:00 p.m. on February 22. His address is 481 King Street, Suite 1206, Phone #61-2-9252-4031. Please contact his office should you have a change of plans. Sterling is docked in Sydney until February 23. I am going to be ashore part of the time while in Sydney. Should you experience any more symptoms related to your concussion, please feel free to contact me on my cell at 212-543-5951.*
> *Dr. Perrine*

Charles had a full day in Sydney before his appointment. He slipped the note into his wallet and spent the afternoon packing his suitcases. It would be strange permanently leaving the ship tomorrow. Who would have thought he would be on a month-long cruise and have the need to see a psychiatrist as soon as he went ashore? When he started the cruise, he fancied himself as the imaginary partner of Sam Spade. After a few days, he created an imaginary playmate named Vicky. Not only that, but he'd had some blonde woman from New Zealand investigated for a possible murder. The only drama it seemed that he had avoided was having anything to do with the missing diamond. Charles checked his phone for the time. It was 5:30 p.m. He was going to say goodbye to Marvin. Charles was hopeful that Marvin would still speak to him after having asked Marvin to call Security on Ann.

Charles entered the Panorama Lounge for the last time. All the temporary tables from the afternoon immigration inspection had been removed. Everything in the lounge appeared normal. Marvin was visiting with a couple seated at the bar. Charles's preferred stool of choice was unoccupied, so he walked straight to it and sat down. As he had done on many occasions before, he pulled his phone out of his pocket and set it on the bar in front of him. Instantly, he hit the application to check his email. Why did he bother? Everything would be back to normal by tomorrow. Back to normal as far as his internet coverage was concerned, anyway.

Marvin approached him. "Good evening, Sir Charles."

"I'm glad you're still willing to talk to me."

Marvin slid a cocktail napkin in front of him. "Of course. You simply added to the excitement on board. Now, may I get you a vodka and soda?"

"Yes. Thank you." Marvin mixed his cocktail and set it on the napkin.

"I guess you heard I was mistaken about Ann?"

"Yes, I heard. She does have a fiery temper, though."

"Believe me, I know."

Charles considered telling him about his Mystery Island incident. No, that wouldn't be prudent. "When Ann learned that I was the individual responsible for her being investigated, she confronted me in the Saloon."

"Really? What happened?"

"She sat down at my table uninvited and informed me,

using less-than-delicate words, exactly what she thought of me. Then, to further emphasize her point, she slammed her fist on the table, spilling my cocktail, and then stormed out."

"Wow, you've had quite a cruise."

"Marvin, it's only the tip of the iceberg of the experiences that I've had on board. I only wanted to get a little reading done and see some interesting sights. Instead, I got myself into all kinds of drama. Perhaps most of it is self-inflicted, but drama for sure."

"Well, tomorrow is Sydney, and when you disembark, your life can get back to normal."

"I'm not so certain about that, Marvin. It's possible some of my experiences on board might stay with me for a while."

Marvin left to wait on a couple who had arrived at the bar. He wondered if Marvin would have another version of Charles Pierce get on board in Sydney to provide him with evening entertainment. Marvin came back over to him. "Would you like one more, Sir Charles?"

Charles looked at his nearly empty glass. "No, I think I'm one and done. So, Marvin, are you going to be able to get off the ship in Sydney?"

"For sure. I'm off work for an entire day."

Charles stood up. "Wonderful. Listen, I'll buy you a cocktail if we run into each other on the shore. I'll be the guy sitting by himself, drinking either a vodka or a chardonnay."

"I think I'll be able to identify you." They both laughed. "Safe travels, Sir Charles."

Charles waved at Marvin and walked out of the Panorama Lounge for the last time.

CHAPTER THIRTY-FOUR

The next morning, Charles woke up early and went down to the dining room for breakfast. He had a lovely final breakfast next to a window as the ship began its approach to Sydney Harbour. As soon as he finished, he headed up to the top deck of the ship. It was a beautiful, sunny day. A crowd had already gathered at the front of the ship to get the first glimpse of the famous opera house and the Sydney Harbour Bridge.

Charles found a chair next to the railing and settled in. Several waiters in dress whites were serving champagne at 10:30 a.m. What a way to end a cruise. The ship docked in Sydney Harbour, with a view of the Sydney Opera House on one side and the Sydney Harbour Bridge on the other.

Charles went up to the pool deck to have a casual lunch. There was only one table remaining that was next to a window. He hurried over to it and sat down. A server noticed him and placed a paper coaster on the table in front of Charles. He asked, "May I bring you something to drink?"

"Yes. How about a glass of pinot grigio?" The waiter left, and Charles perused the simple menu. He thought that he would have it memorized by now. He looked up to see the silhouette of a woman. The sun was directly behind her, filtering around her head.

"Charles Pierce," she said.

"Yes?" He tried to shield his eyes so that he could see her face. Who was this woman?

"May I sit down?"

"Uh, sure. Please have a seat."

It was a two-top table, and she sat across from him. The woman was wearing a light-blue sundress, with her gray hair pulled back under a matching straw beach hat. She wore a gray-tinted pair of sunglasses. Her face was partially concealed, but he could see that she was quite attractive and in her midfifties. He wondered why she wanted to sit with him. He struggled to find something to say. Finally, he said, "There's a shortage of tables. The pool deck is popular today."

"That's not why I asked to sit down."

"I apologize. Have we met before?"

The woman removed her sunglasses. "You don't recognize me?"

Charles closely examined her face. Those eyes. He had seen those ice-blue eyes before. He said, "You do look familiar. But I can't place where I have seen you."

The server returned with Charles's glass of wine. He asked the woman, "May I bring you something to drink?"

"I presume the gentleman is having chardonnay," she said.

The server looked at him, puzzled. Charles stammered, "No, I'm drinking pinot grigio. I normally do order chardonnay, though. How did you guess that?"

The woman was expressionless. She asked the server, "Do you, by chance, have a Renaldo chardonnay?"

"I don't know," he said. "Let me go check."

"Renaldo chardonnay," Charles said. "I've had that chardonnay before, back in Dallas. It has a nice oak flavor."

"Yes, I had some in downtown Dallas as well—at a quaint little wine bar with a funny name. I believe it's called the Wine Therapist."

"I go to the Wine Therapist almost every week. Is that where I remember seeing you?"

"Perhaps. We may have crossed paths there."

The server returned to the table and said, "I'm sorry, ma'am, but we don't have a Renaldo chardonnay."

"OK. I'll just have a glass of pinot grigio."

"So may I ask how you know my name?"

"Charles Pierce, you and I had quite an exchange one morning."

"Exchange? What do you mean?"

"It was one-sided. You kept interrupting everything that I said."

Charles scratched his head. "Are you referring to a trial?"

"Trial. Is that what you call it? I thought it was more like a humiliating grilling."

The server brought the woman her pinot grigio. He asked, "Would you care to order?"

The woman remained silent and glared at Charles. He said to the server, "Maybe in a while. Would you mind giving us about ten minutes?" Charles looked at her, forcing himself to meet her stare. "Did I question you as a witness in a trial?"

"Yes. I'm Jamie Simon. Ring any bells?"

"Jamie Simon? Your name sounds familiar . . ."

"I was the wife of John Simon."

"John Simon. Yes, Mrs. Simon, I do now recall. That was the Mutual Indemnity Insurance Company experimental procedure case."

Mrs. Simon took a drink of wine. "You damn well know that procedure was not the least bit experimental."

"Mrs. Simon, you have my profound and sincere apologies for my part in that trial. I could say that I was just doing my job. But that would be cowardly."

"Pierce, my husband died because of what you did. Do you realize that? We couldn't afford to pay for that procedure without insurance."

"I saw your husband's obituary."

"You kept interrupting me at trial. You denied me my one opportunity to plead my case to the judge. You kept objecting and interrupting me. I got so flustered."

"Yes, I know. Mrs. Simon, that's what lawyers are required to do in representing their clients. I know it doesn't seem fair or even moral. In these types of cases, the laws are really stacked against people like your husband."

"How could you live with yourself, doing that to other people?"

"Mrs. Simon, I couldn't. I retired from practicing law right after your husband's case."

Mrs. Simon took a drink of her wine. "But you had to have that one last scalp before you retired."

"If it wasn't me, it would have been some other lawyer. The case was almost impossible to lose."

"You were so callous and uncaring." Mrs. Simon pulled her purse up to the table. She opened it and fished out an empty vial and placed it next to his drink.

"Pierce, do you know I had you followed?"

Uncomfortable, Charles grabbed his glass of wine and took a drink. "I thought some young man was following me. I had no idea that he worked for you."

"Yes. We learned all about your habits and interests."

"But why?"

"You made my life a living hell. I wanted to make your life a living hell as well. Pierce, do you remember my first name?"

"Yes, of course. Jamie."

"Did you know that your wife thought you were having an affair with me?"

Charles started trembling and set his wineglass down hard. Part of it spilled over the side of the glass, dampening the tablecloth.

"I see by your reaction that this little revelation surprises you. I see she was not able to discuss this matter with you before she died."

"She committed suicide!"

"I am aware of that. I assure you that I intended her no harm. My only objective was for her to divorce you—or otherwise make your life miserable."

The note in Charlotte's hand: "Tell me about Jamie."

"Charlotte had a note in her hand that said, 'Tell me about Jamie.' I was being a jerk, and she thought I was having an affair with you. So that's why she took her life. Oh my God!"

"I should be sorry for your loss, but my hatred for you is too intense."

Charles put his head in his hands.

The server came over to their table. "Are you all right, sir?"

Charles raised his head. His eyes were full of tears. "I'm OK.

Thank you."

The server looked at Mrs. Simon and left. She was gazing at her half-empty glass of pinot grigio.

Charles wiped his eyes with a napkin.

Mrs. Simon picked up the vial off the table. "See this empty bottle? It once contained enough ketamine to kill a throng of people."

"Did you say ketamine?"

Mrs. Simon ignored his question. She pulled the dropper out of the bottle and pretended to empty it into his glass of wine. "Pierce, you have more lives than a cat."

Charles felt his stomach tighten up. "So you were trying to kill me. Instead, you killed that poor young man at the Adolphus Hotel."

"All you had to do was take one sip, and it would have been you."

"So you hired Skylar to distract me?"

"Skylar? Is that the name the prostitute used to lure you? How clever. Skylar, I like that. I bet she had you eating out of her hand."

"What about the woman who was poisoned at the Nasher Sculpture Center? Was that you as well?"

"Yes, the server was supposed to give that glass of char-donnay to you."

"Was he part of your scheme?"

"No, I spiked the glass when he wasn't looking. I have made several attempts to poison you, Pierce. Remember the free drinks delivered to you at the Water Grill?"

"Yes, but we didn't drink from them."

"I was very disappointed in you. I scoured the news for a

week, hoping to see that I was successful. I finally decided to book the same cruise you selected, in case I needed to finish the job."

"Have you tried to poison me on board?"

"That's why my bottle is empty."

The server again appeared at their table. "May I bring you anything?"

Charles said, "Yes, could you take this glass away and bring me a fresh glass of pinot grigio?"

He looked at Mrs. Simon. "Ma'am, would you care for another glass?"

"No. I'm fine."

Charles said, "The police have already tied the Adolphus Hotel death to the poisoning at the Nasher Sculpture Center."

The server returned with the glass of wine and set it on the table in front of Charles.

Mrs. Simon said, "I assumed they would before too long."

"Why did you decide to tell me?"

"I've no more ketamine. Frankly, I'm tired, Pierce. I wanted you to know how you ruined my life. That's why I decided to confront you."

"Mrs. Simon, I couldn't be any more remorseful about what happened to your husband. But don't you think I know what it feels like to lose the love of your life? My wife, Charlotte, meant everything to me."

"I do feel sorry that my actions may have contributed to your wife's suicide. As I said earlier, that was not my intent. I surmise, though, that what I did was just the final straw that broke the camel's back. You were the real reason why she took her life."

Charles finished off his wine and set his glass down. "I know."

"Well, Pierce, I'm flying home this afternoon." Mrs. Simon stood up.

"Aren't you afraid that I'll tell the police?"

"You do what you want. I don't care anymore."

As soon as Mrs. Simon left, the server returned to Charles's table. "Would you care to order now?"

"No, I've lost my appetite. Would you bring me a strong citron vodka and soda, though?"

Should I tell Polhaus that a woman tried to kill me while on board? Hell no! She wouldn't believe me. Like Vicky LeBlanc, Jamie Simon would just be a figment of his imagination. Maybe neither woman existed.

The server arrived with a cocktail and placed it on a napkin in front of Charles.

"Thank you." He took a quick drink and held the glass up to the sun. This drink was the only thing he was certain existed anymore.

CHAPTER THIRTY-FIVE

Charles went to the upper deck to wait until it was time to disembark. When his group was announced, he walked off the ship and collected his luggage. He had arranged for a driver to take him to a hotel. The hotel was part of the post-cruise package. As Charles expected, it was a five-star hotel, complete with a five-star price. *Oh well, I might as well end the trip in style.* As soon as he stepped into the lobby, a porter took his bags and led him over to a private area to check in. The man behind the desk asked, "May I please have your name and a credit card for incidentals, sir?"

"Charles Pierce."

He studied a computer screen for a few minutes. "Excellent. You're going to enjoy the view from your room. In addition, you're welcome to enjoy complimentary wine and cocktails in the VIP lounge on the thirty-third floor every afternoon at five during your stay. Please give the receptionist your name and room number. Your luggage will be delivered to your room in a few minutes. Enjoy your stay."

The man handed Charles a room key.

"Thank you. I'm sure I'll enjoy it."

Charles located his room on the thirty-third floor. The guy

at the desk wasn't exaggerating. The view overlooking Sydney Harbour was phenomenal! Once his luggage was delivered to the room, he headed out onto the streets to explore the city.

It was warm but comfortable as he walked. Charles made his way a few blocks down to the harbor and got his bearings. He headed toward the opera house. It was a pleasant walk, with the water on one side and the other side crowded with restaurant after restaurant with outside seating. Fifteen minutes later, he was standing on the steps leading up to the iconic opera house. It was much larger than he had anticipated. He took a brief, self-guided tour to try to see as much of the facility as possible. Afterward, he walked an indirect route back to the hotel so that he could experience some of the local culture. Charles felt fine. This was a wonderful experience. Perhaps he was only glad the cruise and the drama were behind him.

He arrived back at the hotel, took the elevator to the VIP lounge on the thirty-third floor, and gave the receptionist his name and room number. He poured a glass of chardonnay and sat down by a window to enjoy the view. He decided he would get a small dinner downstairs and go to bed early.

* * *

THE NEXT MORNING WAS ANOTHER warm, sunny day in Sydney. Charles grabbed a map off the concierge desk and studied it to locate the Rocks area. It was touted in his research as a historical must-see place in Sydney. He ventured out of the hotel and through the business district. The landscape suddenly changed from twenty-first-century high-rises to quaint, late-1700s buildings. Most of the buildings were occupied by pubs, restaurants, and small stores. He came across a small pub and restaurant that served an exquisite fish and chips.

After lunch, Charles found the Museum of Contemporary Art Australia on the map. It was a short distance away, near the harbor where the ship was docked. He spent the better part of the afternoon exploring a current exhibition. When he got around to checking the time, it was already 5:30 p.m.

Charles decided to go back to the Rocks and find a pub. Not only did he find a pub, but he found the oldest pub in the Rocks, named the Fortune of War. There was no way he could resist having a drink at the oldest pub. Sam Spade would insist. *Funny, I haven't thought about Sam for quite a while*, Charles realized. He guessed he had been busy creating his own messes and then trying to get himself out of them.

The small pub appeared not to have changed much for a hundred years. It had worn hardwood planks on the floor and a semicircle bar of dark wood. Charles spotted a vacant stool and sat down. The man on a stool next to him turned and said, "We graciously welcome everyone to the Fortune of War."

Charles was a bit startled. "Thank you. How did you know I was a tourist?" He glanced at the man's clothing, which did not look much different than his. They were both wearing faded blue jeans and short-sleeve cotton shirts.

"We locals can always tell."

The bartender approached Charles from behind the bar. "Welcome. What may I bring you?"

He thought a moment. "Do you have chardonnay?"

"Yes, actually, we do." She soon returned with a glass of chardonnay and set it on a paper coaster that had the history of the pub written on it. "Would you like to start a tab?"

"I guess I will," Charles said and handed her a credit card. After she left, he took a drink of chardonnay and read all about the Fortune of War history, printed on the coaster.

The man next to Charles noticed him reading. "What it doesn't tell you is that in the early days, this pub was the recruiting grounds for involuntary sailors."

"I don't think I understand."

The man took a drink from his pint of beer. "In exchange for a small fee, unscrupulous bartenders would get young men drunk on whiskey. When they were about to pass out, the bartender would walk the young men to the back of the bar to supposedly sleep it off. See that staircase? It leads right down to the harbor. When the bartender gave the signal, some guys from the ship would shanghai the poor, unsuspecting souls. The next morning, they would wake up with a horrific headache as sailors on a ship to God only knows where."

Charles took a drink of chardonnay. "Thanks for the story. I'll make sure I don't drink too much." They both laughed. Charles pulled his phone out of his pocket and started checking his email. Finally, being on land in an urban area, he had decent internet speed. He scrolled and deleted emails for several minutes.

"Leave it to you to order chardonnay in a historic brewpub."

Charles glanced to his left. "Dr. Perrine! You did get ashore. I admit that I didn't believe you when you said you were going to take some time off to see Sydney."

Dr. Perrine smiled. "Well, I have my phone, so I'm only a call away from duty, if needed."

"May I buy you a drink?"

She stared at his glass of chardonnay. "Well, I'm certainly not having chardonnay." The bartender approached as Dr. Perrine settled on her stool. "I'd like a pint of blonde ale, please."

The bartender immediately began filling a pint. She placed the full glass with a foamy head on a coaster in front of Dr. Perrine. "This is our most popular."

"Thank you. I'm sure I'll love it." She looked over at Charles with her pint in her hand.

They tapped their glasses together. "Cheers!"

"So, Mr. Pierce, are you enjoying your stay in Sydney?"

"Absolutely! I've squeezed a lot into a day and a half. How about you? Oh, by the way, since I am technically no longer a patient or a passenger, would you mind calling me Charles?"

Dr. Perrine took a drink of her pint, which left a slight trace of foam on her upper lip. She licked it off with her tongue. She was a lovely woman. While getting treatment for his concussion, Charles couldn't see past her white coat. She was just a doctor.

"Sure. Please call me Kristin. To your question, though, I've just been exploring the Rocks this afternoon. I want to go to the opera house tomorrow and see a performance of some kind, if possible."

"You'll be struck by its enormous size. It's deceptively large."

Kristin took a drink from her pint. "That's what I hear. However, I would be remiss if I didn't put my doctor's hat back on for a minute. Do you mind if I ask if you are going to keep your appointment with Dr. Taylor tomorrow?"

Charles considered telling Kristin about Jamie Simon. No, that wouldn't be prudent. "Yes, I am. But I must say that I feel much better now that I'm off the ship. Maybe it's just because I'm enjoying Sydney, but I feel better than I have for a long time. More importantly, I have not seen any women with blue streaks in their hair named Vicky—in person or in my dreams."

Kristin listened intently. "I'm glad to hear you're feeling better. I also think you're wise to see Dr. Taylor. Based on your session, he should be able to determine if you need continued therapy and provide some guidance for when you return to the States."

"I understand. However, I'm sure it won't be the highlight of my visit here."

"You never can tell what's in store when you see a doctor. Would you have imagined during your appointment with me the other day that we would be sharing a drink in a historic pub?"

"You're right about that. I can assure you, I've got no plans to enjoy a drink with Dr. Taylor." They both laughed.

"I have one last doctor question. Have you experienced any symptoms from your concussion?"

Charles shook his head. "No. I've felt great since I've been here."

The bartender came toward them. "Would either of you care for another?"

Charles asked Kristin, "Would you like another?"

"Yes—may I have a glass of chardonnay instead, though?" Kristin said to the bartender.

"Make that two," Charles added.

The bartender left to pour their wine. Kristin checked the messages on her phone. Instinctively, Charles looked down at his phone as well. An appointment reminder flashed across the screen: *Dr. Taylor, 2:00 p.m., February 22.*

The bartender returned with two glasses of chardonnay.

Charles picked his glass up and said, "Here's to drinking char-donnay in the oldest brewpub in Sydney."

Kristin set her phone down and picked up her glass, and they each took a drink of wine. Charles said, "I just got a reminder on my phone about my appointment tomorrow. While you're enjoying a performance in the opera house, I'll be meeting with a psychiatrist."

"It won't be that bad. You'll be finished in no time and able to enjoy the rest of your stay." Kristin's phone chimed. "Excuse me; I need to check this."

He sat silently while she studied her phone. Kristin turned to face him. "One of the crew fell off a scaffold on the ship. My assistant thinks the injuries he sustained may be severe. I must go to the ship and examine him. Thank you so much for the drinks and especially the conversation."

Kristin stood up, and Charles did as well. She gave him a slight hug. "I hope your appointment tomorrow goes well."

"Thank you. This has been the highlight of the trip."

"I doubt that, but thanks. I can always use a compliment." She stopped at the door and waved at him before leaving.

Life could be so strange at times. She didn't know it, but their thirty minutes together in this pub was the highlight of his trip. Life seemed natural and normal again.

CHAPTER THIRTY-SIX

A t 1:00 p.m., Charles pulled out the note that he had received from Kristin concerning his appointment with the psychiatrist. He found the address on the map that the concierge had given him earlier. The office was on King Street, only two blocks from the hotel. He arrived at the office at 1:45 p.m. It was a midrise, contemporary office building.

After an elevator ride to the twelfth floor, Charles found suite 1206 and opened the door. It was a nicely appointed office with expensive, contemporary furniture. The receptionist handed him some forms to complete and asked him to take a seat. He spent the better part of thirty minutes filling out forms concerning his medical history, psychiatric history, and medications. When he had completed them to his satisfaction, he returned them to the receptionist.

She said, "Please take a seat again. Dr. Taylor will be with you soon." Charles returned to his chair and started checking emails and news on his phone.

Another fifteen minutes passed, and then the door opened. A tall, thin man with a neatly trimmed beard took a step into the reception area. "Mr. Pierce?"

"Yes." Charles stood up.

"Hello, I'm Dr. Taylor. Please follow me."

They walked through a narrow hallway past an office. Through the crack in the door, Charles could see magazines and books stacked on a large wooden desk. Several degrees were framed on the wall opposite the door. Dr. Taylor paused by an open door to another room. "Please take a seat in that chair," he said, gesturing for Charles to sit.

Charles made his way over to the chair as directed. The room was neat but austere. A modern-looking sofa and two chairs occupied the room. Dr. Taylor sat in the other chair. "I'm sorry to have kept you waiting, but I wanted to spend a few minutes reading your history before seeing you."

Dr. Taylor had a file in one hand, and an electronic tablet sat on a side table next to his chair.

"No problem. Thank you for seeing me on short notice."

Dr. Taylor smiled. He set the file down on the table, picked up his tablet, and typed a note. "Mr. Pierce, please tell me what prompted you to want to see a psychiatrist."

"I had some bad experiences the past few weeks on this cruise. It started when I met this woman on board while having a cocktail. She confided in me that she thought she might be in danger. The woman, Vicky, said she was having an affair with a married man. She thought the wife might be on board. The wife has some mental issues, apparently. I became worried that something had happened to Vicky. To make a long story short, the ship had no one with a name even distantly similar registered. I even went to the bar where I initially met Vicky. The bartender remembered me, what cocktail I had ordered, and even where I sat that evening. But she didn't remember seeing a woman with me. Well, I thought I had found out who the ex-wife was because

I overheard someone address a blonde woman as Anita. Earlier in the cruise, I had seen Vicky and Anita arguing. Vicky had told me the man's wife was named Anita. Then, later that evening, I witnessed some commotion on a deck below me while I was out getting some fresh air. It was too dark to see much, but I saw the back of a blonde woman's head and then heard a splash as something went overboard. I reported what I saw to Sterling Security, and they investigated. No one was thrown overboard. Also, the woman was not the ex-wife. And Vicky never surfaced again. So I don't know if I imagined Vicky or if she really exists. I kept having these vivid dreams about her, but they weren't ordinary dreams. When I awoke, I was almost certain she had been there."

"Have you ever experienced anything like this in the past?"

"If you mean have I experienced imaginary people, then the answer is no. Listen, I even had sex with this Vicky. She was as real as this wooden table." Charles tapped the top of the side table with his right hand. Dr. Taylor made a few notes on his tablet. "Prior to the cruise, had you been under any stress?"

"Yes, my wife committed suicide. I felt useless and needed a change of scenery, so that's why I went on a monthlong cruise by myself."

Dr. Taylor continued his note-taking. "Prior to her death, how would you describe yourself?" Charles was sure he must have appeared bewildered at the question. "Let me rephrase. Do you enjoy being around people?"

"Yes. I still do. But I'm an introvert. I also don't mind being alone."

Dr. Taylor stared at his tablet. "On this cruise, would you say your social interaction was what you would consider usual for you?"

246 ★ ABERRANT BEHAVIOR

"I think I was more withdrawn than normal. As an example, I was invited to a singles' cocktail reception and had to force myself to go. Then I left early because I insulted one of the women there. What little social interaction that I did have occurred in the ship's bars."

Dr. Taylor wrote more notes on his tablet. "Did you drink more alcohol while you were on the ship than you normally do at home?"

Charles grimaced. "Probably. Everything is complimentary on board. Not to mention, there were so many days at sea. Other than reading or attending lectures, hanging out in bars was my entertainment."

"How much alcohol would you say you consume daily?"

Charles squirmed in his chair. "It varies. I know I drink too much. I sometimes enjoy a glass of wine at lunch. Every night I have a predinner cocktail or two. During dinner, I order at least one glass of wine. After dinner, I usually get another cocktail or two."

"I see." He typed some notes on his tablet. "Let me ask you about your dreams. Did you have them every night that you were on the ship?"

Charles thought a moment before responding. "No, I just had them a few nights. But they were so damn real. I could have sworn I was living the experience and not dreaming. Does that make sense?"

"Were they always about this woman you met?"

"Yes. The theme of each dream was always the same. Vicky was always there and looking so beautiful, vulnerable, and fragile. I pleaded with her to let me help and protect her."

Dr. Taylor took more notes. "Did she ever respond to you

or acknowledge you?"

"No. She was there and then not there. My dreams paralleled what was happening on the ship. After we had three encounters, she just disappeared. How could she disappear on a ship? Were all my experiences with her merely a dream or a hallucination?"

Dr. Taylor stared at his tablet and then looked up. "When you had these dreams, did you drink more than usual? In other words, did you drink excessively before you went to bed?"

Charles thought about the question before answering. "Yes, I would say that is true. There is one more thing I should tell you. But first, I must give you a little background. I used to practice law. My clients were typically large health insurance companies that I represented in lawsuits brought by their insureds. The lawsuits were usually for costly medical procedures that were proposed to be performed, but the insurers refused to pay due to some technicality under the policies. I quit after the last lawsuit that I tried because I couldn't stomach that type of work anymore. It was a particularly egregious case where the insurance company denied coverage for a procedure that it determined was experimental. The expensive procedure had been performed successfully numerous times in Europe. There was enough wiggle room under the policy that the insurer could legally deny coverage. I won the case, and the man suing the insurance company died a few weeks later because he and his wife couldn't afford to pay for the procedure out of their own pockets. Believe it or not, the widow was on the cruise I just completed. She confessed to me on the last day of the cruise that she had made several efforts to poison me—not only during the cruise but even months before."

Dr. Taylor stroked his beard. "Did you say this widow was

on your cruise?"

"Yes. I know it's hard to believe, but it's true."

"Did I hear you correctly that the widow said she had made several attempts to kill you?"

"Yes. I know it sounds far-fetched. But the police back in Dallas were investigating the poisoning of two individuals in two separate cases. The only thing in common in both cases was me."

"I see. Have you only had this one encounter with the widow?"

"Yes, except when she testified at trial."

"And you said it occurred on the last day of your cruise?"

"Yes, she came and sat down with me when I was getting ready to order lunch."

"Had you been drinking that morning?"

"No, I had just ordered a glass of wine when she appeared."

Dr. Taylor typed on the screen of his tablet. "Please describe to me how she appeared to you."

"Well, I looked up from my table and saw a woman standing next to me. The sun was in my eyes, so all I could see was the silhouette of her body. She asked if she could sit down."

"What happened next?"

"She sat down at my table. I think she was surprised that I didn't recognize her. When she told me that her name was Jamie Simon and that her husband's name was John, I remembered her from the case. Mrs. Simon proceeded to tell me how I ruined her life. She held me responsible for her husband's death. Mrs. Simon told me that she had me followed to learn all my habits and interests." Charles abruptly stood up from his chair. "This is the difficult part."

"Mr. Pierce, please sit back down."

He slumped back into the chair. "Mrs. Simon said that she told Charlotte, my wife, that she and I were having an affair."

"Why would she do that?"

"She said she wanted Charlotte to divorce me and make my life as miserable as her life had become. Dr. Taylor, Charlotte was clutching a note when she committed suicide in our living room. It said, 'Tell me about Jamie.' That had to be related to my supposed affair with Jamie Simon. She then told me about all the attempts on my life back in Dallas. They pretty much line up with what I personally experienced and what I learned from the Dallas police."

Charles watched in silence as Dr. Taylor typed on his tablet. "Mr. Pierce, you were on this cruise for a long time, and yet you never saw this woman before the final day?"

"Yes. That was the only time that I recall seeing her since the trial."

"Why do you suppose this woman who has been trying to kill you suddenly appears and decides to admit to committing all these untoward deeds?"

"She showed me an empty vial that she said had previously contained the poison. As I recall, she said that she was not able to get any more of it. I asked her if she was afraid that I would tell the police. She responded that she was tired and that I should do what I must do."

"Mr. Pierce, do you think it is possible that your encounter with Mrs. Simon was perhaps a dream, similar to your dreams about Vicky?"

Charles started to answer and then paused. "I was going to assert that I was positive that my encounter with Jamie Simon was not a dream. But now, I'm starting to doubt myself."

"Let me change the course here. How do you feel since you have been off the ship?"

"Actually, I've felt pretty great. I love Sydney, and everyone is so friendly. You live in a wonderful city."

Dr. Taylor smiled. "I'm glad you're enjoying your visit." Dr. Taylor leaned back in his chair. "Mr. Pierce, when was the last time you had a comprehensive physical?"

"I had one last year."

"I would like for you to contact your internist when you get back home. Please tell him everything that you shared with me today. For me or any psychiatrist to make an accurate diagnosis, we must rule out any physical problems that may have led to your symptoms. Once we are certain that we are dealing with a potential—and I emphasize the word potential—psychiatric problem, then we can determine the best course of treatment. The hallucinations that you describe experiencing are unusual. I have had many patients who experience mild hallucinations, such as imagining for a few seconds that they see insects crawling on their hands. The kind you describe, though, are much more personal and intense. You had conversations, physical contact, and even a name for this woman or possibly women in your hallucinations. Most people suffering from schizophrenia experience hallucinations or some type of aberrant behavior. They can be visual, auditory, or even involve the smell or taste of things that are not there. Have you experienced any of these other types of hallucinations at any time in your life?"

Did he say schizophrenia? Aberrant behavior?

"I'm sorry, do you think I might suffer from schizophrenia?"

Dr. Taylor shook his head. "No, I'm not making a diagnosis.

All I'm saying is that various hallucinations are symptoms of schizophrenia. Many people who suffer from alcoholism also suffer from schizophrenia. There is no empirical evidence that alcoholism leads to schizophrenia, or vice versa. However, you do have an alcohol problem, and I can tell by your responses that you recognize that."

"Yes."

"Let me ask again: Have you had any other type of hallucination?"

"No. I've never had any other type of hallucination."

Dr. Taylor made some notes on his tablet. "Mr. Pierce, do you have any questions that you would like to ask me?"

"If I am eventually diagnosed with schizophrenia, how is it treated?"

"Depending upon the severity, schizophrenia may be treated with therapy and medication. After several sessions, your psychiatrist should be able to determine what is appropriate for your case."

"Is there a cure?"

"There is no cure. We can only treat the symptoms." Dr. Taylor looked at his watch. "Any more questions?"

"I guess not."

Dr. Taylor stood up. "When are you leaving Sydney?"

Charles stood up as well. "Tomorrow afternoon."

"Should there be a need, you may contact my office at any time before you go."

Charles turned around and started to leave.

"Safe travels, Mr. Pierce."

Safe travels, really? The trip home was the least of his concerns. He thought psychiatrists were supposed to make patients feel better. But damn, he felt like crap! How depressing! Just over an hour ago, he'd felt so much better about himself.

Charles walked back to his hotel and up to his room. Once inside, he did a swan dive onto the bed. In less than a month, he'd gone from being a moderately depressed man to a hallucinating schizophrenic. At least he was heading home tomorrow. He got out of bed and peered out the window at the view of Sydney Harbour. For all he knew, that view didn't even exist. But it was gorgeous! He decided to walk down to the harbor one last time.

It was crowded with people taking pictures and enjoying the beautiful day. For no reason, Charles started walking toward the Sydney Opera House. He wondered if Kristin was able to see a performance. When he reached the steps leading up to the opera house, he stopped in his tracks. What if he ran into her? She would probably think he was stalking her. *Maybe I should turn around and go back to the hotel.* Charles changed course and started retracing his steps. An early evening dinner crowd was filling in the outdoor dining areas of the various restaurants. From behind him, he heard someone shout, "Sir Charles!" He spun around. Marvin came jogging up to him.

"Marvin, I'm so glad to see you! So you were able to get off the ship."

"Absolutely. I took a tour of the opera house."

Charles patted him on the shoulder. "Good for you. Marvin, I said if we ran into each other on the shore, I would buy you a drink. Do you have time for one now?"

Marvin glanced at his watch. "I'm meeting some friends at the Rocks in half an hour."

"It's a mere ten-minute walk from here. What do you say?"

"Of course."

Charles pointed at a pub a few yards away. "How about there?"

He and Marvin walked into the pub and found two stools at the bar. A bartender quickly came over to them. He asked Marvin, "What are you having?"

"A Tooheys New, please."

The bartender looked at Charles. "I'm not sure what that is," Charles said, "but make it two."

The bartender returned with two bottles of the Australian beer.

"So, Sir Charles, I didn't know you were capable of drinking anything other than chardonnay and vodka."

"Well, a woman on board—who is apparently a figment of my imagination—once said to me that sometimes you have to live dangerously."

Marvin took a drink of his beer. "Did you say a figment of your imagination? Is that in *The Maltese Falcon* or something?"

"No, I wish it were. This has been the most surreal trip for me."

Marvin studied his face to determine if he was joking. "In what way?"

"I won't bore you with all the details, but this is the extremely abbreviated version. You remember the brunette with the blue streak I always asked about?"

"Yes, the mysterious woman."

"Well, I'm not sure she existed. That's the strangest part of my trip. Second, as you know, I had that blonde woman, Ann, investigated for potentially being a threat to the brunette woman. Third, I was knocked out on Mystery Island. Someone threw a rock at me. I didn't see who threw it, but I know that the blonde and her friends were on the island at the time. She had threatened me earlier. The rock missed me, but I lost my balance and was knocked unconscious. Dr. Perrine examined me and believes that I sustained a concussion." He paused to take a drink of beer. "I then told her about all that had happened to me on board, and she set up an appointment for me to meet with a psychiatrist in Sydney. And listen to this, Marvin. The last day I was on the ship, a woman confessed to trying to poison me. Sounds like I'm crazy, doesn't it?"

Marvin took a drink of his beer. "Are you kidding me?"

"Unfortunately, I'm telling you the truth. At least, that's the truth as I know it."

"Even the last part about the woman confessing she had been trying to poison you?"

"Yes."

"Honestly, Sir Charles, that's a little hard to swallow."

"I wish I was kidding you, Marvin. But no, it's all the dead-level truth."

"Did you see the psychiatrist in Sydney?"

"Yes, this afternoon."

"How did that go?"

"I honestly don't know. The psychiatrist couldn't make a diagnosis after one session. I'll probably start seeing a psychiatrist when I get back to the States. Marvin, I know you run into a lot of strange people on the ship, but I think I may be the strangest you have ever seen or will ever meet."

Marvin lifted his beer bottle. "Sir Charles, here's to better times." They clanged beer bottles. Marvin looked at his watch. "I had better get along. Thanks for the beer."

"My pleasure, Marvin. I always enjoyed visiting with you. Good luck in the future."

Charles watched as Marvin walked away. It was a strange feeling to know that he would never see Marvin or Kristin again. *People come into your life and then just leave.* He finished his beer and slowly walked back to the hotel.

CHAPTER THIRTY-SEVEN

For his last night in Sydney, Charles found a pub in the Rocks and enjoyed a casual dinner of fish and chips. It was a pleasant, clear night. He took an indirect route back to the hotel so that he could get a little exercise and enjoy being outside. By the time he arrived back at the hotel, it was 9:00 p.m. He decided to visit the hotel bar for a final cocktail. After all, it was his last night in Australia.

The bar was decorated with blond woods and accent lighting. Charles easily found a stool and set his phone on the bar. A bartender approached him.

"Good evening. May I bring you a cocktail?"

"Yes. Do you have a citron vodka, by chance?" The bartender turned around to check his vodka supply. He grabbed a bottle and held it before him. "This is the only kind in stock."

Charles squinted to read the label. "Sure, it's fine. Could you mix it with soda?"

He mixed the drink and set it on a napkin in front of Charles.

"Thanks very much."

"Not a problem."

Charles took a taste and then started accessing his email on his phone. Out of his peripheral vision, he saw someone sitting down on the stool to his right.

"Choosing not to live dangerously tonight, eh?"

Charles felt as if he had been struck by lightning. A chill shot down his spine. He jerked his head up to see who had asked the question. The first glimpse he caught was of a blue streak.

It was Vicky, sitting next to him, staring directly ahead. She turned to face Charles and smiled. "No White Russian? I'd have thought that you would love living dangerously by now."

Charles just sat and stared into her eyes. "I was beginning to think that you were just a figment of my imagination," he stuttered.

Vicky laughed.

The bartender approached them. "Care for a cocktail?"

She shifted her attention to the bartender. "Just a glass of champagne, please."

Vicky then turned back to face Charles and put a hand on his arm. "I'm very real."

The bartender returned with a glass of champagne. Vicky raised her glass. "Cheers."

"Your name is not Vicky LeBlanc, is it?"

Vicky lifted her hand from his arm. "No. Actually, it's Brigid."

"Why did you tell me your name was Vicky?"

Brigid looked down at her glass of champagne. "Don't you think that I look like a Vicky, with the blue streak and all?"

"Why did you just disappear?"

"I didn't disappear."

"But I never saw you again."

"Of course you did. We made eye contact several times."

Charles was confused.

"Charles, did you ever see that movie *Catch Me if You Can*?"

"I think so. Why?"

"Do you remember the scene where Frank Abagnale is trying to make a point to his son, Frank Abagnale Jr.?"

Charles shook his head. "Not sure."

Brigid took a drink of her champagne. "The father says to the son, 'You know why the Yankees always win, Frank?' Frank Jr. replies, 'Because they have Mickey Mantle?' The father says, 'No, it's because the other teams can't stop staring at those damn pinstripes!'"

"So what's the connection?"

Brigid set her glass down and smiled. "It's all about branding. The Yankees created the pinstripes. They were the gold standard of baseball. You either loved them or hated them. Regardless, you saw those pinstripes. Do you remember the first night that we met at the Cove Bar?"

"Of course, yes."

Brigid moved closer to him. "What's the first thing that you noticed about me?"

Charles stared at her hair. "The blue streak in your hair."

"Precisely. I knew I had you hooked from the moment we first met. You were so vulnerable. I could sense that you desperately needed some human contact and purpose. After we visited for a few minutes, I gave you that purpose. I confided in you about my affair with . . . now, what was his name? Oh yes, Miles, a married man. And when I said, 'Let's continue this conversation later,' you were hooked. Your expression changed completely. I planted the seed of passion back in your life. Do you recall the second time we met, in the Saloon? I checked every bar on board that night, searching for you. When I walked into the Saloon and saw you sitting alone, I was ecstatic. I was now able to execute my plan. You should have seen your face when I first suggested that we meet in my stateroom later that evening. Your eyes twinkled, and your face flushed red. You were like a young schoolboy asking a girl out on a first date. It was so cute."

"May I ask why you picked me, of all the men on board?"

"Simple. You were the only single man who attended the singles' cocktail reception. I wanted to talk to you that evening, but that blonde woman, Anita, monopolized your attention."

"So you knew that I would eventually think that Anita was the unhinged wife of the guy with whom you were having an affair?"

"Of course. She was a critical part of my plan. Once I confided in you that I thought the wife of my lover was on board and a danger to me, I needed someone to be her. I thought Ann would be the perfect woman to play a mentally disturbed wife. Don't you agree?"

Charles didn't respond.

"Since she and I were both single, I got to know her quite well. I quickly learned that she had a bad temper. I thought she would be very convincing to you as the wife."

Charles leaned back in his chair. "Was Ann in on what you call 'your plan'?"

Brigid shook her head. "No, she was an unwitting pawn, just like you."

The bartender approached them. "Either of you care for another drink?"

Without waiting for Brigid to respond, Charles blurted out,

"I definitely would!"

He turned to Brigid. She said, "Sure. Why not?"

Charles sat in silence, watching the bartender mix his cocktail. He returned and placed the drink in front of Charles and poured a glass of champagne for Brigid. Charles stared at her. "Why did you need Ann and me as pawns in your plan?"

She took a sip of her champagne. "An alibi."

"An alibi for what?"

Brigid glimpsed around the bar. "You remember my earlier reference to Frank Abagnale Jr.?"

Charles nodded.

"Frank was a confidence trickster, an impostor—and an excellent thief. Well, I'm better than Frank. I'm also a master magician. Sterling contacted my agent and invited me to perform on this cruise. That's when I learned about the Volk Yellow Diamond being featured in the boutique. I wanted to be on this cruise—but incognito. So I referred Sterling to my son, Jasper. He's an up-and-coming magician. Sterling didn't care about credentials; they just wanted someone to perform magic."

"You're the one who stole the diamond?"

Brigid put her finger to her lips. "Shhh."

They both looked around, but no one was near them. Brigid put her hand on his arm again.

"Yes, I took it. I had to wait for the right opportunity. Do you recall when they let passengers hold and examine the diamond? Well, I made sure that I was the last one in line. When my turn came, I took the diamond and replaced it with a very realistic-looking fake one. It's a very simple sleight-of-hand trick to perform. The poor gemologist was staring at my blue streak like the teams stared at the Yankees' pinstripes while I

261 261 261 261 261 261 261 261 261 261 261 261 261 261 261 261 261 261 261 261 261 261 261 261 261 261 261 261 261 261 261 261

was switching stones on him right under his nose. I'm surprised it took him several days to discover the diamond was missing."

"So how could I be an alibi for the theft of the diamond?"

She set her glass down. "I ran through several possible scenarios of how you could be useful to me. Fortunately for you, I just had to employ one. I knew you would come looking for me after you witnessed my little spat with Ann at the pool."

His mouth dropped open. "How did you know I would see that?"

"I was visiting with Ann and keeping an eye on you. When I saw you were waking up from a nap, I goaded Ann into an argument. She was so easy to manipulate. I took a calculated risk that you would see us. When I stormed off the deck, away from Ann, I knew she would follow me. When we entered the ship, I suggested that we go into the ladies' room to talk. I immediately apologized to her, and all was forgiven."

Charles took a drink of his cocktail. "Well, it worked. I did come looking for you and then inquired about you at the ship's reception desk."

Brigid patted his cheek. "Poor baby, you wondered what had happened to your fragile Vicky LeBlanc, didn't you?"

"Yes, and then I even thought that Ann and some men might have tossed you overboard."

"That was a brilliant trick, wasn't it? I assume you remember the muscular young man who always doted on Ann?"

Charles nodded his head.

"He was on my team. We followed you to the seventh deck the night the golf bag went overboard. Then we hurried downstairs to the golf area on the sixth deck. When Jon saw you peer over the edge below, he called out to me, 'Get her.' We pretended to fight, and then he threw one of the golf bags overboard."

"But I saw a blonde woman below!"

"You certainly did. I wore a blonde wig for the duration of the cruise. That's also why you never saw me again—you were always looking for my pinstripes, a.k.a. the blue streak."

"So earlier in the evening, you had this Jon guy address Ann as Anita in front of me in the Saloon, is that right?"

"It worked beautifully. I thought a bright fellow like you would put two and two together and conclude that Ann was the evil, dangerous wife. So scenario one was that I wanted you to distract Security with this woman-overboard story, or how you had fallen in love with a woman who had disappeared. The more they concentrated on finding me, the less time they would devote to finding the missing diamond. If Security ever got close to discovering that I was the thief, I planned to come out of hiding. You would be so thrilled to have me back. Together, we could convince Security that I was just an innocent woman having an affair and was afraid for my life. There was no way that I could be a thief."

"What if we weren't successful in convincing Security, and they thought you were the thief?"

"Well, then that would have been an unfortunate scenario as far as you were concerned. I would have set you up to take the fall. If I can switch a diamond in front of a gemologist and God knows how many security cameras without being caught, I could easily plant the diamond on you or in your stateroom. But, Charles, I'm so happy it didn't come to that, aren't you? If that had occurred, you would be in some prison in Sydney, and I'd be having a glass of champagne by myself."

"Why are you telling me this now?"

Brigid kissed him on the lips. "I like you, Charles. Besides, I did you a favor. You were a sad, pathetic soul lost on a ship for a month. I put passion back into your life."

Charles stared down at his drink. "You're not afraid that I'll tell the authorities what you've just told me?"

"No. You're grateful to have had the experience, and I think you're in love with me. You don't strike me as the kind of man who would hurt someone he loves." Brigid looked at her watch. "It's late. I must be going."

Charles picked up his phone and checked the time. It was 11:00 p.m.

"Goodbye, my love." Brigid kissed him on the lips and walked away.

"Goodbye, Vicky," he whispered.

Charles snapped a photo of her profile with his phone as she turned to walk toward the door.

CHAPTER THIRTY-EIGHT

Charles got up early the next morning. His flight was scheduled to leave at 2:00 p.m. It would be wise to get to the airport no later than noon. He had a light breakfast, checked out, and caught a cab to the airport. The queue waiting to proceed through security was relatively short. He reached his gate at 12:15 p.m. and relaxed into a chair in the waiting area.

Instinctively, Charles took out his phone and began to check his email and the latest news. He then accessed his photos. The first image to come up was the photo he took of Brigid as she was leaving the bar last night. It was sharp and vivid. Even in the muted light of the bar, you could make out the blue streak in her hair.

What a strange, surreal encounter. As soon as he had convinced himself that he was hallucinating, his hallucination came to life. He had the photo to prove that Vicky, or Brigid, or whatever her real name was, did exist. Was she telling him the truth last night about being a thief and using him as a pawn in her scheme? She could just be psychotic and enjoy watching people squirm as she weaved her web of lies. However, she was wrong about one thing. He was not in love with her, and he was no one's pawn. He fumbled through his wallet and found the note from Kristin Perrine.

He emailed a message to her:

> Dr. Perrine, please see the attached photo. I took it last night in the bar at the Regent Hotel in Sydney. This is the woman I mentioned having met on board. You will note the blue streak in her hair. Trust me, she is very real. Although she didn't say, I assume she is staying at the Regent Hotel. As you may recall, she told me on the ship that her name was Vicky LeBlanc. Last night, she told me her first name is really Brigid. She also said she was a master magician and the mother of the young magician who performed on board—I believe his name is Jasper Gutman. I am not sure if Gutman is her last name. Brigid informed me last night that she stole the diamond from the Sterling Boutique. She was the last passenger to hold and examine the diamond. Through a little sleight of hand, Brigid replaced the real diamond with a fake. Maybe the security cameras can verify her story. She used me as an unwitting alibi in her plan to commit the theft. Obviously, I was very gullible. I know this story may be hard to believe. Please rest assured, I have pondered thoroughly why she would confess to me last night about stealing the diamond. It's not logical and seems awfully careless. The only rationale that I could fathom is that she does not think I would do anything with this knowledge because I am either too weak or too infatuated with her. But she is wrong!

Maybe this Brigid really does like living dangerously.
If you are so inclined, please alert Chief Polhaus.
Perhaps with a little due diligence, she will finally
nab her thief. Thank you for your care and support! I
am about to board my plane to return home. Safe
travels!

Thirty minutes into the flight, an attendant approached
Charles. "Mr. Pierce, would you like a cocktail or something
to drink?"

He smiled. "A glass of water would be nice."

The plane touched down sixteen hours later at Dallas/Fort
Worth International Airport. He had slept most of the flight.
Due to crossing back over the International Date Line, his flight
had left at 3:00 p.m. and arrived at 4:00 p.m. the same day.
While waiting for the plane to taxi to the gate, Charles switched
on his phone. He watched as dozens of emails suddenly emerged
in the in-box. There was an email from Dr. Perrine. It read:

Thank you for contacting me, Charles. I hope by the
time you receive this text, you will have landed safely
back home. As you requested, I alerted Chief Polhaus
about our "friend" with the blue streak. I can assure
you that she took the matter seriously. I don't think
I would recommend seeing a psychiatrist after all. :)
All the best! Kristin.

Charles took a cab back to his apartment. It was strange
being back home after a month away. His apartment was neat
and appeared unchanged. He left his luggage inside the door,

walked into his bedroom, and dove into bed fully dressed. It was comforting to be in familiar surroundings. While lying down, he took his phone out of his coat pocket and scrolled through some news websites. Under international news was this headline:

WOMAN NABBED IN DIAMOND HEIST

When Charles accessed the article, there was an image of Brigid, complete with a blue streak in her hair. She was hand-cuffed and in the company of a Sydney uniformed police officer. Charles smiled.

Well, Vicky, you did say that you were sailing to Sydney to meet a man. You just didn't know that it was going to be a policeman.

Sam Spade would be proud!

CHAPTER THIRTY-NINE

"Jamie Simon opened the door to the clinic and said, "Good morning, Frida."

"Good morning, Jamie," Frida replied. "How are you doing?"

"I'm doing fine. How about you?"

"Pretty well."

"I take it Dr. Graves isn't working you too hard?"

"No, just the usual sixty-hour workweeks," Frida joked.

"Is she tied up with a patient?"

"No, she is doing some paperwork in her office. She told me to tell you to come on back when you arrived."

"Thank you, Frida." Mrs. Simon opened the door to the lab, which connected the reception area with Dr. Graves's office in the rear. She scanned the lab. It had been completely rearranged since she had worked there. Mrs. Simon knocked on Dr. Graves's office door.

Dr. Graves said, "Come in."

Mrs. Simon opened the door slightly and peered in. "I hope I'm not interrupting anything."

"Of course not. How are you doing, Jamie?"

"I'm doing OK, but I'm a little bored."

The two women hugged. Dr. Graves said, "Please have a seat."

Mrs. Simon took a seat in one of the client chairs, and Dr. Graves returned to her chair behind the desk.

Dr. Graves said, "Jamie, you just cruised halfway around the world. I would suspect that anything after that trip would be a little boring."

"It was an interesting trip, full of all kinds of suspense." Mrs. Simon described the diamond being stolen from the ship's boutique and the following Code Red for the duration of the trip. She did not mention her meeting with Charles Pierce.

"Wow, that sounds exciting. You got more than you bargained for when you booked that cruise."

"I certainly did."

"Did you meet any men?"

"Samantha, you know I'm not interested in meeting men."

"I know, dear. But you can't grieve for John for the rest of your life."

"I know you're right, but I'm still hurting."

"OK, let's change the subject, then. What brings you in to see me?"

"I said earlier that I was bored. Please feel no pressure, but I wanted to see if there is a chance I could work a day or two a week."

"I'm sorry, Jamie, but I've filled your part-time position with an intern. He gets school credit for working here, and I don't have to pay him."

"I understand. Would you consider letting me work one day a week on a volunteer basis? I don't need money. I just want to feel useful and productive."

Dr. Graves leaned forward and rested her elbows on the desk. "Are you sure?"

"Yes. It's the least I could do after all the support you have provided me in the past."

"OK, Jamie. Why don't you come in on Wednesday afternoons? You can assist the intern. His name is Dan. I think you two will get along fine."

"Thank you, Samantha. I would love to do that. I noticed when I passed through the lab that it looked rearranged from what I remembered."

"Yes, Dan is meticulous in making sure everything is in its place."

"You don't think I will get in his way, do you? I could come sometime when he's not here."

"Perhaps you're right. Are you free at eleven on Tuesdays?"

"Yes."

"Would you mind filling in for Frida for two hours each week?"

"Not at all."

"Perfect. Frida has class every Tuesday morning. She's getting her certification as a veterinarian's technician."

"Great. I'll be here next Tuesday at ten forty-five."

"Let's go out to reception and let Frida know what we've decided."

Dr. Graves led Mrs. Simon back through the lab to the reception area. Mrs. Simon's eyes darted around the lab. Dr. Graves opened the door to the reception area and said, "Frida, Jamie is going to cover for you every week while you're in class. That way, you don't have to rush back to the office right afterward."

Frida said, "Wonderful. Thank you so much!"

"Please give Jamie one of the spare keys to the office in case I'm not here," Dr. Graves said.

"Will do."

Dr. Graves turned to Mrs. Simon. "Welcome back."

Mrs. Simon said, "Thank you so much, Samantha. This will be a lifesaver."

CHAPTER FORTY

Tuesday morning, Jamie Simon pulled her car up to Dr. Graves's clinic. The parking lot was empty. She parked her car in visitor parking and walked up to the front door. Mrs. Simon jiggled the handle of the door, but it was locked. She fished her key to the clinic out of her purse, unlocked the front door, and entered the reception area. Immediately, she locked the door behind her and set her purse on Frida's desk. She needed only a few minutes and didn't dare get caught.

Thirty minutes later, Mrs. Simon heard keys being inserted in the front door lock. She quickly sat down behind Frida's desk.

Dr. Graves entered the reception area and said, "Good morning, Jamie."

"Good morning, Samantha."

"Jamie, I should have mentioned that you should leave the door unlocked after you arrive in the morning. We might have walk-in patients."

"I apologize. It's just a habit I have of locking doors behind me. I'll remember next time."

"No problem. Were there any phone calls?"

"The phone did ring twice, but it went to voice mail."

"OK, I'll check on that when I get back to my office."

Mrs. Simon sat still as Dr. Graves made her way back through the lab to her office.

No one came to the clinic until 1:00 p.m., when Frida opened the door and stepped inside the reception area.

"Oh, Jamie, you startled me. I forgot you were covering for me."

Mrs. Simon stood up. "Hi, Frida. How was class?"

"It was a little dull today. The good news is that I'm almost finished with the course."

"Soon you will be certified and can ask Dr. Graves for a raise."

"Exactly. Anything exciting happen while I was gone?"

Mrs. Simon gathered up her purse. "No. Like your class, it was pretty dull. I will see you next week, Frida. Please tell Dr. Graves goodbye for me."

"I assume she's in her office?"

"Yes."

"By the way, did you happen to go back into the lab?"

"No. I've been in the reception area the whole time I've been here. Why do you ask?"

"Good. Dan, our ambitious intern, gets a tad anxious if someone messes with how the lab is organized. He's a nice young man but a little anal-retentive."

"I will have to meet this Dan someday."

"Goodbye, Jamie."

"See you next week, Frida."

CHAPTER FORTY-ONE

"Hello?"

"Hello, Mr. Pierce, this is Detective Gonzalez."

"Yes, Detective?"

"I wanted to let you know that the ketamine poisoning cases have been officially classified as inactive. We have exhausted all leads. Whoever was responsible has gone into hiding, back under his or her rock."

"I see." Charles wondered if he should tell Detective Gonzalez about Jamie Simon. No, he'd already decided that they were even. They had destroyed one another's lives.

"How was your trip, Mr. Pierce?"

Boy, if you only knew. "It was therapeutic and relaxing."

"Well, that's good. I don't suppose you've thought of anything you've forgotten to tell us about the case, have you?"

"No, sir. I haven't thought about it in over a month."

"OK, Mr. Pierce. Have a good evening."

"Thank you, Detective. You too."

* * *

ACROSS TOWN, DAN KNOCKED on Dr. Graves's office door.

"Come in."

"Dr. Graves, do you have a moment?"

"Yes, Dan. What is it?"

"May I show you something in the lab?"

Dr. Graves followed Dan back into the lab. He opened a cabinet and pointed at a half-empty bottle. "This bottle of ketamine was not in its proper location. Also, the bottle was completely full yesterday."

"Dan, are you quite sure you aren't mistaken?"

"Positive. Here's my spreadsheet listing every drug in the lab by type of drug, exact quantities, and location."

"This isn't good."

* * *

THREE HOURS LATER, CHARLES GLANCED at his phone. He needed to get a move on if he didn't want to be late. The traffic was terrible. He should have just walked. It would have been faster. Finally, he rounded the corner and pulled up to the valet stand in front of the Nasher Sculpture Center. A Nasher employee held the door open for him. Charles could see a crowd milling around in the sculpture garden outside. Another Nasher employee asked, "May I have your name, sir?"

"Yes. It's Charles Pierce."

She scribbled on a sheet of paper attached to a clipboard. "Yes. Here you are. Please feel free to go out to the garden. The reception is outside this evening."

Charles exited the building and headed into the garden. It was a still-cool March evening in Dallas. A server approached with a tray of champagne and white wine. "Sir, would you care for something to drink?"

Charles refrained from taking a glass of wine. The last place he'd had any alcohol was over eight thousand miles away in Sydney, Australia. No way was he going to fall off the wagon for house wine. He said, "No thank you."

Someone tugged at his coat. "Hello, Charles."

He spun around. "Felicia. What are you doing here?"

"Well, ever since we attended the lecture on minimalism, I've become a modern art aficionado."

Charles studied her face to see if she was teasing. "No way."

Felicia burst out laughing. "You're right. My law firm is one of the sponsors of tonight's event. I volunteered to attend to help represent the firm. Besides, maybe we will get to witness an attempted murder."

"What? Attempted murder?"

"Wasn't some woman poisoned at one of the events you attended here last year?"

Charles nodded his head. "Yes. In fact, I haven't been here since then." *Should I tell Felicia about Jamie Simon?* Probably not. She was history anyway.

Felicia gestured with her glass of champagne. "Aren't you drinking chardonnay tonight, Charles?"

"No. Not tonight."

"You're not afraid someone is going to poison you, are you?"

He laughed. "No, I'm not worried about being poisoned. I hit the alcohol pretty heavily on my trip and decided to give my liver a break."

* * *

AN EMPLOYEE HELD OPEN THE front door to the Nasher Sculpture Center as a woman entered. Her blonde hair was pulled back in a bun. She was wearing tinted glasses and a black pantsuit. Another employee greeted her. "Good evening, ma'am. May I have your name?"

"Mrs. Jamie Simon."

ABOUT THE AUTHOR

Jim Lively is currently the Artist and Curator at Martsolf Lively Contemporary in Richardson, Texas. After practicing law for many years, Jim decided to pursue his passion full time as a visual artist, film maker and author. He received the 2016 Merrimack Media Outstanding Writer Award for his second novel, *Punitive Damages*.

His artwork and art films have been recognized in numerous juried competitions, publications and film festivals. He has exhibited his artwork in several group and solo exhibitions across North America and Europe.

Thirteen of Jim's films have been selected to various film festivals around the world. His art film, *The Soul of Vinyl, Abbey Road Side 2*, screened at the 2016 New York City Independent Film Festival. Jim's film, *The Case of the Deranged Sommelier* won Best Experimental Film in the 2016 Directors Circle of Shorts Film Festival and the 2017 Lion's Head Film Festival. His film, *Still Mad as Hell* screened at the 2017 New York City Independent Film Festival. His latest film, *Seduction* screened at the 2020 Manhattan Hinge International Film Festival.

Jim's education includes a Bachelor of Arts from The University of Texas at Austin and a Juris Doctor from Southern Methodist University in Dallas.